DEADLY TEXAS SUMMER

Colleen Thompson

⟨H⟩ HARLEQUIN

ROMANTIC
SUSPENSE

HARLEQUIN®
ROMANTIC SUSPENSE™

Recycling programs
for this product may
not exist in your area.

ISBN-13: 978-1-335-62647-9

Deadly Texas Summer

Copyright © 2020 by Colleen Thompson

This edition published by arrangement with Harlequin Books S.A.

For questions and comments about the quality of this book, please contact us at CustomerService@Harlequin.com.

Harlequin Enterprises ULC
22 Adelaide St. West, 40th Floor
Toronto, Ontario M5H 4E3, Canada
www.Harlequin.com

Printed in U.S.A.

The Texas-based author of more than thirty novels and novellas, **Colleen Thompson** is a former teacher with a passion for reading, hiking, kayaking and the last-chance rescue dogs she and her husband have welcomed into their home. With a National Readers' Choice Award and multiple nominations for the RITA® Award, she has also appeared on the Amazon, BookScan and Barnes & Noble bestseller lists. Visit her online at www.colleen-thompson.com.

Books by Colleen Thompson

Harlequin Romantic Suspense

Passion to Protect
The Colton Heir
Lone Star Redemption
Lone Star Survivor
Deadly Texas Summer

Cowboy Christmas Rescue
"Rescuing the Bride"

Silhouette Romantic Suspense

Deadlier Than the Male
"Lethal Lessons"

Harlequin Intrigue

Capturing the Commando
Phantom of the French Quarter
Relentless Protector

Visit the Author Profile page at Harlequin.com for more titles.

To all the teachers who inspire, challenge and demand better of their students, including those educators I worked with and those who once upon a time gave me the tools to reach for my dreams.

Chapter 1

Wildlife biologist Emma Copley gritted her teeth as her silver Jeep bounced along the gravel road, raising a cloud of dust that hazed the stark blue southeast Texas sky. Already running late that humid August morning, she ran through a mental checklist, troubleshooting the device she and her graduate assistant had spent most of the summer testing—a machine meant to reduce the number of protected birds of prey killed each year by the towering wind turbines that dotted the grassy coastal hills.

If she could only figure out why it kept randomly shutting down individual windmills, forcing the two of them to scramble to reset it by hand on four of the past six mornings. "Camera must be picking up on insect swarms," she murmured, trying out a new idea, "or maybe bats heading back to their roosts for the day."

From the back seat, River, the young golden retriever mix she'd adopted after last year's breakup, responded with a sound, half yawn and half yodel, that made Emma smile…

At least until her cell rang, though reception could be hit-or-miss here. Emma grabbed the phone from her cup holder, her heart skipping a beat when she saw the caller was her mother, who was supposed to be in Amsterdam with Emma's stepdad, on the first leg of the two-week European river cruise they'd been dreaming of for years.

"Everything okay, Mom?" Though her mother had been given the green light for travel, she was still regaining her strength after completing chemo treatments. "Are you feeling all—"

"Hey, there. Remember me?" came an unexpected male voice. The shock of hearing it, all these months later, had Emma braking so hard that River yelped and scrambled to remain on the seat. "Or are you so busy screwing everything in pants, you've forgotten all about the only man who'll ever really love you?"

As a punch of nausea struck hard, nerve endings fired icy harpoons from the back of Emma's neck and down the length of her spine. But it reminded her, too, she had a backbone. Pulling over on the empty road, she said, "You've spoofed her number, haven't you? My mother's, this time."

Late one night a few weeks earlier, her ex-husband of four months had pulled the same stunt, using some sleazy caller ID–altering program to trick her into believing it was her best friend phoning. Instead, Emma had been treated to a clearly drunken round of accusations: how she'd destroyed their marriage, how he would make her pay. Since his method left neither an electronic trail nor witnesses to produce hard evidence that her ex-husband had violated the no-contact order, she'd had no way to stop his abusive language and his threats short of powering off her phone.

"Would you have picked up otherwise?" Jeremy asked, his voice slurred again, though it was only nine fifteen in the morning. Normally at this time, he'd be working, for the uncle in Waco who'd been kind enough to offer him a fresh start in a new city when others had been hesitant to employ a man on probation.

"You have to stop calling me. You know that." For all the hell he'd put her through, she didn't want to see him foul up this second chance.

She was interrupted by the same scoffing noise he'd once made when she'd warned that he'd get caught cutting class in high school. Back when he'd been the exciting sort of dangerous, the kind she'd foolishly imagined her good example could reform. For a while, it seemed she had succeeded, her hard work and academic honors inspiring him to seriously step up his game. After a few years of working alongside his father, he'd established his own home contracting business, then set about—with a focused determination that had left the shy bookworm she'd once been both charmed and flattered—convincing her that, for all their many differences, he was still great husband material.

Had he been playing the long con even then? Or had the loving, attentive man she'd married been the real Jeremy, the man he could still be if he hadn't let his insecurities— and his attempts to self-medicate them into silence—take over his life?

"I want you to know that, on my attorney's advice, I'm recording this conversation," she warned, though she couldn't get the app to start, probably because of this rural area's weak cell signal.

In desperation, she bluffed. "The judge's already

warned you that if you violate again, you'll end up doing jail time."

"You're doing him, too, aren't you?" Jeremy accused, the irrational anger taking hold again. "I saw the looks he kept sneaking your way in the courtroom. And you think I didn't notice your slutty little signals? You're nothing but a whoring bit—"

"Not this again. We're done here." Blinking back the haze burning her eyes, she disconnected, sick of his endless accusations, which had started not long after his business had gone under just as her professional star began to rise. Sick of who she'd been for too long, with her increasingly desperate efforts to reassure him and convince him to go to counseling and at least scale back his drinking. The whole nightmare had come to a head the day he'd burst into the office of her seventy-four-year-old dean shouting obscene accusations. Fearing the poor man would have a stroke, she'd rushed in and tried to intervene. Jeremy turned on her, shoving her hard into a bank of cabinets before storming out the door. Leaving her to— As her fingers drifted to her lower abdomen, she fought back the darkest memories.

The phone rang again, the call coming this time from an unknown number, likely from some burner phone he'd picked up. She let it go to voice mail, telling herself that Jeremy had no idea that she was working hours from her home in Austin for the summer. Otherwise, he wouldn't bother with these pathetic phone calls.

"Well, we have better things to do than listen. Right, River?" Emma half hoped that her ex might be tanked enough to leave a message that would result in actual jail time. Though he might've talked a good game in the courtroom, tearfully apologizing for "my part in what happened"—as if she were equally to blame—and vowing to attend court-ordered counseling, Emma trusted these raw glimpses of his unguarded anger far more than she would ever believe his rehearsed performances.

When the same caller tried again, she blocked the number. Afterward, she switched off her phone's ringer just in case before stroking the dog's broad golden head and whispering, "It's over now."

Still agitated, she spun her wheels before they suddenly caught. As the Jeep lurched forward, she fought to shake off her lingering dread. But she scarcely registered the cattle she passed, the grazing animals' hides a rich red brown against the wispy, sunburned grasses. Scarcely noticed the silhouettes of dozens of wind turbines rising above the coastal hills.

Slowing for her turn, she made a right, only to hear the rhythmic thump of River's fringed tail against the seat back and the sound of her excited panting.

"That's right, girl. We're almost there," said Emma. "And I'll bet your friend Russell will throw your squeaky duck a few times."

At the mention of her beloved toy, River barked.

Laughing at the dog's excitement, Emma felt a little of the tightness in her rib cage loosen. As late as she was to meet her grad assistant, Russell Jorgenson, who was as passionate as she was about reducing the blade strikes that had killed so many hawks and eagles, she knew he'd be eager for a game of fetch. Anything to put off donning safety harnesses and helmets and undertaking the long, steep climb up the interior steel ladder leading to the top of Turbine Number 43, an ascent that safety regulations forbade either one of them from making solo.

Don't kid yourself. His willingness wasn't about delaying the inevitable—or the chance to play with her dog, either.

Her assistant for this summer project, a confident twenty-four-year-old with a winning smile, had made it increasingly clear that he was interested in her, despite the fact that she was nine years older. Emma had done her best to nip it in the bud, telling him in no uncertain terms that she didn't get involved with students—or anyone she worked with—as soon as she had realized that his attention was more than academic.

To her surprise, he'd only grinned. *Then how do you expect to ever meet somebody new?*

She'd shut him down with a cool look, but her instincts, along with his puppylike attentiveness to her every word and action, warned her that he hadn't given up. And part of her—a part she hated—couldn't help worrying that word of her student's hopeless crush would somehow get back to Jeremy, who seemed to consider their divorce, like the no-contact order, a mere technicality.

Slowing, she pulled under a gate marked, like practically every pasture in the area, with the name and famous running-K brand of the historic Kingston Ranch. As her wheels bumped over the metal grid of the cattle guard, she vowed to leave behind all thoughts of her ex-husband, along with the lingering fears that hearing his voice had managed to re-trigger.

Filled with fresh determination, she entered the enormous spread, which leased land to Green Horizon Energy for its wind turbines. At Number 43, she pulled up beside her grad assistant's old blue pickup. Though she'd texted earlier to let Russell know that she was on her way, he wasn't waiting for her behind the wheel as she'd expected. Nor did she see him sitting on the tailgate or near the massive turbine's base. Had he tired of waiting and taken a short walk?

She felt a nervous flutter—tiny birds' wings in her stomach. Exiting her vehicle, she called out his name. The ever-present wind off the Gulf of Mexico, about a dozen miles to the east, snatched the word from her mouth and carried it away. Her hair, too, was blown around, light sandy-colored wisps flapping flag-like in her face.

What she didn't hear was any answer, though more than three hundred feet above, the normal hum of the turbine remained silent, the stillness of its blades proof that the strike deterrent system remained offline.

She opened the Jeep's rear door and let out River.

"Find Russell. Go and find him!" Emma pitched her voice high, making it sound like the world's most exciting game.

The young dog leaped and play-bowed in her direction, not catching on until Emma pulled out the day pack containing the beloved duck and repeated the command.

With a deep chuff of joy, the retriever bounded off, running in widening circles. Meanwhile, Emma grabbed her phone and tried another text.

I'm at your truck. Where are you?

The hummingbirds' wings returned, beating even harder with every passing minute that the text message went unanswered. She thought again of Jeremy's call, his enduring obsession with the delusion that she was sleeping with someone. How could she even be sure that he was still in Waco? What if he *had* found her, had tracked her to this location and transferred his rage to—

"Stop it," she told herself. Surely Russell would walk up any second to show her a falcon's feather he'd found or tell her about an armadillo or a family of piglike javelina he'd spotted on his walk.

Holding the image in her mind, she went to his pickup and opened the unlocked driver's side door. Reaching over, she grabbed his unzipped backpack from the passenger seat, where she spotted a familiar compact tool kit and sighed in relief. Even if Russell had grown impatient enough to break the rule against climbing up the turbine alone, he never would've done so without taking what he needed to attempt repairs.

Uncertain of what else to try, she hit the horn twice—two long blasts that ought to get her assistant's attention if his cell's battery had run down. When he still didn't appear, she closed the truck's door, listening as the warm wind rushed around the parked vehicles, scouring their paint jobs—and her exposed skin—with abrasive grains of sand and somehow heightening her sense of isolation. Her vulnerability, out here in the open, so far from the things people so often took for granted. Things like witnesses and help.

Something tugged hard at her shoulder. Sucking in a sharp breath, she spun around, heart slamming her sternum, before looking down.

"Darn you, dog! Don't sneak up on a person like that," Emma said, realizing that River had returned and grasped the day pack in her strong jaws. Returned alone, and was now backing up, her long tongue lolling and pure duck-lust gleaming in her deep brown eyes.

Knowing she would get no peace until she turned over the squeaky toy, Emma pulled it from the pack and threw it. While River bounded off, Emma tried phoning Russell instead of texting, needing the reassurance of his voice.

The call rolled over to his voice mail. Frustrating as that was, Emma was distracted to see River drop her squeaky duck and race barking to a spot about twenty feet out from the windmill's base.

A bird. She's run across another turbine blade-strike victim. One Russell hasn't found yet. Trained to alert but not disturb, River should run to it and then lie down. Instead, she ran in tight circles before looking up and all around herself, as if in confusion.

Trotting closer, Emma was confused, too, to find no telltale mound of feathers. Nor did she glimpse Russell's reddish hair or spot his body half-hidden in the dry gold grasses. Instead, she was jolted to spot his smartphone, a crack across its screen. As she picked it up, she made out the missed call from her number and the list of several unread messages on the mostly readable display.

"So how'd your phone get broken?" she asked aloud. "And how'd it end up down here?"

Her heart pumped faster, harder, the horror dawning in her body before her mind could grasp it. She looked beyond the phone's screen, her gaze funneling toward the turbine's base, catching that spot near its curved edge where the service door stood slightly ajar.

"Oh, Russell. Oh, no." Her stomach plummeting, her voice tightened. "Please tell me you didn't—you didn't go...*up.*"

With her legs shaking so hard she could barely remain standing, she swallowed a whimper. Forced herself to tilt her head back. To look high above her, at the dark shape silhouetted against the impossible stark blue.

At the sight of his body, limp and dangling just beneath the housing of the turbine, something broke inside her.

Emma's shrill scream joined the wind's howl, and she crashed down to her knees.

Emma didn't remember calling 911, but she clearly must have done so. By the time she'd climbed back down from the turbine, sobbing and bleeding from the fresh blisters she'd torn open, the first responders had begun arriving. She spotted sheriff's department vehicles, volunteer firefighters offering manpower and a pair of EMTs leaving their ambulance.

As two of the latter had tried to persuade her to let them check her over, a stocky man in a Western hat and khaki uniform shirt waved them off and introduced himself while chewing on a toothpick half-hidden by his drooping, gray-blond mustache. Sheriff Wallace Fleming, he'd had to say twice before Emma's shell-shocked brain could make sense of the words. Walking her over to his vehicle, he asked bluntly, "What happened here?"

"It's Jeremy. Jeremy Hansen, my ex-husband. I—I think he's killed Russell." The whole story gushed from her, from this morning's unsettling phone call to the moment she'd found her assistant dangling. The only time she slowed down was when she handed the sheriff Russell's phone, with its cracked screen. She then passed over her own unlocked cell as well, and showed him the call log that would corroborate what she had told him about this morning's calls.

As he looked down at the screen, she continued filling in Fleming on Jeremy's troubled history. River pressed close beside her, whining and licking at the top of Emma's free hand in a clear attempt to soothe her.

"That's enough," Emma told the dog, gently pushing her muzzle away as it finally sank in that the sheriff's eyes were anything but sympathetic.

Confused by the man's obvious disapproval, she struggled to formulate a question. "Will you put out an APB?" she finally ventured. "Find Jeremy before he can do more damage?"

"I was wondering—" Fleming sounded droll as the

toothpick bobbed to the other side of his whiskered mouth "—when you might finally come up for air. First off, I think you mean a BOLO, for 'be on the lookout.' That's what those of us in law enforcement like to call 'em. And generally, we like 'em to be *our* idea—*once* we've determined that an actual crime has been committed."

"Of course a crime's been committed." Hadn't he listened to a single word she'd said? How could he really imagine this might be some sort of accident? "Russell knew how serious the company was about safety—and how fast they'd shut down our research project if we gave them an excuse by climbing up alone."

Fleming gave a sloppy shrug, the late morning sun glittering off his silver badge. "People get in a hurry, even bright young men who you'd swear knew better. They get things on their minds. They make mistakes. I've seen it plenty."

"Not Russell. He would never—"

"*You* went up alone, right? Without gloves or proper safety equipment."

"I *had* to. Because Russell was—he was hanging up there, and I didn't—I couldn't know for sure that he was…*gone*." Emma's voice broke on the awful word. Because Russell was still up above them, as far as she knew, his limbs stiffening like tree branches and his safety harness, which looked to have either slipped or broken, somehow caught up around his neck. She wanted to glance skyward, to confirm the terrible, impossible reality, but she kept her gaze locked on the sheriff's hard blue eyes.

"Maybe he thought he had good reason, too," said Fleming. "In a hurry to get that contraption fixed and the turbine back up and runnin'."

"Not without his tools," she countered. "I'm telling you, this is no coincidence, after Jeremy's calls this morning—"

"Calls your phone's log can't identify, from a man you're telling me is five hours away in Waco. That's where your ex-husband works, right?"

"*If* he showed up there this morning. He could've found me somehow, called from somewhere nearby."

Another sloppy shrug. "That's easy enough to check out. You have his employer's contact information?"

"You'll find it in my phone there, under RK Construction. But it's his uncle's business. Who's to say he won't cover for his nephew?" Emma shook her head, frustration boiling over. "I can guarantee you Jeremy's spent all summer convincing anyone who'll listen how he's the victim in all this, and I'm just some scheming tramp who twisted the authorities around my finger. You're going to have to dig deeper if you want the truth, find witnesses who aren't related. Maybe call the—"

The sheriff's hand shot out, clamping down on her wrist with such surprising speed that she gasped.

"This is Kingston County," he said around the toothpick, now clamped down hard between his molars. "*My* county. And no lady bird professor outta Austin's gonna run my investigation. Hear me?"

The normally gentle River exploded into barking, the hackles on her back raised and her lips peeled back as she leaped toward him. Releasing Emma, Fleming stepped back and drew his gun.

Terror ripping through her, she shouted, "River, *down! Down—stay!*"

The retriever hesitated before her training—or the urgency in her mistress's voice—kicked in. Lowering herself slowly, River kept her dark eyes locked on the sheriff, her muscles quivering and the low rumble of her growl vibrating like an idling truck engine.

"Please, no! She'd never bite you," Emma cried, her voice shaking even harder than her knees. "Please don't shoot my dog."

A stillness followed, thin as crystal. A silence filled by the pounding of her heart and interrupted by an unexpected voice off to her right.

"Charming your constituents again, Wallace?" said a man she hadn't heard approaching, a pair of plastic water bottles in his hands. Taller and leaner than the sheriff, he was darker as well, from his tanned skin to the challenge in his deep brown eyes and the black waves peeking out from beneath a finely made straw cowboy hat. Along with a light blue chambray shirt, he wore a pair of faded jeans, molded to his long legs. "Or maybe *bullying*'s the right word. You were always good at that."

The sheriff turned his head to glare at the intruder. "This is *my* scene, Kingston. Which means I'm in charge here—"

"Well, as the owner of the land it's sittin' on, on one of the hottest days this summer, I thought I'd bring by some cold drinks for everybody working—and condolences for the lady here." Ignoring the drawn gun completely, he nodded in Emma's direction. "I'm Beau Kingston, and we here at the ranch were so sorry when the news about your loss came over the scanner."

As the sheriff awkwardly holstered his weapon, Beau Kingston pressed one of the waters, blessedly cold and slick with condensation, into her shaking hand. The relief of it, the simple human consideration, had her choking back tears.

"If there's anything we can do to help," he told her, his voice softened with kindness, "all you have to do is ask."

With that, Kingston offered the second bottle to the sheriff, who had two dark sweat rings blooming in the armpits of his rumpled uniform shirt. "Here you go, coz. You look like you could use to cool down yourself."

"You're no cousin of mine," the sheriff grumbled as he swiped the bottle from the younger man's hand. Turning, he stalked away, muttering, "I've got work to do. Damned mongrel."

Emma wasn't entirely certain whether he was referring to Beau Kingston or her dog.

Before Fleming had made it three steps, he whipped around and pointed at her, his hand forming an approximation of a pointed gun. "*You.* Don't go too far. I'll get back to you as soon as I get my—my personnel coordinated."

Clearly, he was embarrassed to have been thrown off his game, diminished in front of her. And furious that she'd been there to witness the moment. Her instincts warned her the sheriff would remember it, just as Jeremy had remembered every insult. Would Fleming, too, take his humiliation out on her, especially if she didn't quickly distance herself from the man at her side?

As one of the deputies flagged down his superior, Beau Kingston snorted and shook his head in Fleming's direction before returning his attention to her. "How 'bout I crack that open for you?" he offered. "You look like you've been through hell and back."

"I—I've got it. Thank you, Mr. Kingston." Though she broke another blister doing it, she unscrewed the cap and took a long drink, emptying most of the bottle before coming up for air.

"It's Beau, and there's plenty more back at my truck." He hooked a thumb toward a deep-blue-and-chrome pickup bearing a license plate that read KINGSTN. "Come on over. You can wash your face and cool down."

"I don't think I should…" Though his offer seemed kindly meant, she had more than the sheriff's hurt pride to worry about in standing so close to this handsome man—and she'd have to be blind, not just traumatized, not to register the masculine appeal of the rancher's hard, clean-shaven jaw, the proud, straight nose and intelligent, dark eyes of a man in his prime. What if her ex was still somewhere nearby, watching her next move? After the horrific lengths he'd gone to in order to punish poor Russell for his harmless crush, would Jeremy lash out at this stranger for his thoughtfulness? Or kill her, too, for yielding to it, now that he'd crossed the irrevocable line between threats and homicide?

Emma's stomach swooped, and her abraded fingers dropped to cup the flesh below her navel. The confidence she'd spent the past ten months so carefully rebuilding crumbled into dust.

"C'mon, Miss…" the rancher began, his dark eyebrows rising in a query.

She pulled herself together to respond to Beau Kingston's unspoken question. To behave like a normal person instead of breaking down. "It's Emma. Emma Copley."

"At least come over in the shade while I get your dog some water." Beau nodded down toward River, whose panting continued unabated. "You don't want her getting heat exhaustion, do you?"

Responding to his reasonable tone, she took a steadying breath. As oxygen seeped past her panic, she assured herself that Jeremy was smart enough to leave the immediate area. Surely he'd realize that law enforcement would soon be climbing up the turbine, giving them a commanding view of the vicinity.

When Beau started walking, she found herself drawn in his wake. For River's sake, she told herself.

"I can't believe Wallace, keeping you out here baking in the hot sun," the rancher said as they approached his vehicle. "But then, nobody's ever accused my cousin of getting dealt a full hand when it comes to human kindness."

Or the animal type, either, she thought, shivering at the memory of Fleming drawing his weapon on poor River.

A pair of strapping firefighters arrived and lifted a large cooler from the pickup's bed. "Thanks for the drinks, Mr. Kingston," said a square-jawed man in his midthirties with curly golden-brown hair.

"Sure thing, fellas, and I'm still Beau to you, Patrick, same as back in high school. And we at the ranch appreciate all of you fellas, especially after that range fire you put out last month."

"Your donation was very much appreciated," said Patrick before nodding toward his younger comrade, a kid of no more than twenty whose flashing smile, smooth, golden-tan complexion and raven-haired good looks undoubtedly had young women from here to El Paso taking note. "And that barbecue you had the rookie here bring over. That was some serious brisket, man."

"I'd never send my ranch manager's son with anything but the best." Beau exchanged a quick grin with the younger man. "And anyway, it's the least I could do after all the head of cattle your crew's quick thinking and hard work saved me."

The two firefighters exchanged a look before setting down the cooler. Only then did they shake Beau's hand and offer their condolences to Emma, who had apparently become visible now that she had the blessing of a man who was clearly Kingston County royalty.

Once the firefighters left, Beau said, "Don't worry. I've got plenty more water in here." He reached inside a second, smaller cooler in the pickup bed.

"So, you and the sheriff," Emma asked, circling back to what Beau had said about his *cousin*, "you really are related?"

"Every family's got its black sheep." Beau shrugged, a spark of amusement in his eyes. "I'll leave it to you to figure out which of us is which."

On another day, she might've returned his smile. Even now, she felt the tug of it, the way the shifting seasons called vast flocks to warmer climes. But at the thought of Russell still up on that turbine, nausea quickly followed, with horror, disbelief and guilt close on its heels. Shaking her head, she said, "I should—I should go to my Jeep. I have a bowl for River in there."

"I'm sure I've got one in here," he said, then looked down at River. "C'mon, pup. How about that drink now?"

River fanned her fringed tail and went to him. Standing in the shade of the truck's cab, Emma hung back, watching as the dog lapped her way through his offering before slobbering all over his jeans as she accepted an ear scratch.

"We mongrels have to stick together, don't we?" he told her, an effort at good humor edged with what sounded very much like bitterness.

It made Emma wonder about his real reasons for stepping in after Fleming drew his gun. But whatever Beau's agenda, she didn't have the strength to refuse when he offered her a second bottle, already cracked open. Next came a neatly folded, dampened bandanna he'd retrieved from the truck's cab.

After wringing it out, he passed it to her. "This'll make you feel better. Take my word for it."

Numbly, Emma nodded and then washed her face, neck and hands. After she had finished, he produced a second, dry cloth.

"This one's clean, too," he said, "in case you want to dry off. And I've got a little first aid kit here. How about some antiseptic for those palms?"

"Thanks," she said, rubbing the salve on the broken skin as he'd suggested. And feeling the relief of the warm wind blowing against her cool, still slightly damp skin.

"Why are you—why are you doing all this?" As she crumpled up the dry cloth, suspicion filtered through her pain and grief. "This isn't about some childhood beef you have with Sheriff Fleming?"

"Oh, it's a heck of a lot more than just some kid stuff," Beau said before adding, "unless you want to count what that fool's ugly talk is doin' To *my* kids…"

"It's not that I don't appreciate what you've done for me, but whatever kind of feud you two have going," she continued, too overwhelmed by thoughts of Russell and of Jeremy to ask questions, "I can't afford to end up in the middle of it."

Beau frowned and shook his head. "You're absolutely right. That's not your worry—and it's not the reason I came, either. I'm here because a man died on my land today, a young man who was part of a team—*your* team—that I personally signed off on working on my property, Dr. Copley."

Surprised by his use of the honorific, she said, "You—you saw to that personally? I'd just assumed some assistant or ranch manager—" *Maybe your wife*, she'd been about to add, recalling the reference to his children, but she hadn't seen a wedding band, nor even a strip of paler skin to mark where he had worn one.

"That was me, before my father's death this past April. Which made me feel I ought to be the one to come today."

"That's very kind of you, but what happened here—it's not your fault."

"I know it's not my fault," he said, his dark eyes studying her so intently that she began to feel self-conscious. "Do *you* know it's not yours?"

A flush of heat engulfed her, making her want to drop her gaze. Instead she faced him squarely, her heart stuttering at the question she hadn't yet dared to ask herself.

"Why on earth would you ask me that?" She sounded more than a little defensive, even to her own ears. *How on earth did he guess I'm to blame?*

Reaching down to scratch her dog's ears once more, he stood there looking at her, the saddest smile she'd ever seen contrasting with the warmth of his bronzed skin. "I could tell you it's because he was your student. But the truth of it is that guilt's written on your face as plain as day for anyone to see...or maybe only anyone who's been there."

Chapter 2

Beau was as surprised as Emma Copley looked by the words he'd blurted. Most days, he did a better job keeping the painful memories of Melissa's death three years before locked down tight. Lately, he'd had an easier time of it, so busy raising two lively young boys and running the ranch his father had left him to dwell on things that no amount of self-recrimination would ever change.

But there was something about the fresh wound of this woman's devastation that brought it all back. Something that made him want to assure her that no matter how horrific or overwhelming things seemed, it was possible to go on breathing.

"I didn't kill him," Emma protested, a tear breaking free from long, damp lashes to track its way down a face he found lovely, despite its current grief-blotched puffiness. "I would never think of hurting anyone."

He wanted to reassure her that that wasn't what he'd

meant. But instinct had him saying nothing, sensing there was more to come. Feeling it in the same way he might anticipate the next move of a flighty half-broke filly he was gentling or a spooked calf trying to charge around his mount to race back to its mother. To give her space to breathe, he grabbed his own dog's lead from the cab, found tucked beneath his youngest's booster seat, to lend her.

When Beau looked again, Emma's thin shoulders slumped, and he heard the faint sound of her sigh.

"But I do think—" she said, pushing back bedraggled tawny hair behind her shoulder. Like the rest of her, her once-white V-neck T-shirt and olive cargo pants bore a thick layer of grime. "I believe my ex-husband's done this because he thought— He's dangerously unstable."

"You said *ex*-husband, didn't you?"

She nodded stiffly. "I had to divorce Jeremy, for everybody's safety. Not only mine, but everyone I knew. Something happened to his mind." She shook her head. "I'll never understand what went wrong, but he wouldn't listen to reason, wouldn't let me get him help."

In her pale green eyes, Beau saw that she was haunted, just as he was, by the choices she'd been forced to make.

"Sounds like he didn't leave you much choice," he said.

"I thought—I thought divorce would be the end of it, that we could both move on with our lives. But lately, he's started up again with all the same old nonsense. Forget the no-contact order."

"But what makes you think that this—" Beau nodded in the direction of the turbine's base—and immediately regretted inadvertently directing her attention to the spot where two of the firefighters were moving a sheet-draped body on a stretcher to a gurney. "What makes you think your ex-husband could've forced a grown man up there?

Or shoved him off the top? If he'd wanted your assistant dead, don't you think he would've found some simpler way to do it? One that didn't involve two people climbing all those ladders?"

Her hand rising to cover her mouth, she watched the scene beside the turbine unfold. Not hearing a word he said, if he was reading her correctly.

"Look at me," Beau directed. "Or better yet, focus on your dog here. It's River, right?"

She didn't answer.

"Come on, Dr. Copley," he coaxed. "Emma?"

Her gaze snapped to meet his before her eyes narrowed in a look of fierce concentration. "The sheriff never went up." Color flamed in her cheeks, and her voice shook with anger. "He couldn't have, so quickly. And neither of the deputies is wearing a safety harness, either. Which means your *cousin* didn't take me seriously. Didn't even bother investigating to see if this *could've* been a murder."

Beau looked around and saw that she was right. Wallace was leaning his lazy ass against his vehicle, talking on his cell phone while using his free hand to mop sweat from his forehead with a wadded handkerchief.

Beau noticed, too, a couple of men he hadn't spotted earlier emerging from the turbine's base, both wearing green-embroidered white coveralls identifying them as Green Horizons technicians. He'd bet his last heifer that they, likely the only experienced climbers on-site knowledgeable about the company's equipment and procedures, had been the ones who'd actually gone up to get the body.

"Hey, wait up," he called as Emma made a beeline straight for Wallace, her head lowered and arms swinging. With the still-untethered dog bounding after her, Beau followed, too, adding, "Hold on, I don't think this is a good idea."

She stopped abruptly and pinned him with an annoyed look. "It's not that I don't appreciate your help before, but I don't remember asking your opinion."

"He grabbed you," Beau reminded her, "drew his gun."

Her brows rose. "Honestly, I hadn't thought that mattered to you half as much as your grudge."

"Why do you think I came running? He might have the voters around here fooled—" Beau's own father had had a hand in that, ignoring Beau's opinion to support his nephew's campaign to unseat the former sheriff "—but my cousin's a damned hothead, and he's hated dogs ever since he got torn up by a stray back as a kid. Had to go through rabies shots and everything."

"Maybe you'd better hold River, then. She'll be fine with you. I just have to make Sheriff Fleming understand that he can bluster all he wants to. I'm not going to sit down and shut up while he takes the path of least resistance on this. And there's no way I'm letting my ex-husband get away with murder. Or sitting around and wondering who'll be next."

Leaning forward, Beau told the dog, "It's okay, girl." When her trusting brown eyes turned to him and her tail waved at his reassuring tone, he snapped the leash onto her collar and told Emma, "I've got her. Now *you'd* better get a firm grip on your temper. My cousin most likely isn't going to shoot you, but unless you wanta get bit, I'd suggest you treat him like a bear with a bad toothache."

"You mean the way *you* did?" she asked irritably.

"Only because as much as my cousin would probably love to shoot, I'm the one who got the Kingston name, not him."

"So that's, like, what around here? A big, gold-plated get-out-of-jail-free card?" she asked.

"It has its benefits," he admitted, liking that as an outsider, she had no idea how unlikely a recipient he was of family legacy. And no clue that his old man, wherever he was, was having the last laugh imagining the surprise Beau had gotten when he'd found the ranch's second set of books…

The *real* books, which showed a number of dubious investments in the years prior to his father's death and a shocking amount of debt. Debt that made the income from the new turbines to be constructed next spring—an expansion that Beau himself had negotiated with the company in exchange for Green Horizon's prepayment of the thirty-year lease money—absolutely crucial to ensuring the ranch's survival.

"Okay, okay," said Emma, drawing herself to her full height—which couldn't be more than five six—as she visibly struggled for control. "I might not have the Kingston name in my back pocket," she said, "but I've navigated enough male egos in academia to know how to make my point without leaving too many footprints on their fragile feelings."

"Not on a day as upsetting as this one, I'll bet you haven't," Beau said before movement attracted his attention. It was followed by the solid *chunk* of Wallace's Tahoe's door as the sheriff slammed it and then spun on his heel to face them.

"Hell's bells," Beau burst out, recognizing the hard set of his cousin's jaw as he pocketed his phone and strode purposefully in their direction. "Looks like I won't have to worry overmuch about *you* agitating Wallace. Whatever he's heading here to tell us, that bear looks good'n poked already."

"Hold her tight," Emma urged Beau as River lunged forward, her deep barks ringing as the sheriff zeroed in. Emma could hardly blame her dog since the stern set of his jaw and his reddened face had her own heart pounding.

"That's enough. Sit, River," Beau kept his voice low and his grip firm on leash.

The dog responded to his assertive tone, dropping to her haunches. Still, she was quivering with energy, her gaze latched onto the lawman.

"Stay," Emma added, worried that not even the strong rancher could keep the seventy-pound retriever from lunging if the sheriff made any threatening moves.

"Thought you oughta know," Fleming said, his gaze burning into her. "I just spoke to your husband out in—"

"My *ex*-husband," she pointed out.

"Your ex-husband then," Fleming continued, scowling at the interruption "*In Waco*—and he didn't seem one bit surprised you'd try to push this off on him."

She recoiled, her cheeks blazing. *"What?"*

"His boss told me the same thing." The ever-present toothpick tilted, caught up in a smile that didn't touch the sheriff's hard blue eyes. "Says it's just another of those divorce deals. Woman scorned and all that, you're desperate enough to make up any kind of nonsense just to get back at him."

Two men walked up behind Fleming, the first deputy she'd spoken to and one of the Green Horizons techs.

Refusing to give either a chance to interrupt, Emma said, "First off, Sheriff." Her voice vibrated with humiliation. Fury. Frustration at his ready acceptance of a man's, a stranger's, word above her own. "*I* was the one to divorce Jeremy Hansen, the one to ask for and receive a no-contact order after he—"

"I don't think it's necessary," the sheriff said, signaling

the two newcomers to hold up for a minute, "to get into the sordid details of your marriage here, Miz Copley."

"*Doctor* Copley." Though Emma wasn't normally one to pull the PhD card, she wasn't about to let this man shame her into silence. "And these are hardly irrelevant trifles."

"Whatever you want to call yourself," he said dismissively, "what we need to focus on right now is what happened today with your assistant."

"You can look it up yourself," she said. "There are police reports, court records. Jeremy's on probation for assault and terroristic threats against people that I've worked with. And he called me again this morning, sounding drunk and angry, shortly before I—before I found…" Her heart stuttered as she remembered that dizzying moment when she'd looked up, the world's axis tilting slightly as the reality slammed down on her hard.

She hadn't realized she was swaying until she felt a steadying hand on her shoulder. Beau Kingston's hand, from where he'd moved up to stand behind her. Only his touch felt as big and firm and comforting as Fleming's had felt wrong before.

A wave of dizziness followed; the sight of all the emergency vehicles, of the uniformed men—and one female EMT—washed over her like the hot and humid breath of August.

"He sounded stone-cold sober on the phone to me, Dr. Copley, so whatever you want to believe, you need to listen to me on this. Your husband *wasn't* here. He couldn't have been," Fleming insisted. "I spoke to his boss, too, and he's swearing they've been installing custom cabinets since first thing this morning, with at least three other witnesses—all of 'em willin' to vouch that Mr. Hansen's been there the whole time. Not making any nasty phone calls. Not going anywhere."

"They're *lying*," she insisted, her vision hazing with tears. Because maybe, as Beau Kingston, who gently squeezed her shoulder from behind, had suggested, it was too much to believe that Jeremy had somehow driven here, onto her and Russell's turf, and forced an athletic young man, an experienced climber, off a three-hundred-plus-foot tower. But that didn't—couldn't—mean that Jeremy was blameless. "He *did* call me. I swear he did. You saw it on my phone's log."

Fleming passed her back her cell. "I saw that *someone* called, sure. But you could've been confused about who it was," he allowed, his tone softening, "overwhelmed by everything that's happened. You've had a helluva day, after all. Once you've calmed down a little, had a little rest, might be you'll remember things a little different."

"I know my ex's voice. I *know* it," she insisted, looking around as her desperation grew to be believed by any of the men around her. "And even if he didn't come here, who's to say he couldn't have arranged this, talked one of his crazy friends into driving down and taking out what he saw as the competition? Or maybe Jeremy scraped together enough money to hire some lowlife to do it for him. I've seen things like that on the news, where somebody gets caught on camera trying to have a wife or girlfriend or a rival murdered."

"Do you hear yourself?" the sheriff asked. "Hear how much energy you're willing to put into twisting facts whichever way you have to just to pin what's sure to be an accident on a man that any fool can see you've got a grudge against?"

She blinked, her heart jackhammering against her rib cage. *Had* she pushed things too far, looking for an explanation that meshed with the instincts screaming that Russell's *accident*, as Fleming was already putting it, on the heels of Jeremy's phone call, had been anything but a coincidence?

The other deputy looked down, while the Green Horizons technician in his coveralls blew out a deep breath and looked away when she tried to catch his eye. A glance back at Beau, at the chagrin, the even more distressing pity in his dark eyes, confirmed her worst fears.

No one here believed her, nor were any of them likely to ever listen to anything more she had to say on the subject. To them, she was hysterical—a shrill, spurned woman who refused to accept their superior male judgment. Or to understand that all of Russell's intelligence and training, strength and youth were no match against a moment's inattention.

Even when her heart cried out that the sheriff—that everyone who'd gathered in this godforsaken hellhole—had the facts completely wrong.

Chapter 3

Five days later

As he sat seething in the third row of the local memorial service for Russell Jorgenson, Beau carefully uncurled his fist and fought to slow his breathing. With a glance to his left, he spotted the reproachfully arched eyebrow of his petite blonde aunt Alicia, whose many years spent looking after Beau had gifted her with the ability to foresee and head off trouble. The look served as a reminder that he hadn't come this evening for the purpose of flattening his least favorite cousin. Or giving Wallace the verbal flaying he had coming, either.

But the sheriff's smug expression as he strutted into the rear of a community center named for their common ancestor wasn't making things any easier. Especially when he made a point of looking Beau straight in the eye and smirking, clearly reveling in the knowledge that, just this morning, Beau had been served with papers informing him of the lawsuit Wallace filed against him. A lawsuit that would likely expose Beau's two sons, the small boys sitting to his right, to the same sort of name-calling and abuse that had made Beau's own childhood a living hell.

No one wants you around. Don't you get that, little bastard? Beau could still hear Wallace, the leader of the pack of blue-eyed cousins, could still see him sneering downward as if Beau were lower than a cockroach. With Beau's older half brother, who'd considered him an insufferable pest but hated Wallace's two-bit punk act more, away, Beau's real friends, the Spanish-speaking hands' sons, banned from the house, and his aunt inside wrangling sandwiches, there'd been no one to come to Beau's defense. And no one to stop the teen, who'd had seven years and seventy pounds on the scrawny, deeply-tanned eight-year-old Beau had been back in those days, from shoving him, the way Wallace had shoved him so many times before. Except that push, beside the pool, had been hard enough to lift Beau from his feet and send him flying backward. Beau remembered his skinny arms windmilling as he'd come down on the flagstone—and then *nothing* after the back of his skull struck a landscaping rock. The incident had cost him more than twenty stitches and a week out of school before he'd quit seeing double. It had also earned him, rather than his father's sympathy, a look of pure disgust as he had told Beau, *High time you quit whining like a baby and learned to stand up for your own damned self.*

His own two boys, Beau swore, were never going to suffer like that. And they were never going to wonder for a single second if their father had their back. Or if a part of him—a part his own father would never admit aloud but had indicated in a thousand different ways—believed the rumors about the dark-eyed, raven-haired child his second wife had left him. The child that Beau's mother, a sweet-faced blonde he remembered only from a few surviving photos, had told everyone who'd listen was the spitting image of her Sicilian grandfather.

This evening, as the reverend spoke from the podium of the promise of heaven, Beau shot Wallace a final look that foretold the personal hell Beau intended to rain down on him. Gratified when the jackass broke eye contact first, Beau turned to make certain that neither of the boys had found some mischief to get up to. Six-year-old Leland, who would soon start first grade, had disappeared into his own world, playing with a small toy car he'd discreetly pulled from a pocket. On the other side of him, eight-year-old Cort rested his elbows on his knobby knees and kept his dark head bowed. Like his brother, he was clearly marking off the seconds until he could finally escape this boring adult function and head over to the Crazy Cow—a new shop that was all the rage with the elementary set—for the ice cream sundaes they'd been promised if they could manage to keep still.

Beau smiled, relieved that the boys hadn't seemed to equate the family duty they'd been dragged to this evening with the funeral they'd attended a few short months ago. There, the same minister, the distinguished-looking Reverend Turner, had spoken of their grandfather in equally solemn tones.

Today, however, there was no coffin in front of the rows of padded folding chairs, just a blown-up photo on a stand between two tasteful floral displays. The picture, taken against a backdrop of snowcapped mountains, showed a youthful red-haired man with a backpack slung over one broad shoulder and a cocky grin across his sunburned face. While the funeral itself would be held in Russell's home state of Washington, this memorial service had been arranged for the benefit of the fellow students who'd driven down to the town of Pinto Creek from the university in Austin, two representatives of Green Horizons Energy, and a dozen or so locals who wanted to pay their respects. Along with Emma Copley in the front row, the woman he had met on what had surely been one of the worst days of her life.

Beau looked up in time to catch the flutter of her black skirt that, despite its modest length, revealed a glimpse of shapely legs as Emma moved up the steps to the low platform. Against her simple white blouse, her face was drawn and her pale green eyes puffy, the mascara slightly smeared. But it was her obvious struggle to compose herself that captured his attention—that and the flick of her slim wrist as she flipped a lock of sun-streaked, light brown hair off her face and behind her shoulder and looked around the room.

For a split second, her gaze touched on his; he saw a glimmer of recognition before she abruptly looked away. It didn't surprise him, given how completely she'd closed off to him after Wallace had shut down her accusations against her ex-husband that terrible afternoon. She'd also failed to respond to the note Beau had sent to the motel where she was staying later asking if he might send a meal or assist with any of the necessary arrangements.

He'd taken the hint. She hadn't forgiven him for failing to swoop in and defend her theory that Russell Jorgenson had been murdered. But he reminded himself that as sorry as he felt for her sudden loss, he didn't really know her. Told himself that with two kids, a ranch and scores of employees to worry about, he had neither the time nor the energy to get wrapped up in a stranger's troubles. Especially when, as much at he hated Wallace, Beau had to admit his cousin had had a point about her twisting reason into knots to cast her ex-husband as a murderer.

Beau wouldn't have been here at all tonight if not for his aunt, a firm traditionalist who spoke passionately—and often—about the responsibilities their family owed the community. She'd reminded him this morning that the family would be expected to put in an appearance at today's memorial service—*unless you want Wallace*, she'd added with a disdainful sniff, *to imagine he has you worried with this lawsuit nonsense of his.*

After that, there'd been no question that his family would be here. Just as there was no way Beau could take his eyes off Emma Copley, who looked as if she'd give anything to be elsewhere.

"Thank you all for coming...to pay your respects," she said, her gaze lingering on the young people sitting near the front before moving on to look over the other twenty or so gathered. "Russell Jorgenson was one of the most personable, hardworking and dedicated young biologists I've had the—the pleasure of working with during my tenure at the university."

She went on for a few minutes, her voice gathering strength and warmth as she continued recounting her dead student's virtues. As Beau took in the pain etched into her delicate features, he recalled giving the elegy for a father who'd run hot and cold with him his whole life—his struggle to find kind words about a man who had offered him so few.

But he'd somehow gotten through it, unlike Emma, whose voice had sputtered to a stop mid-sentence. Her eyes closing, she gripped the lectern, splotches of color rising to her cheeks as those assembled exchanged concerned looks and the awkward silence stretched on.

Beau was gripped with the impulse to get up from his seat and whisk her away to someplace private, where the raw wreckage of her emotions wouldn't be on display. He checked himself, reminding himself that stepping in and rescuing her from one bad situation didn't make her his responsibility for life.

Leland looked up from his toy car. "What's wrong with the pretty lady?" he asked, his lisping voice, thanks to a missing front tooth, too loud for the room's breathless stillness.

"Shh. Just give her a moment," Beau said, hoping she would recover on her own.

As the delay drew out, Reverend Turner went to her side and quietly offered, "Please, miss, let me help you back to your seat."

When she shook her head, the whispers started, and two young people, clearly college students, given the girl's piercings and rainbow-streaked blond pixie cut and the dark-skinned young man's expensively torn denim, got up and hurried toward her.

"Dr. Copley?" the girl said, as she trotted up the two steps. "It's okay. We can take it from—"

Emma raised a palm to stop their progress. But her gaze moved toward the room's rear, where Wallace had moved to sit in the back row.

Was she about to blow up at him, here and now? Accuse him of somehow influencing the medical examiner's report? Or would she once more bring up her outlandish theory about her ex-husband and hired assassins?

Or was her ire directed this time at the two men in dark green polo shirts embroidered with the Green Horizons logo that Wallace was seated next to? Beau had been, as the landowner, copied on an email that the company sent saying that until their engineers completed a thorough review of safety procedures and equipment at the wind farm, no one—particularly Emma and her students—was permitted to climb any of the towers for any reason.

Reading the pain in her expression, he felt a pang of guilt, remembering how, on receiving that message, he hadn't thought first of the victim of this horrific accident. Instead, Beau had worried only that the investigation might delay this spring's construction of the new wind turbines—and the payment he was counting on to ensure the ranch's future.

Still, he felt certain she'd regret making a scene at her student's service, so Beau impulsively faked a cough—one loud enough to prompt an annoyed look from his aunt. But the ploy appeared to distract Emma and wipe away whatever dark thoughts had held her in place.

"Sorry, everyone," she offered, waving her hand and adding, "I'm afraid I haven't been myself these last few days. But thank you all again for coming. Russell... Russell would've been so touched to see you here."

His eyes full of relief, Reverend Turner smiled his approval and reached to help her off the platform. Ignoring his outstretched hand, Emma deftly ducked around him and trotted down the two steps. She paused to grab a small purse she'd left on the front seat, before—without slowing her stride a bit—she rushed down the center aisle. Shoulders tight, she darted straight past the sheriff and the Green Horizons engineers and through the rear exit without a backward glance.

Though it was nearly eight in the evening, the late August sun was only now kissing the horizon. Red-orange streamers of the dying light cast long shadows, which pointed like fingers from the parked vehicles and back toward the one-story beige brick Josiah Kingston Community Center, which Emma had just fled. By the time she reached her Jeep, she was breathing hard, the silky material of her white blouse sticking to her back from a combination of the sticky heat and nervous perspiration. A wave of dizziness made her wonder when she'd last eaten, or snatched more than a fitful hour or two of sleep.

No wonder her nerves were fraying. Otherwise, she'd never have fled the memorial service instead of remaining, as she should have, to greet those who'd come to honor Russell and offering comfort to those students who'd made the hours-long drive from Austin to be here for their friend.

But when she'd looked up to see Sheriff Fleming in the back, all she could think of was how for days on end, he'd been ignoring her messages, having his receptionist cancel appointment after appointment, and even slipping out the back to avoid her the day she had followed him inside after spotting him parking his marked Tahoe. A wave of pure frustration broke over her, followed by fury that he would dare show up here and act as if he'd done anything beyond rushing to close the books on Russell's death as quickly as he could. Presumably so he could get back to his pressing work of issuing parking tickets and loose livestock citations.

She'd thought of calling him out on it right then and there, letting his constituents know what kind of useless slacker they'd elected. But Beau Kingston had happened to cough at that moment. The sight of him sitting with his little family, along with the concern she read in his handsome face, was enough to make her lose her nerve. So instead, she'd wrapped up as best she could and fled, escaping the staring eyes and buzzing voices.

It had probably made Fleming's day, seeing her unnerved, defeated. Did he imagine she was about to pack her things, just as she'd been asked to gather the personal effects from Russell's motel room to be sent back to his grieving family, and head out of town—and out of his hair forever?

At the thought, she swallowed hard, remembering how many times she'd done exactly that. Backed off instead of standing her ground, let things drop she never should have. Pretended to see Jeremy's side of things in an effort to cheer him up—or at least to avoid giving his resentment and jealousy of her professional success more ammunition.

Too long. Her hand reached down to cup the empty hollow where a new life had once taken root. A possibility she'd never planned for, hadn't even, with the state of her marriage, dreamed she'd wanted. Yet she still mourned its loss keenly ten months later.

And now, seeing Russell, too, cut down so cruelly, imagining him another victim to Jeremy's cruelty and her weakness…

You have a backbone still. So use it.

Abruptly, Emma cranked the steering wheel and pulled her Jeep behind the building, in the shadows of a large metal trash receptacle. Steeling her resolve, she climbed out and peered around the building's corner, praying that Sheriff Fleming might hang around a while as the gathering broke up, maybe to shake the hands of some of his constituents before heading for his Tahoe.

Only Emma would be waiting for him, breaking from cover to cut off his return. And once she had him there, in this semipublic space, she would finally make him listen. And tell him that, though she'd accepted it was possible she'd been wrong about Jeremy's involvement, she was more convinced than ever that her instincts about Russell's so-called "accident" had been right on one count.

He hadn't been a careless young man. Not in any aspect of his work, nor in the documentation he'd been secretly gathering, proof she'd found hidden in his motel room, that created a multimillion-dollar motive for someone to want him dead.

As she watched the first attendees begin leaving the community center, Emma heard something clatter against side of the metal trash bin, followed by the thump of footsteps just behind her.

Someone hiding back there. Jumping out and rushing toward me.

Raw terror propelled her toward the open, where someone leaving the service would be sure to see her. Would hear her screaming—except a pair of hands grabbed her neck from behind, clamped down on her windpipe.

Unable to make a sound, she fought like a snared bobcat, kicking backward with her heel, flinging an elbow, and then clawing at the iron grip cutting off her airway. Her blood roared in her ears. She felt a nail rip. Felt a sandal come off as inky blackness swarmed her vision...

A darkness filled with terror and her own impending death.

Chapter 4

After shaking a few hands and telling the university students how sorry he'd been to hear of the loss of their friend, Beau noticed his freckled eight-year-old shifting restlessly from foot to foot and darting glances toward the door. Checking on the smaller Leland, Beau found the boy staring, transfixed, at the raised platform, with its photos and flowers—and especially the lectern and microphone in front.

"We'd best get moving," he whispered to his aunt, "before one of these hooligans makes a break for freedom—or life on the stage." Though Cort would rather vanish into one of his books than call attention to himself, it would be just like Beau's younger son to spontaneously decide to try his hand at singing—or perhaps stand-up comedy—at a stranger's memorial service. Especially considering his recent fascination with one of those TV talent competitions that had featured a couple of performing kids.

"Honestly, those two." Aunt Alicia emitted a sigh of

exasperation, though one corner of her perfectly lipsticked mouth curved upward. She was leaning more heavily than usual on her violet cane—color-coordinated, as always, with one of her many pantsuits. It was just one more sign that a long day of "herding the wild and woolly," as she called the childcare duties she wouldn't hear of allowing Beau to ease by hiring a nanny, was getting to be a bit much for her these days.

"I'll take them from here," he said, feeling guilty about having to rely on her so much lately. "You go on home and put your feet up. Relax for a change." Since he'd had to meet with his attorney about Wallace's ridiculous lawsuit earlier, she'd driven the boys here in her vintage Cadillac.

Her penciled eyebrows shot upward. "And miss out on my ice cream sundae? Perish the thought."

The two shared a smile and ushered both boys toward the exit. As Beau held open the door for them, Wallace approached, maneuvering his way past Beau and his sons to the family's unofficial matriarch. "You're looking well, Aunt Alicia."

Normally, she would she would say something minimally polite in response, ever reluctant to publicly air the clan's dirty laundry. But this time, when she glared up at Wallace, Beau thought for a moment she might raise her violet cane and crack it down over her nephew's head.

Drawing herself up to her full height of five feet, she hissed, "We have nothing to say to each other, *Wally*."

Wallace—who'd long bristled at any mention of the childhood nickname—reddened and let her go, only to glare at Beau with blue eyes burning with resentment. Blue eyes that matched those of Beau's aunt and his late father—every member of the family except Beau and his sons.

For a moment, the two men stood face-to-face, Beau looking down at a man who had never seemed smaller. But Beau himself would be smaller still if he were to start something with the grasping, jealous tool now, so instead, he gave a snort of disgust before breezing past— or starting to.

He stopped short along with his boys, all of their heads turning toward the sound of a sharp cry from outside. Even Aunt Alicia, who didn't hear as well, turned to stare toward the rear to the building, where an even louder shriek rose. A sound Beau instantly recognized as a woman's mortal terror.

"Get them back inside, now!" he told his aunt as his training from his military years came rushing back, and he was instantly off in a crouching run, keeping to the building's perimeter and heading for the trouble.

"Right behind you," Wallace called.

A glance back confirmed it, just as the all-business look on his cousin's face assured Beau that he had heard the scream, too. Wallace's gun was drawn and for one chilling moment, Beau realized how easily, how permanently, their rivalry might be settled in the early evening gloom by an "accidental" discharge.

But the sounds from behind the brick building—a thud, a clang, a grunt and the words, "Get *off*!"—left him no room for indecision. For strained as the voice was, it sent a shock of recognition through Beau.

"Emma! Emma Copley!" he yelled as he closed on the rear corner of the building, caring more about breaking off an attack in progress than he did about surprising the assailant.

"Sheriff's department," Wallace boomed in his deepest cop voice, though he had fallen about a dozen yards behind Beau's longer strides. "Hands where we can see 'em! Freeze!"

Beau might have held up for a few steps, allowing his armed cousin to bypass and precede him. But it wasn't only his marine corps training but the memory of Emma's struggle for composure and the hint of tears in her green eyes before she'd left the podium inside that had him blasting around the corner, his heart pounding out the message: *help her, help her now, before it's too late.*

He spotted her alone, standing in the deepest shadow, bracing herself between the wall and the dumpster. Blood poured down her forehead and the right side of her face, and the silky white blouse she had been wearing was torn and hanging off one shoulder. Ignoring the impulse to go to her aid, he swept the rear of the building with his gaze and checked behind and inside the receptacle for further threats.

As Wallace joined them, Emma gestured wildly toward the opposite corner of the building. Teeth chattering, she fought to tell them, "He—he ran off. W-went that—that—"

Beau moved in to keep her from falling as her knees gave out. "It's all right," he told her, hoping it was only from the aftermath of the massive adrenaline rush and not a serious injury, maybe a head wound judging from the gash high on her forehead. "Let's just get you off your feet."

When he tried to pick her up, she abruptly straightened, hobbling away on a single sandal. "I can stand. Don't touch me!"

She made it a few steps before pitching sideways, and this time, he did scoop her up, saying, "Let me, please. We're here to help you," and lifting her above the oily residue and broken glass littering the concrete.

He felt the tension in her muscles and her body's violent shaking, but his words must have registered, because she said, "Okay."

Taking it as permission, he carried her toward the grassy edge of the open land behind the center. He paused, however, looking out over the twilit expanse of an overgrown pasture choked with tall scrub trees and drought-scorched grasses. The perfect hiding place for Emma's attacker if he'd only jumped a string or two of barbed wire, rather than running around the building's edge where she had indicated.

Or could she have been wrong about that, shocked and injured as she appeared to be?

"Stay here and see to her," Wallace told Beau, his drawn gun slanted downward and his breathing heavy. Other footsteps preceded the arrival of a younger man with buzzed blond hair, whom Beau recognized as an off-duty deputy who sometimes assisted Reverend Turner at the church.

Pointing at him, the sheriff ordered, "With me. We need to run down the man who did this. He armed?" he asked Emma.

Still trembling, she shook her head as her remaining sandal dropped to the ground. "I don't—I didn't see. It was all too fast. I—I don't even know *who*—"

But Wallace and his deputy were already running, the younger man quickly outpacing his superior after bending forward to pull a backup weapon from an ankle holster. Beau wanted to go after them, to make damned sure that whoever had hurt Emma was apprehended—but not before sustaining some injuries of his own. Instead, he turned his attention to the woman in his arms.

"Let's get you out of here," he told her, carrying her away from the weed-choked pasture and across the parking lot toward his pickup.

More people were emerging from the service now, and an exclamation of alarm rose as several caught sight of Emma in his arms. She turned her face against his shoulder, her body shrinking against him as a handful of individuals ran toward them, peppering them with questions.

"Gracious me! What happened?"

"Should I get an ambulance?"

"Have you called 911 yet? Never mind. I've got 'em on the line!"

Emma's words rose from the level of his chest. "Please get me out of here. Right now. I don't want my students—*anybody*—seeing me like this."

Her halting words brought back what she'd told him earlier about having to divorce her jealous husband for *everybody's safety*. This, he thought, was a woman who had hid her battered face before. A woman abused by the same man she had so stubbornly insisted had killed her graduate assistant.

Had the spineless SOB tracked her here, stalking and attacking her this afternoon? Could she be right, too, to think her student had been murdered?

Before he could process the question—or wonder if Emma had been truthful when she'd claimed she hadn't seen the man who'd hurt her—Beau spotted his aunt and the boys. "Can you take them over to the Crazy Cow?" he called to Aunt Alicia. "I'm running Dr. Copley to the ER to get her checked out. I'll see you all back home."

His aunt nodded before turning away Cort and Leland, who were straining to get an eyeful and trying to shoehorn in their own questions about what happened to the pretty lady among the clamor, and hurrying them toward her car.

Moments later, Beau placed Emma in his truck's passenger seat and buckled her in after asking her students to give her some air.

"I need you two to let the sheriff know we'll be at the ER," he told the student with the ripped jeans and his friend with the rainbow hair before turning his attention to Emma.

"Here you go," he said in the same tone he'd use to calm one of his sons after a nightmare as he handed Emma a clean towel he'd found in the rear seat.

"Press this against your forehead as tight as you can stand it to slow down the bleeding. Then we'll get you out of here and away from all these people."

The pain in her eyes eased, replaced by a look of gratitude. Wadding up one end of the towel, she did as he'd suggested and allowed the rest of the material to drape down to hide her face. Was she hiding the shame of a once-loving relationship that had spiraled out of her control, or was he misreading this? Was there something else she was concealing?

Waving off further questions, he climbed behind the wheel. As they sped away, Beau glanced at her, noticing her bruised legs and recalling the way her shirt was torn open.

"You weren't—? He didn't—" Beau stopped himself abruptly, unable to choke out any reference to sexual assault. Though he'd dealt with a number of such incidents during his military career, the idea of such a thing happening here in Pinto Creek, to her, in the few minutes after she had left the community center, had his stomach flipping.

"No, thank God," she said, apparently following his train of thought. "He didn't have the chance to… I don't even know what he wanted. I only know he g-grabbed my neck, and then I broke away, fell forward. He tried to get hold of me again, but I—I screamed and kicked, and then I guess he heard you coming. All I know is he was gone, and there w-was all this blood."

As he slowed for an intersection, he caught her full-body shudder out of the corner of his eye.

"It doesn't look too bad," he tried to reassure her. "Facial cuts can bleed a lot, but a stitch or two, and you'll be—"

Bending forward, she was sick, and his foot mashed down on the accelerator harder.

"You're still here?" Emma said as Beau peeked his head around the curtained-off emergency department exam area hours later. "I told you when they brought me back, you didn't need to wait around. I'm fine, or I will be."

It was only partially a lie. Following an exam, a CT scan and four sutures just below her hairline, the doctor had confirmed that she would soon recover. But Emma couldn't stop shaking every time her brain replayed the sound of her attacker's fast-approaching footsteps, or the feeling of his iron grip on her throat. Whoever had attacked her had surely meant to leave her as dead as Russell. She could not imagine that the two acts weren't related.

Her pulse fluttered, and her stomach tightened. What if he came after her again?

"You're sure you're all right? You look a little queasy." Beau shifted his suit jacket, which he'd removed, to drape it casually over one well-muscled forearm, bared now since he'd rolled his sleeves up.

"The doctor says there's nothing serious."

"So, no concussion?" he asked. "I was worried, with the vomiting."

She winced. "Sorry about your truck."

He shook his head and raised a hand. "Already taken care of, so please don't worry about it. My main concern is how you're doing."

"It was just like you said before," she told him, remembering his assurances on the way over, "a few stitches, a bit of a headache, and there's bound to be some bruising."

"You do look better since they got you cleaned up," he said, nodding toward her freshly washed face and the hospital gown that a nurse had assisted her getting into.

"That helped a lot," she said, feeling less like a horror movie extra with most of the blood cleaned off and her wound covered with a neat white bandage.

The tension written in his face eased, and she could see he really had been worried for her. "Your students will be so relieved," he said. "They got your earlier message that you'd be okay, but those two have been driving the staff crazy trying to get someone to let them back here to check on you in person."

"So how did *you*?" she asked before his fleeting half smile raised her suspicions. "Wait a minute. Let me guess. This is another of those special Kingston privileges, right?"

"I wouldn't exactly say that," he told her, though his offhand shrug spoke volumes. "But I've always figured it's better to seek forgiveness than prior approval—especially when everyone's momentarily distracted by some drunk guy yelling at the triage desk."

A laugh slipped out before the wrongness of it in these circumstances hit her. Blinking tears away, she said, "It's not funny. None of this is."

His eyes went somber. "I know, Emma. But sometimes you have to smile, or even laugh out loud, to get through the rough stuff."

A shadow darkened his expression, reminding her that he knew of what he spoke. Or at least that's what she'd overheard yesterday when she'd stopped to pick up a to-go breakfast from the café. Though the bells on the door had jingled with her entry, the two waitresses, a curvy little brunette with exaggerated cat's-eye makeup and a willowy redhead with the legs of a Las Vegas showgirl, were too engrossed in their gossip to notice. So Emma had waited at the counter while they'd idly wiped condiment containers on the tables and chatted about how Beau Kingston had been mourning the wife lost in a car crash back on a snowy Colorado mountainside for *almost three whole years already*—and how one of them *had better do something about it before some damned gold digger beats us to the mother lode*.

The poor man. "Thanks," she managed, noticing that he looked a bit rumpled this evening, with his thick black hair slightly ruffled and a hint of stubble darkening his cheeks. His collar unbuttoned; he'd taken off his tie, too, and she saw that his blue dress shirt was smeared with red streaks near the collar. Her blood, she realized, imagining she must have gotten it all over him when he'd picked her up.

"I—I hope your suit's not ruined." She thought of how freshly combed and handsome he'd looked sitting with his family earlier during Russell's service. "I can pay for cleaning."

"Don't be ridiculous," Beau said in a voice that brooked no argument. What she'd imagined as fatigue fell away, replaced by an intensity that took her breath away. "If anyone pays, it's going to be your ex."

"My...*what*?" She shook her head, pain blossoming anew. "Why would you say that? I never said that Jeremy was the one who—who hurt me."

She'd been so intent on the evidence she'd brought to show the sheriff, she hadn't once thought of her ex-husband.

"You're sure about that?" Beau asked. "Because after the way you were acting and what you said before about your divorce—"

He must have noticed the way she was looking at him because he explained, "I served a couple of tours with the marine corps MPs right out of high school. Military police. Sometimes, during our, um, domestic investigations, the women didn't want to speak up."

She looked up sharply. "I don't know *who* it was. One moment, I was back there, waiting near the rear of the building to try to catch the sheriff when he came out, and the next second I heard footsteps before someone grabbed me."

"A man?" he asked. "It was definitely a man who jumped you?"

An impression of power and speed convinced her. "I'm pretty sure of that much, but as for everything else… And anyway, why are you asking me these questions? Shouldn't the sheriff or someone be here by now? Someone from the department?"

"I'm guessing they're still tied up looking for that suspect. Meanwhile, it wouldn't hurt to gather some facts for him while they're still fresh on your mind." Beau might be a rancher and no longer an MP, but the cop behind his gaze loomed large.

She shrugged. "I'm sure it wouldn't hurt, if I knew anything to tell you."

"Was he tall or short? Young, old? Did you maybe notice skin tone, hair, eye color?"

"I—I couldn't say." She shook her throbbing head. "It happened so fast."

"Did he say anything?"

She tried to think back, her heart accelerating and her stomach knotting with the memory. "No words I could make out. But I don't really think—it just didn't *feel* like my ex-husband." Fragments spun through her mind, impossible to nail down.

"Any idea of what he was wearing? What about tattoos? Scars?"

Frustration mounting, she lashed out. "If I could tell you for certain who had done this, don't you think I would? *Especially* if it was my ex, of all people?"

Beau blew out a sigh. "I don't know you well enough to say for sure what you'd do. But I do know that for some victims of abuse, feelings can get in the way."

Bristling, she sat upright on the emergency department bed. "Let's get one thing straight, Mr. Kingston. I appreciate your help. I do, but whatever's happened to me, I'm nobody's *victim*. I'm a fighter, so don't stand there looking down at me like I'm some pitiful broken thing it's your job to protect."

He raised his palms. "I stand corrected, Dr. Copley. I didn't mean to push it. Or to offend you, either."

She blew out a breath, forcing herself not to take her roiling emotions out on the near stranger who had helped her. The man she'd thanked by making a mess of both his suit and his truck.

"You should call me Emma," she said by way of apology for the anger she still heard crackling in her voice. "I owe you at least that much for bailing me out again and hanging around here all evening. It must be ten o'clock by now, at least." With the emergency department crowded, she'd ended up waiting around for what seemed like an eternity while a number of food poisoning cases from a family barbecue gone wrong were treated.

"You don't owe me anything. I just happened to be at the right place at the right time, and I did what anyone would. It's only common decency."

"I'm not sure decency's quite as common as you think," she said, "but thank you. And thanks, too, for—for getting me out of there so quickly. My students, though. Maybe we should bring them in here."

"I sent them on a mission, partly to keep them busy for a little while. The young man's driving the girl with all the colors in her hair—I think her name is Lacey?"

"Lucie," Emma corrected, her heart aching to imagine what both her students must be thinking, with their professor attacked so closely on the heels of their friend's death.

"I called the motel manager—Nadine's an old friend—to ask her to let the girl into your room to take care of your dog and pick up a change of clothing for you," Beau said. "I'm afraid the sheriff's office is going to need to collect what you had on tonight."

"For evidence, I'm told." A shudder started deep inside Emma before rippling across the surface of her flesh. It wasn't as if she wanted any of the torn and bloodstained garments back again. It was the thought of what had happened to them—and the purse she'd been carrying when she'd left the community center earlier.

Her pulse fluttered in her throat. "What about my handbag? Did you happen to see it? I must've dropped it somewhere when I was—"

He frowned and shook his head. "I remember spotting your other sandal, but I don't recall any kind of bag."

"A small shoulder bag. It can't be gone. It *can't* be."

"Maybe someone found it. One of the deputies or—"

She hugged herself. "You don't understand."

"No, I don't." His gaze locked onto hers. "Why would

you have been waiting behind the building for the sheriff anyway? And what was in that purse?"

She hesitated, weighing how far she should trust him. But what difference did it make at this point if he knew? "Fleming's been avoiding me for days, ducking my visits, ignoring my messages. Only this time, I had proof. Proof of why someone might have wanted Russell silenced."

With a swish of the curtain, the sheriff crowded into the space beside Beau and frowned down at Emma. His face gleamed with perspiration, and his uniform shirt, smudged with grime, had come untucked on one side. Removing his hat, he raked his fingers through dark blond hair several shades less gray than his drooping mustache. "What's this nonsense about me ducking you? It's been a busy week, that's all. Tonight, for example, we ran halfway across town on foot before a lady pointed out where she'd heard her neighbor's door slam just a minute or two prior."

He puffed his chest out, thrusting his jaw forward. "That's when we nabbed our man sneakin' out the back way, scratches all down his face."

"I don't remember scratching him." Confusion swirled through Emma's mind as she tried to make the pieces fit. "He grabbed me from behind. I never got the chance to—"

"Registered sex offender, this fella. Thought ol' Jorge might actually keep his nose clean and his fly zipped this time, but he's known to collect empties outta trash bins to recycle, and I guess the sight of a pair of pretty legs in a short skirt was too much for him, and he decided today was the day to graduate from flashing. If we can't get a confession outta him, maybe we'll get lucky on some of the blood found on your clothing or underneath your nails."

So that was why the older nurse assigned to her had clipped Emma's nails and taken scrapings from underneath them. *Just in case you caught him without realizing it in the struggle*, the woman had said, patting Emma's arm gently before and after the procedure and the exam that followed.

Emma asked the sheriff, "Did you find my purse back there? I'm sure I had it with me by the dumpster."

"Can't say that I did," the sheriff said, "but it might just turn up yet."

Desperation clawing at her, she described it for him. "Small, black nylon, with three silver zippers across the front."

"We'll find it if he's got it," Wallace told her, "unless he ditched it somewhere on his way back to that old house he lives in and someone grabbed it. Soon as you can, though, you'd best put a call in to your bank and any card providers, just in case some associate of his is off and runnin' with your credit cards."

"I don't care about the cards," she cried. "Or my cell phone or my Jeep keys, either. Those can be replaced, but not— There were papers in there. Handwritten notes I found when I packed up Russell's clothing to clear out his motel room."

The sheriff shook his head. "A deputy and I thoroughly searched and cleared that room the day after Mr. Jorgenson's death. Didn't see anything but his clothes and shoes left, and a few personal whatnots. No kind of papers I remember."

"I didn't find them at first, either," she said, "not until I heard this crinkling sound when I was packing up his duffel. It led me to a false bottom and a little packet of pages hidden underneath it."

"And you were alone at the time?" he asked.

"I was," she said, ignoring the skeptical set of his mouth.

"So what was in these papers?" Beau asked. "And what did you mean about them being something that could've gotten him killed?"

"*I'm* asking the questions here," Wallace warned before returning his attention to Emma. "He, um, he didn't have any passwords written, did he? Because I'd like to take a look at Jorgenson's laptop, just as a formality, before I turn it back over to his family."

Emma shook her head, a chill rippling through her as she recalled unfolding the gridded pages, which she suspected had been torn from the small field notebook her assistant had always carried in his pocket. In Russell's neat, small print, she'd found several long, handwritten columns.

"No password. What I found instead was data," she said as her mind spun with the repercussions, "documentation of far more bird strike deaths than we've recorded in our study's database. Enough deaths of protected species, if they've been intentionally hidden, to get Green Horizons Wind Farm shut down forever—"

"And cost a hell of a lot of local jobs," the rancher finished for her, his handsome face looking stricken.

Wallace snorted, flinging a disdainful look in his direction. "Cost you a pretty penny, too, now wouldn't it, what with all that money you're about to rake in with that new turbine construction?"

"What construction?" Emma asked.

"How'd you know about—"

"Your new pal here didn't tell you?" the sheriff scoffed before thumbing a gesture at his cousin. "This one's in tight with those Green Horizons fellas. Talked 'em into nearly doublin' the project's size, building turbines galore once they get past the *little inconvenience* of your damned birds—and writing him a big, fat check for—"

Beau made a scoffing noise, as if the amount meant nothing to a man in possession of the land and cattle he was. "It's not about the money, but this is clean, sustainable energy, bringing good-paying jobs to an area of the state that desperately needs them."

"At this point," Emma insisted, "I don't give a damn about who loses what jobs or how much money. All I care about is figuring out who *murdered* my graduate assistant—and if I'm next on his list."

Wallace screwed up his face in that stubborn way that Beau remembered from years back, so it didn't surprise him a bit when his cousin held up a hand to shut down Emma. "Wait a minute. Hold up. Last thing I remember, you were at the turbine spoutin' nonsense about how you were sure your ex had gone after your boyfriend."

"*Boyfriend?* Where on earth did you get that?" Her face flushed an angry red. "Russell was my *student*, and I won't have you slandering his reputation or mine, either, suggesting that I've overstepped professional boundaries."

"Well, the way you've carried on about him, tellin' me about your former husband being jealous, I thought that maybe—"

"Then think again," she spat out. "Because I'm telling you, you're way off base with that idea."

Beau believed her, since she'd never radiated anything more than a professional concern, along with an educator's protectiveness, when speaking of Jorgenson.

"All right, your *student* then," said Wallace, backing off so easily that Beau figured he'd been only half-heartedly probing to see if her reaction might yield pay dirt. "But before, you were certain your ex had something to do with his death."

"I was, and for good reason since he'd called and threatened me that very morning. And Jeremy *did* make that phone call. I'm standing by that claim."

Unable to stay silent any longer, Beau interjected. "But now you're figuring that Russell's death's more likely got something to do with these papers you had in your purse, right? And that somehow this is wrapped up with what happened to you this afternoon."

"It *has* to be. Don't you see it? This can't be a coincidence."

Beau wasn't sure about that, but he could see how badly Emma wanted to believe it. Just the way she'd wanted, perhaps needed from the start, to believe that the unthinkable—a senseless accident—could not have possibly taken the life of a capable, vibrant young assistant.

"Listen to me, please," she went on, her beautiful green eyes looking from one man to the other, "if we can prove those unrecorded bird deaths my assistant documented really happened, it'll mean big trouble for a lot of people. What I can't understand is why Russell would've kept something like this from me. He cared as deeply as I do about saving hawks, falcons and eagles, and he'd have to know that we could end up with huge problems, too, if the government ever figured we were intentionally misreporting…"

"So let's suppose these papers really do exist—" started Wallace.

"Those records are *real*," Emma insisted. "I just wish I knew what Russell was up to. Maybe he felt the need to double-check his data before coming to me, or…"

"Or maybe he threatened the wrong party," Beau finished for her. "Is that what you're thinking?"

"I warned you to stay out of this." Wallace glared at him. "So why don't you slink back to that fancy mansion you're squattin' in and let me do my job?"

"I don't think you want to go there right now, *cousin.*" Voice dropping to a low growl, Beau felt his hackles rise. "Not unless you want that badge my father bought you kicked so far up your—"

"Russell was a dedicated wildlife researcher, passionate about the raptors we were here to save," Emma interrupted. "It's possible he was so infuriated by what he discovered, he said the wrong thing to the wrong person. Someone who assumed that I must know, too."

Still, the two men's gazes remained locked, years of grievances crowding the tight space between the ER bed and curtain. Grievances that had re-flared the day Beau's father had, out of guilt or compassion or in response to Aunt Alicia's pleas, extended an olive branch and invited his prodigal son to return home with the remains of his shattered family. Recovering from the same rollover that had cost his wife her life, Beau was too broken, physically and emotionally, to refuse the offer...or the chance to heal the rift with the family he'd walked out on so many years before.

All except the cousin who'd apparently figured that, with both Kingston sons estranged from their father, he had stood to profit. Just thinking of Wallace's calculation, of the years he had spent scheming and the accusations he was making now in his damn fool lawsuit, had Beau aching to rearrange his cousin's dental work. But Emma, who had been through so much, deserved far better than a ringside seat to a family blowup.

Wallace, however, had apparently come to a different conclusion, for he abruptly turned his scowl on Emma. "You forget, we already have a man in custody, a two-time loser sex offender with his face all scratched to pieces and you there with at least one broken nail that I'm bettin' has his blood and skin under it. Yet still here you sit, carrying on about some crazy, convoluted plot to kill you over a few damned birds."

"*Murder* me. Like Russell," she said flatly.

"His death was ruled an *accident*. By the medical examiner."

"*You* made your decision from the ground," she accused. "You didn't even wait to see the body before you'd closed your mind to anything I had to say."

"First off, I viewed the scene from live-feed video, examined photos of the body carefully before I cleared it for removal in a way that would ensure that no one else ended up hurt."

"Removal by technicians from the company—"

"Your ex-husband's uncle filled me in on the way you are," said Wallace, "and now, as far as I'm concerned, you're crying wolf again."

"I'm not crying wolf! If you'll get out there and find my purse—"

The curtain was pulled back, and a imposing woman with a mass of tiny black braids gathered like a crown and a nurse's badge clipped to her blue scrubs frowned at them over the rims of her half-glasses. "Excuse me, Sheriff, but it's getting a bit loud in here," she said, quietly but firmly. "And we do have other patients. But if you need to continue this discussion elsewhere, we'll be discharging her shortly."

"Sorry, Trixie," Wallace said, sounding as if he might actually mean it. "We'll keep things down from here on in."

He waited for the nurse to leave before returning his attention to Emma.

"We'll do our level best to find your purse," he said

more quietly as he shoved his hat back onto his head. "In the meantime, you've been through an upsetting experience, getting pawed at by some pervert. Why don't you get a good rest tonight," he went on, "maybe take the edge off with whatever they're giving you for pain? Then we'll talk again tomorrow, once you've had the chance to catch your breath."

She narrowed her eyes at him. "So does that mean that this time, when I stop by, you won't sneak out the back door?"

Wallace flushed an angry shade of red that had Beau snorting in amusement. She'd been telling him the truth before. She might've been through hell, but she didn't have it in her to play the passive victim.

"Oh, I'll be there, all right—" a fat vein pulsed at the sheriff's temple "—ready to get this case sewn up and you and your Austin entourage on your way out of my county."

As Wallace made his exit, Emma grimaced before asking drily, "Why is it I get the feeling that he's not my biggest fan?"

"I can't imagine," Beau said, "especially when he's so very fond of me."

She snorted before the brightness in her eyes dimmed. Shoulders sagging, she pressed her fingers to her forehead, carefully avoiding the bandaged area.

"You okay?" he asked.

"Not really, no. Today was—it's been a nightmare. And I don't know what to tell my students. I can't keep lying to them, letting them believe that Russell's death was accidental."

"You don't know it wasn't. Not for certain. And they've been through a lot, too. They were his closest friends, right?" At her nod, he continued. "Do you really want to upset them late at night, before you've had the chance to think this all through?"

She looked up at him, her expression stricken. "You don't believe me either, do you? You don't think I can prove that Russell was onto something real?"

"I'm reserving judgment," he said, keeping his words as steady as he could, "until I see more evidence. And you might want to consider holding back on any more accusations until you've recovered from this shock—and you have that proof in hand."

"Oh, I'll find the proof. I have a good idea where, too. All I have to do is get back to the turbines as soon as possible and find the—"

"No way," he said sharply. "You're not going out there. You saw the email, right? About Green Horizons' safety review?"

She gave him a disgusted look. "Of course they want to keep everyone away. If they're somehow involved in all this, they'll drag out their review forever. And leave any evidence cleaned and sanitized for their own protection."

"*Or* they're trying to keep from being on the hook for any further accidents. Either way, I said *no*, Emma. I don't want you or your students taking any unnecessary chances."

"I'd never involve them. *Never.* After Russell, there's no way I would chance that." She shook her head, tears filling her eyes. "I was—I was the one to call Russell's parents. I insisted on it. It nearly killed me, breaking that news to them."

"Then you'll understand how I feel," Beau said, "when I tell you I'm not making that call to *your* folks, your boss or anyone else when you go getting yourself hurt again. Or worse."

She made a scoffing sound. "You've helped me out a

couple times, sure. That doesn't make me your responsibility."

"That's where you're wrong, Dr. Copley. I take everyone who lives on, works on or sets foot on my spread as my responsibility," he said, sincerity ringing in his every word, "which is why, from this point forward, I'm barring you from Kingston property. And telling everyone who works the ranch you're absolutely not to set foot beyond those gates."

Chapter 5

Arrogant. Controlling. As Emma tossed and turned throughout the long night and dragged her sore body to the shower in her motel room the next morning, her thoughts kept returning to how Beau had gone from supporting her so completely to flatly refusing to further discuss his decision to bar her from his property. As if he expected her to meekly accept that the head Kingston had the final word.

More irritating still, when Josh and Lucie had been allowed back in to see her, Beau had shaken their hands before advising them, "Best not to leave her alone tonight if you can swing it."

Was it because he really cared that she might have a concussion, or did he imagine that if left to her own devices, she'd grab the spare Jeep key she kept as a backup and attempt to defy his order?

"You don't have to worry," Josh had said, restless energy giving his warm brown skin a light sheen of perspiration. A graduate student who had roomed with Russell back in Austin, he looked as if he'd aged years since his friend's death. "I know the sheriff said they got the guy, but we aren't planning on leaving her a minute. No offense, but I don't trust this jerkwater little town of yours one bit."

"Under the circumstances, I can't say as I blame you," Beau had told him. "I just want to be sure Emma has someone there with her just in case."

Shifting the day pack with Emma's clothing from one hand to the other, the younger Lucie had nodded, her eyes red-rimmed and her multicolored pixie cut sticking up in places like a tropical bird's crest. With little money and even less family support for her studies, she had often referred to Josh and Russell, who'd taken her under their wing, as her big brothers. "We've got it covered, Mr. Kingston," she had said. "Josh took the vacant room next to Dr. Copley's, and I asked the manager to move a cot into her room so I can be there if she needs me. We're not letting her out of our sight until we get her back to Austin."

Emma had grimaced, knowing that her students had meant well but not at all liking the idea of being "managed" like this. Watched over…and then herded as far as possible from the proof she needed to blow wide open whatever secrets had cost Russell his life—and possibly resulted in her attack as well.

As she picked at the breakfast Josh had dropped off while she was in the shower, Emma startled when the old-fashioned black phone in her room rang loudly. With her cell missing with the stolen purse, it hadn't occurred that anyone would try to reach her on a landline.

Her stomach tightened and her thoughts flew to Jeremy and the recent lengths he'd gone to in order to trick her into answering his calls. But she was closer to the phone than Lucie, so Emma held her breath and answered—and sighed with relief to hear it was the university's director of human resources calling to check on her.

"Are you all right?" Mrs. Reddy asked, concern tingeing her faint Indian accent. "I understand there was some more…unpleasantness in Kingston County last night."

"I'll be fine, but how did you hear about what happened to me down here?" Emma asked before glancing toward Lucie, who was adding salsa to her egg-and-bacon taco at the room's small table while River sat near her feet drooling hopefully.

Not from me, Lucie mouthed in response, the silver stud on her nose winking in the light as she shook her head.

"First thing this morning, there was an email from your department chair," Mrs. Reddy said.

"But I haven't had the chance to reach out to him yet—or call anybody."

"The important thing," the HR director hurried on, clearly eager to get to the real purpose of her call, "is that we get you back home to facilitate your recovery, and to cover some freshman-level sections when the new semester starts in two weeks. Professor Paulsen's had to take an unanticipated leave of absence this semester."

Sorry as Emma was for her colleague, whom she'd heard was dealing with a spouse in hospice, alarm bells blared in her brain. "But what about my research?" She'd lobbied hard to block off time and secure funding for a project intended to protect endangered amphibians from agricultural runoff. As much as she valued the semesters she spent in the classroom, this project, like the turbine study, was work she'd always dreamed of doing. Work that could go industry-wide to save living animals in practice, not just theory.

Only now she was being relegated to teaching section

after section of the one freshman-level class the aging Paulsen still taught—a watered-down version for non-science majors checking off their life studies requirement. For Emma's burned-out colleague, coasting toward retirement, it was a tedious but unchallenging assignment. For anyone motivated to make a difference, it could only be seen as torture. Or a punishment.

"No one's told you?" Mrs. Reddy sounded surprised. "That project's on hold for now, some sort of issue with a grant. And considering everything that's happened, for your own mental and physical health and safety, we feel it's best for you to return to the more…structured campus environment. As soon as possible."

"I don't understand," Emma said, but Mrs. Reddy quickly made it clear she had only called to impart the university's wishes, not its explanations. As she ended the call, questions swirled through Emma's mind. Was she being blamed for a student's death?

Or was there some sort of behind-the-scenes conspiracy to get her out of Kingston County as quickly as possible—and keep her too occupied to stir up further trouble?

It was a question still on her mind later that morning when Josh came to the room, his dark curls damp from the shower he'd taken after making their breakfast run. But the way he was holding another white paper bag, supporting its weight from the bottom, made her think he had something heavier than egg tacos in it. As did the troubled expression on his face.

"What's wrong?" Lucie asked him. "You didn't accidentally grab a meat one, did you?" Josh was always trying to convince anyone who'd listen of the benefits of a vegetarian diet.

Walking past her, he ignored River's attempt to greet

him. "A bad scare is what I got. When I was getting out of the shower, I heard this thump from underneath the sink. I ended up pulling out drawers to look, and this is what I found."

He opened the bag and showed them the pistol inside: black and rather small, partially wrapped up in a piece of silver duct tape, along with one of the motel's cheap white hand towels, which Josh had used to cushion it.

"What the—where did that come from?" asked Lucie, her eyes widening. "Should we call the police or something?"

"I don't know where it's from, but I thought—I thought maybe..." His gaze dialed in on Emma. "That room was Russell's, wasn't it? Did he ever mention anything to you about a weapon?"

Emma shook her head, shivering at the sight. *So much for the sheriff's* thorough *search of the room earlier.* "For all we know, it could've belonged to a different guest," she told the two, though the more she thought of it, the more she doubted that was true. It seemed unlikely that someone would care enough about the gun to secure it out of sight, only to simply check out and forget it.

She found it easier to believe that Russell had known those records he'd been keeping might prove dangerous in the long run. Perhaps he hadn't felt he was in immediate danger, but maybe he'd liked the idea of having it close at hand just in case someone figured out what he was up to.

But if she told Josh and Lucie what she suspected, Emma knew they would insist on staying, and she wasn't about to risk drawing the pair into a clearly dangerous situation. After a moment's thought, she asked for the bag and tucked it inside her day pack, explaining, "I'll just take it with me to the sheriff's office when I give my statement later. I'm sure they'll know how to handle it, and it'll be a lot faster than calling someone over here to hold you up with a hundred questions." She cast a meaningful look toward Josh, who would soon be graduating. "You really have to be back in Austin for your interview this afternoon. It's at four thirty, isn't it?"

"I could probably reschedule," he said uncertainly before stroking River's golden head. "You know what, I'll cancel it. Another job will come along."

"This isn't *just* a job. You know that." She frowned, reminded of the strings she'd pulled to get Josh a face-to-face with the conservation nonprofit that would be the perfect match for his interests and talents. "You *deserve* to be there after all your hard work. I absolutely insist on it. Just give me a lift back to my Jeep and both of you can be on the road within an hour. Then I won't have to rush getting my business taken care of."

"But you *will* leave Pinto Creek before nightfall?" asked Lucie, who needed to get back, too, to the part-time bartending job that allowed her to stay in school. "You can't think of staying here another night alone, not after what happened."

"Definitely," Emma told them, infusing her voice with every atom of sincerity she could muster. "That's one thing you don't have to worry about, I promise."

And holding their gazes long enough to watch them weaken, unable to imagine that the professor who'd expanded their dreams, nurtured their ambitions, and taught them to be honest and critical researchers would look straight into their faces and tell an outright lie, even to protect them.

Beau knew as he caught his first glimpse of the foreman he'd promoted to ranch manager cresting the hilltop in his pickup a little after noon that whatever had brought Fernando Galvez here had to be important. Before heading over with the boys this morning to this tiny slice of heaven Beau had known since childhood as the frog pond, he'd left strict instructions that he and his sons were not to be disturbed. Not for any emergencies involving cattle, the vaqueros—the cowboys of Mexican descent who had worked for his family for generations— and most especially not a damned thing to do with the bankers or the lawyers that had lately kept Beau from Cort and Leland far too often.

Their summer vacation was nearly over, passing in a blaze of abandoned ideas and glossed-over promises. Time and time again, Beau had been forced to shuffle his sons off to his aunt with some excuse about how he couldn't go with them to the beach or take them fishing on the family boat, which had remained docked every damned day of the season, despite his promises before his father's death.

Maybe it was the attack on Emma Copley, or more likely, the memorial service for her young assistant, that had reminded Beau so painfully of how quickly, how irrevocably, life could change forever. This morning, he'd awakened to thoughts of his own father: all the promises broken, all the priorities his disregard had branded into the hearts of his two sons. Two sons he'd eventually lost: Beau, for many years, and Beau's older half brother, Jake Jr., forever, after he'd turned away from this ranch, and his whole family, years before. After living abroad for years, J.J., as he'd been known, had been killed in a motorcycle accident—a loss that had almost certainly contributed to his father's eventual decision to welcome Beau and his two sons back to the ranch.

Though Beau had never really connected with the man who'd always kept him at emotional arm's length, his fa-

ther's grief for the lost chance of a ninth-inning recon-
ciliation with his namesake had for years clung like an
unwelcome shadow. Maybe that awareness, and not the
ranch he'd never meant to go to Beau, had been his true
legacy: the lesson of how neither land nor cattle nor the
money and power that came with the Kingston name
were enough to keep a man from dying broken and, for
all intents and purposes, alone.

That ends here, with this generation, Beau swore as he
watched the freckled Cort, who for once wasn't off hiding in the pages of one of his books, but instead grinned
ear to ear as his younger brother raced close to the water's edge to catch the soft toy football his father had just
lobbed his way. Skinny Leland's tennis shoes squelched
along the muddy edge, where the weeds grew thick from
the runoff between two grassy hillsides.

"Watch out," Cort warned Leland when Maverick, the
dopey, half-grown mongrel Beau had found wandering,
nothing but flopping ears, jutting bones and every para-
site known to dog-kind, in a remote draw months before,
ran leaping after the toy. Planting huge paws on Leland's
chest, the bluetick Maverick, a mix of hound, cattle dog
and possibly elephant, given the way that he was growing,
twisted skyward. In a single acrobatic moment, the oversize pup snatched away his prize and sent the squealing
six-year-old splashing down into water dappled green-
gold by the sun.

Beau ran to help up his laughing younger boy, only
to have the already-excited Maverick grab on to his own
arm and yank him, too, off-balance. His boot slipping in
a patch of muck, Beau ended up going down with an even
bigger splash, but it was worth the mess—and maybe a
bruise or two—to look up to see Cort snapping picture
after picture on the little digital camera he'd been given

as a birthday gift last spring but had never used before today.

"Blackmail ammunition!" the eight-year-old crowed. "If you don't let us stay up late on school nights, I'm gonna show everybody how you were taken down by Doofus Dog!"

At the sound of the truck door closing above them, Beau stopped laughing. Glancing upward, he saw Fernando standing in front of his truck. His dark brown eyes were shaded by his fine Panama hat, but his impressive black-and-silver mustache twitched as he shook his head in mock disapproval. But then, even before his most recent promotion, the solidly built ranch manager had always maintained an unflappable dignity as he trod the middle path between the common hands from whom he'd risen and the position of authority he'd held for decades. Though Fernando avoided behaving in an overly familiar manner, Beau remembered from his childhood the man's simple kindnesses, from his subtle warnings on days it would be best for Beau to stay out of his father's path to the times Fernando had quietly passed along some skill that Big Jake had grumbled that *any Kingston worth a damn* would know how to do already.

As such, Fernando had been the one to teach Beau, with a steady patience and the occasional word of praise that meant everything to a boy starved for a man's approval, to put a polish on his boots, to treat a horse's cracked hoof and to cinch up his own saddle—when he'd been so young, he'd had to climb up onto a block to reach it.

"Careful of your manners now, my young friends," Fernando advised, the subtle cadence of his first language making a form of music of his words. "We have a lady among us."

As he crossed the front of his truck, Beau stood, chagrined, and helped his younger son out of the slime.

"What's Aunt Alicia doing out here?" whispered a dripping Leland as Maverick bounded triumphantly around them with the football in his jaws.

"Grown-up business, I expect," Beau said as all of them stared uphill toward the frail woman on Fernando's arm. *Bad business*, Beau imagined, that would bring her across the rough track leading to an area she'd so often dismissed as a "muddy hole in the ground good for nothing more than dirtying clothes and getting boys in trouble." This, of course, along with the general lack of adult supervision, was exactly why generations of Kingston kids had all loved the place so much.

"Don't try to climb down here, Aunt Alicia," he called, worried about the arthritis that had limited her mobility. "I'll come up and talk."

"I had no intention, but thank you for the offer," his aunt said from beneath the wide straw sun hat shading her face. The frailty of her voice and way she was leaning on Fernando's strength made Beau more anxious than ever.

What the hell's gone wrong now?

As Beau approached, Fernando nodded his approval. "And you will perhaps allow me to go down and show the two young gentleman my secret spot for catching the biggest *ranas toros*?"

Beau smiled and told his sons, "He's talkin' bullfrogs, boys. You'd better let him show you—and take Maverick along, too. I imagine he's going to turn out to be one champion froggin' hound."

Beau kept his voice deliberately cheerful, watching as his boys eagerly followed to see what mysteries Fernando would reveal along the weed-choked shoreline. When the three were out of earshot, Beau headed up, his gaze catching a glimpse of the top of one of the turbines in the distance. The turbines that might be a relatively new addition to the Kingston enterprise but now stood sentry over a past he was committed to preserving.

He reached his aunt, offering his arm.

"Oh, don't you dare," she said, casting an appalled look at his muddy clothing. "My goodness, but one would've thought you'd outgrown that sort of hooligan-ism by now."

"Yes, ma'am," he said, wishing she'd just tell him what had drawn her from the comfort of the home they shared. "One would've figured. But how about we head back to my truck? I've got a few folding chairs set up off the tail-gate in the shade there."

When she agreed, he picked the smoothest way back to lead her to the spot where he and the boys had eaten sandwiches beneath the interlocking boughs of several cottonwoods that grew only in this relatively damp spot. After showing her to a seat and handing her a paper cup of lemonade, by now somewhat watered down by melting ice, he lowered himself to the chair opposite and waited for the other shoe to drop.

Instead, she plucked a slimy green strand of some water plant off the side of his face. "Bad influence aside," she said, "you're a good father to those boys of yours. A far sight better than your father ever was either of his."

"I figure my paltry attempts are the least I owe 'em." The pang of remorse that hit him was like a spike driven through his sternum. They might not come quite as often these days, with the day-to-day demands of fatherhood and ranch management keeping him so busy, but the pain still had the power to hit hard, triggered by things as simple as a glimpse of the hummingbirds Melissa had always loved—or a compliment on his so-called parental efforts. "Since I cost them a damned fine mother."

"You know that wasn't your fault. The state police out in Colorado said as much."

He only looked at her in answer, unwilling to debate it.

"It's pointless, you know, punishing yourself forever. You could be happy again, Beau, and I'd be so happy for you, if you'd only find a way to—"

Stomach souring, he cut her off before she could broach a subject that they both knew was going nowhere. "I know you didn't come to watch the boys and Maverick and me roll around in the mud, and I pray you're not about to mention another single daughter of a friend of yours. So tell me, was there something else?"

Frowning, she smoothed nonexistent wrinkles from the slacks of today's pantsuit, a match for the light peach-colored cane she'd laid across her knees. "Impatient as your father, aren't you?" she asked irritably before sighing and producing a folded white envelope from a pocket. "All right, then."

As she straightened it, he saw the words *AUNT ALICIA* scrawled hastily across the front. She gingerly pulled a page from inside the neatly slitted top, explaining, "After I went to town this morning for my weekly wash-and-set—" she lightly patted the freshly fluffed and hair-sprayed champagne-colored curls she'd worn for as long as Beau could recall "—I found this tucked beneath the windshield wiper of the Caddy."

Beau scowled. "Wallace, sucking up again?"

Her forehead furrowed as she considered, "Wallace, reminding me that his mama Lynnie was my baby sister—mine and your daddy's—"

"Oh, for crying out—"

"He never got over it, you know, the hurt of his own

father leaving. The shame of learning that he'd started a new family a few towns down the coast."

"So he latched onto the richest substitute the family had to offer. And set out to make my life a living—"

"I'm not excusing what he did. What he's done. I'm only saying that what we should all be worried over is keeping the family together."

Beau spoke through gritted teeth. "He only wants to *remind* you that he's *real* family and I'm not. I imagine he included photos of his daughters, didn't he?" Because that was what it was all about to Wallace: the fair skin and hair and blue eyes he and his girls had inherited through his Kingston mother, a birthright that would allow him to play the big man around these parts and to rule over the Hispanic employees without taxing his brain by respecting those whose stock-handling skills and unparalleled knowledge of the land had so long played a crucial role in the ranch's success. Even if he had to prove Beau a bastard to do it.

"He was only reminding me that none of this misunderstanding is the fault of Sara Ann or Marlie," Aunt Alicia said, her own blue eyes welling with unshed tears at the thought of the grandnieces the family feud had kept her away from, "and if you'd just go ahead and *have* the DNA test like he's asking, we could settle all these questions and put this ugliness behind us."

"Absolutely not," he said, angry that she would suggest it. "I've got the Kingston name, and I'm listed on the damned will. Not him, whether or not I look like some Sicilian ancestor or what that idiot thinks of as poor Mexican labor—as if every one of our vaqueros isn't worth a dozen of his useless ass."

"There's no need to be coarse, Beau," Aunt Alicia

scolded. "And I don't think that it's that your cousin's prejudiced, exactly…"

Beau gritted his teeth and let it pass, thinking of all the times Wallace had just so happened to mutter words like *mongrel* and *bastard* in his hearing, along with the ugly slurs he'd applied to those of Mexican descent.

"It's just that he's a little confused," Aunt Alicia went on, attempting to play the role of family peacemaker as she had so many times before. "You see, while you were away, you and your brother both, he spent quite a bit of time here, talking to your father, taking an interest in the ranch. He had his dreams, I think, ideas for how he might—"

"I've heard all about his grand ideas," Beau said, recalling his father's impatience with what he'd once referred to as Wallace's "fool notions." "But that doesn't mean I'm going to allow Wallace to pretend that my coloring and my sons' makes us one bit less worthy. And besides, he's barking up the wrong tree with this idea about some DNA test. Ed tells me," he said, referring to Ed Franklin, his father's longtime friend and attorney, "it wouldn't even matter, since I was born when my mother and father were married to each other, and since the old man was too proud or stubborn to renounce me. I'm *legally* a Kingston, just like it says on my birth certificate."

Closing her eyes, she sighed again, the loving aunt who'd raised him at war with her role as family peacemaker. "Of course you are, in every way that matters. I've always believed it. It's just that Wallace says—"

"I don't give a damn about anything that ass says. I thought I'd made that very clear."

"It's not his words I'm worried about, Beau," Aunt Alicia told him, trembling as she leaned forward. "It's what he *has* that had me asking Fernando to drive me straight out to this godforsaken mudhole. Wallace says he's found your father's *actual* attorney of record, a Houston lawyer named J. Armstrong Pinckney—"

"Why would my father hire some pompous-sounding lawyer out of Houston?"

"Jake did used to fly out there quite a lot on business in the years before you came home," his aunt explained. "They must've connected somehow, because this Pinckney's shown Wallace another will, one signed and notarized—and dated *after* the one we filed with the county."

"Another will?" Beau shook his head, struggling to read the looming disaster written in the creases on her forehead. "My father's, you mean?"

"Your father's," she repeated, her stare as heavy as lead, "naming Wallace as sole heir."

Just over an hour after Emma left her motel, Sheriff Wallace Fleming strode into the small conference room where she was sitting. "We found it just like I said," he boasted, raising her black purse, now somewhat dirty and misshapen, in his meaty hand.

Flinching at the abruptness of his intrusion, Emma looked up from the six-pack of photos of potential suspects that the deputy seated across from her had shown her. Though she'd understood that one of the men's faces among the headshots must be that of the sex offender currently in custody—and that it would make everyone's job easier if she'd gotten a good look at her assailant—she'd had to explain that none of the faces was at all familiar.

She hadn't yet had the chance to bring up the hand-gun Josh had found, which she'd left inside her Jeep for fear of carrying a loaded weapon into a sheriff's office without warning. But now her full attention was on her bag, which the sheriff triumphantly laid down before her.

"There you go," he said. "Why don't you check it out? Tell me if anything is missing."

"Th-thanks." Emma's stomach squirmed with this big man looming over her while Deputy Kendall, an equally imposing figure with close-cropped prematurely silver hair and a faint fishhook-shaped scar beneath his left eye, watched her from across the table. Up until now, he'd treated her kindly, asking how she was feeling and bringing her a cup of surprisingly good coffee before gently drawing her story from her. With his boss standing over him, however, he watched her with cool gray eyes. Eyes that measured and assessed her as carefully as any cop might a potential suspect.

"Well, go on. Don't be shy," the sheriff urged, crossing his arms above a slight paunch. "Another of my deputies found it early this morning behind some trash cans in an alleyway between the community center and our suspect's house. Looks like whoever snatched it got scared and tossed the thing, maybe hopin' To throw us off his trail. But your keys are still inside, I saw. Your cell and wallet, too, with your driver's license. Everything else present?"

"The credit and debit cards are still here—even all the cash, I think," she confirmed before unzipping the interior pocket she cared most about. The completely empty pocket. "They're gone. They're—"

After rooting through the purse's other sections, she stared up at the sheriff. "Did you take them out? Those papers I mentioned?"

"What papers?" Fleming asked, his face hardening, his vibrant blue eyes shuttered.

He remembers exactly what we talked about.

Planting her palms on the tabletop, she pushed herself to her feet. "The ones from Russell's room. The ones that prove that his death was no accident and that my attack—there's no way it was random."

When the deputy rose, too, one big hand reaching for her, Fleming held up a palm to stop him. "It's all right, Jim. She's okay. Miss Copley—excuse me—*Dr.* Copley—has had a really rough week. Had a couple of things go down, one right on top of the other, that any human being would struggle to make sense of."

"Not you, though." Emma stared a challenge at him, not buying his patronizing show of sympathy for a minute. "You explained it all away with lightning speed. And now, when I had written proof, proof that would make hash of your theories, it *just so happens* to go missing."

"Because if this *proof* of yours ever existed in the first place," Fleming said, his face darkening behind the drooping mustache, "you were fool enough to go skulking around some dumpster with it looking for trouble instead of bringin' it straight here the way any sensible woman would have. And now you're pointin' fingers, never stopping to think for a second that behind the scenes, we've been working our tails off, putting in overtime galore on this death investigation, much less thank us."

She paused, confused—and wondered if it was remotely possible that she might have misjudged him. "So you're telling me you really *have* been looking into Russell's murd—his death?" She adjusted her wording, along with her tone, so as not to incite another argument. Because an honest investigation was all she'd wanted from the start. And justice for Russell if it turned out she was right. "*Really* looking into it, I mean? Including the possibility that someone wanted him silenced before he could release his data?"

Fleming straightened his spine, his gaze hard and cold as steel. "We might not have your fancy university degrees, Dr. Copley, and we might not hail from the state capital, but that doesn't mean we're all a bunch of ignorant hayseeds."

"No one ever said that."

"Glad to hear it, Professor, 'cause when you start hangin' with the wrong sort, listening to what comes out of the big mouth that pretends like he's somethin' more than a stain on his family honor, an outsider like you can maybe start to get the wrong ideas about the way that things get done around this county."

A stain on his family honor? Heat blasted through her, followed by an impulse to rush to the defense of a man her instincts told her was worth a dozen Wallace Flemings. She managed to hold her tongue, reminding herself that she needed the sheriff's cooperation—no matter how repellent she found his attitude.

"Then maybe you can clue me in about the way you do things instead of leaving me to wonder."

He turned up his hands. "You have to understand, Doc, that with any pending investigation, there are things we simply can't share, certain details we have to hold back from the community at large. But I can assure you that if my deputies and I uncover one shred of hard evidence that Russell Jorgenson's death might've been anything other than accidental—or that what happened to you yesterday could be at all related—I'll reopen the case faster than Jimmy here can shoot the head off a rabid skunk."

She glanced at the deputy. "I take it that's pretty fast, then?"

He smiled in answer, his gray eyes hinting there was

an amusing story—one not shared with civilians—somewhere behind the sheriff's boast.

"Meanwhile," the sheriff told Emma, "for your own mental and physical health and safety, I believe it would be in your best interest to leave this all to my department while you return to your—"

"*What* did you just say?" she asked, her breath catching at his phrasing. It struck Emma as well that when Mrs. Reddy had used those *exact same words* earlier this morning when she'd called from the university, she'd done so after dialing the motel's number—a number she might easily have gotten from someone local.

Likely, from someone who knew about Emma's assault and had made it clear from the start that his life would be far easier if she would quickly pack up and leave town.

It was only then that Emma decided for certain what her instincts had been trying to tell her all along. There was no need to mention the handgun hidden out in her Jeep—not if she didn't want that particular piece of evidence to disappear just like the pages.

Instead, she'd hold on to it for the time being, if only to ensure that she was not the next to vanish, too.

Chapter 6

Personal belongings packed in the rear of her Jeep, Emma pulled past a motel exit framed with the trunks of several spindly palm trees, their fronds yellowed and drooping. Though their long shadows pointed the way east, she instead drove toward where the sun kissed the horizon, a beacon leading westward toward the Kingston Ranch.

Guiltily, she thought of the promise she'd made to Josh and Lucie to leave Pinto Creek before nightfall.

"It was only half a lie," she told River, who stared in what Emma imagined to be silent judgment from the back seat. "I *am* leaving the city limits, so please stop looking at me that way."

As the small town's center gave way to residential neighborhoods, Emma thought about the local high school and junior college science students she and Russell had trained to assist them, all volunteers who'd expressed an interest in wildlife preservation. In exchange for course credit, teams of them had turned out five mornings each week to walk a grid pattern at designated turbines to search for any dead birds. Whenever a feathered mound was found, the fatality was photographed, tagged and collected so the bird's species and probable cause of death could be recorded for the study.

If any raptor deaths weren't being reported, there were two possibilities. Either some of their volunteers were hiding carcasses, which seemed unlikely with so many enthusiastic witnesses about, or someone was beating them to the designated spots to remove the birds of prey whose plights they were recording. Each time Emma tried to imagine how Russell might have come up with solid evidence, her mind led her to the same conclusion. He had to have been using the game cameras, a case of which had mysteriously gone missing after last spring's butterfly study, near the bases of the Green Horizons turbines. Capable of taking still shots day or night, the cameras would mark each digital image with a time and date stamp and save it to a memory card.

But did any of the cameras remain, awaiting her discovery? And had those who might be implicated in the photos come to the same conclusion? Could they be aware, too, that one or more of these might have captured evidence from the date and time surrounding Russell's death? For all she knew, the game cams could have long since been removed or, worse yet, destroyed. But as disappointing as it would be to come up empty-handed, she worried more about running into someone desperate to find them out here.

As she passed a grain silo near the railroad tracks, Emma shuddered, imagining herself forced up the turbine as Russell might have been and either hanged, as she feared he'd been, or flung from the maintenance platform. She thought about his gun, which she'd brought along for safety, but the prospect of actually using it left her dry-mouthed and shaky.

"Surely it won't come to that," she murmured, pulling alongside a desolate stretch of ranch road some thirty minutes later and checking the mirrors for signs that anyone might be coming up behind her.

With the sun long gone and dusk deepening with every minute, she spotted nothing but the faint outline of the dusty road and the indistinct silhouettes of fence posts behind her. Noting the emergence of the first few stars, she jumped when River growled from the back seat. Emma jerked her head toward a movement beyond the passenger window and gasped, startled by the movement of a deer behind the ranch gate to her right.

As what turned out to be a white-tailed buck and a couple of does disappeared in the failing light, she told River, "It's okay. They won't bother us," her voice thin and shaky.

Steadying herself, she left her vehicle with a flashlight, taking the day pack with the loaded weapon and River to alert her to the approach of any other unexpected animals or strangers. As she started off in the direction of Turbine Number 43 on foot, she passed the gate. Her pants caught on a thorny shrub just as her phone vibrated in her pocket. Snapping the stick to free her leg, she pulled out the cell, remembering Lucie's promise to call to check on her, though it would mean another white lie.

But a glance at the caller ID told her that her department head was calling, the same Dr. Lee who'd evidently conspired with Human Resources after someone, probably the sheriff, had tipped him off last night.

Upset by his betrayal, Emma answered. "I've been wondering when you'd call and explain why I'll be filling in for Paulsen instead of doing research this semester." Her own voice echoed back over a weak connection. "So which is it? Am I being punished by the dean—or was all this your idea?"

"You damned sure deserve punishment," another voice said, distorted almost—but not quite—beyond recognition. "And you're going to freaking get it any time now because I'm comin' for you, darling."

"J-Jeremy?" Her heart leaped in her chest at the realization that he was spoofing another number he'd stolen from her phone just to terrorize her. Or could she have been right before? Could his jealousy and hatred have pushed him as far as murder?

That can't be right, she reminded herself. *He was in Waco working, not here when Russell died. Wasn't he?*

"You've ruined my life. Ruined me," Jeremy accused, self-pity mixed with anger.

And you nearly broke me. Destroyed my chance to be a mother, and her chance...at everything.

Emma clamped down on the bottomless grief that struck her every time that she remembered. "I don't have time for any more of your garbage right now," she said.

Turning back to look at her, River cocked her head and whined.

"You got me *fired*," Jeremy shouted, the connection abruptly clearing so that he sounded as if he were shouting in her ear. "Are you happy now? My uncle Rob was furious over having to lie for me to the law about me sneakin' out and makin' one harmless little phone call. When I stupidly copped to that much, he completely lost his mind."

"Maybe you should've thought through the consequences for once," she said, though now that she could really hear Jeremy, he sounded as if he had been drinking, dropping the chances to somewhere south of zero that he'd accept responsibility for his own poor decisions.

"Fired," he repeated, "and homeless, too, now, while you're out screwing around like the slut you always were."

It struck her again that this Jeremy sounded nothing like the man who'd worked so hard to overcome a chaotic childhood and an undiagnosed learning disability that had made school a struggle to prove that he was smart and steady enough to build a successful business and win her heart with his drive and dedication. And nothing like the man she'd seen with tears running down his grinning face the day she'd shown him her home pregnancy test, the shock of its unmistakable plus sign seeming like the magical solution to their troubled marriage. But that Jeremy was long gone, drowned in a bitter brew of alcohol and disappointment. And leaving behind something far more dangerous in its wake.

"Did you decide to punish me by going after my student?" she demanded, knowing she might never get another chance to ask him directly. A chance she had to take if she ever hoped to quiet the nightmares she kept having, where Russell's friends and family packed her classroom, pointing as they shouted, *It was your fault! Yours!* "Or did you pay someone to—to come hurt him?"

"When Uncle Rob cut me loose, I—I put my fist right through a window where I was living. Got me tossed me out like I was trash, a criminal. No notice, nowhere to go, and absolutely *nothing left to lose.*"

His words sent chills ripping through her, prompting Emma to reach for her dog for support. As darkness cloaked the rolling coastal prairie, the cry of a lone night bird pierced the emptiness around them.

"Where are you, Jeremy?" she managed, hating how small and shaky her voice sounded. Because a man with nothing left to anchor him might well be on the road already, especially one who'd threatened her before. "Where are you right now?"

"I'm right behind you. *Boo, bitch*—" Her ex's laughter cut off abruptly, leaving her only with a dead connection and the gooseflesh that had broken out from head to toe.

While Beau watched helplessly, Wallace sneered at Cort and Leland, who were sobbing as they shoved their toys into pillowcases in preparation to leave the home their family was about to be kicked out of. The home that Wallace had lusted after since the days when he'd been invited to the mansion for family get-togethers as a kid.

"Be sure you don't leave any of your fleas behind now, little mongrels," he said, the silver star on his chest winking in the light. "We got some gen-u-wine purebreds comin' in now." With that, he gestured toward his elegant blonde daughters, who were wearing tiaras with pink evening gowns as they glided in waving like parade queens.

Seething with fury, Beau struggled to confront his cousin, only to realize he was trapped in the same wheelchair where he'd spent months after the accident that cost Melissa her life. Fury turning to horror, he lurched against the straps—

"No!" Not bindings, but blankets tangled around him as he fought free of the nightmare. On his bedside nightstand, where he'd left his phone to charge, it buzzed, vibrating against the rich and glossy wood.

He sucked in a deep breath to clear his head and sat up in the bed to answer, though a glance at the digital clock told him it was only 4:34 a.m.

Fernando Galvez's deep voice came in a rush. "Sorry to wake you, jefe, but my Antonio was coming home from another shift at that fire station he insists on playing at this morning." At the mention of his youngest's position in the all-volunteer department, which Antonio hoped would one day lead to a paid position in one of the state's larger cities, disapproval darkened Fernando's tone. As he'd grumbled on many an occasion, he saw no reason why the path that he had thrived on—the same that each of Antonio's older vaquero brothers had so wisely chosen—wasn't good enough for this son, too, or why Antonio would want to venture anywhere beyond the ranch and community that were home to all of his extensive *familia*.

"He was stinking of the filthy smoke and soot again instead of the honest smells of horse and cattle," Fernando went on, getting in one last complaint about the boy he'd spent so many hours teaching the finer points of his work, "when he spotted the Jeep you asked us to watch for. It was the same silver Wrangler, parked in the brush behind that turbine where that young man met his fate, may God and all the angels have mercy on his soul."

Turbine Number 43. An image of a slender female body hanging broken from its platform sent adrenaline crashing through Beau's system, followed by a punch of white-hot anger.

"Emma Copley's back? After I specifically told her not to come here?" Beau swore under his breath, cursing himself for falling into the trap, after only a few months officially on the job, of expecting unquestioning obedience to his orders concerning all ranch matters. As if that headstrong woman gave a damn about his status in this county—or anything but the evidence she was convinced that she could find.

"Antonio looked around but didn't see her," Fernando told him, "and the turbine remains padlocked. Should I take him out there with me again, maybe gather some other men as well to find her?"

"No. Tell Tony thanks," Beau said, "and thank you for calling to let me know about it, but when it comes to Dr. Copley, I prefer to go and set her straight myself."

It was still pitch-dark, at least two hours before sunrise, when Beau left the house after letting his aunt know he'd been called out on ranch business. Before pulling out of the drive, he had loaded his truck with a rechargeable lantern, a larger first aid kit, water and blankets... because in the time it had taken him to pull on jeans and boots and button up a work shirt, his fury with Emma's stubbornness had given way to raw anxiety.

What if she'd hurt herself out there, traipsing around in the dark? Would she have brought bolt cutters and tried climbing the locked turbine? Or what if there'd been any truth to those theories she'd been spouting and someone had followed her onto his land, seeing the late hour and remote location as the perfect opportunity to rid himself of a nagging problem?

It had been this last thought that had moved him to unlock the gun safe that had been his father's. And that sense of protectiveness he felt whenever he recalled that moment when he'd found her shaken, her blouse torn and her face bloody, that explained the rifle he had riding next to him.

Beau told himself this wasn't personal, that he would do the same for anybody, especially any woman. But as aggravating as it was to have Emma ignore what he had told her, he couldn't help admiring the way that she'd stood up to Wallace, even if he did suspect that she'd lost all perspective. Coming out here in the dead of night, all alone, especially after she'd told both him and Wallace that she feared someone might be out to kill her, proved it.

By the time he found her Jeep, Beau wasn't sure whether he wanted more to shake the woman or to hug her. But the first step was to figure out if she was somewhere nearby.

"Emma?" he called quietly, not wanting to startle her. Raising the LED lantern, he kept the rifle tucked beneath his right arm pointed at the ground. "Emma, it's Beau Kingston. I've come to check on you."

With the turbine still shut down pending the completion of the safety investigation, he heard a light breeze sifting through dried grasses and the rhythmic chirruping of insects. Other than that, nothing. Not a whisper of a human voice, not a single footfall.

"Emma, you all right?" He raised his voice a little. "There's no need to hide from me. I just need to know you're okay."

He strained his ears, but once more, there came no answer. Only the faint hooting of some kind of owl from somewhere in the distance.

Stepping forward, Beau felt the Jeep's hood, found it cool to the touch. *It's been parked here for hours, maybe all night long.*

The hood was unlatched, too, sitting slightly ajar. Leaning the rifle against the front bumper, he raised the hood, holding the lantern over the engine as he ran his gaze over—

"What the hell?" he blurted out, feeling the pumping of his own heart, the heated tightness of his skin. Because the slack serpentine belt he spotted looked as if it had been sliced, not broken, as if someone had deliberately disabled the vehicle.

Allowing the hood to fall, he grabbed his gun, turned his steps toward the turbine's base, and at first jogged, then flat-out ran in the direction of the door there. Because he couldn't get past the suspicion that if, unlike Tony, he took the time to rattle the chain on it, he would find it unlocked or cut through—and Emma lifeless high above.

He was sweating bullets by the time he reached the entry door. Pulling at the chain, he sighed, relieved beyond measure to find it padlocked tightly, just as he'd been assured.

"Come out now, Emma, please. It's Beau," he shouted, praying she was capable of responding. "You've got me pretty worried."

As the echo of his shout died, he heard a whine, followed by the scrabble of approaching footsteps. With the lantern's wire bail over his left forearm, he raised the barrel of the rifle.

"Identify yourself," he ordered.

A split second later, he realized the individual was incapable of speech.

"River?" he asked as the dog entered the circle of light, her head lowered and her tail tucked between her legs. "It's okay, River. Here, girl."

Crouching, he laid the rifle on the dusty ground and reached out, his arms wide and welcoming. When he spotted the leash that she was trailing, his gut clenched. The dog surely hadn't simply wandered off on her own.

His lowered voice and body language quickly drew her to him, and within seconds he was stroking the silky golden coat, running his hands over her trembling body.

Turning over his palms, he moved them closer to the light and found them sticky with a rusty darkness. Blood—his racing pulse redoubled.

And it didn't take him long to determine it wasn't from the dog.

Chapter 7

Six hours earlier

After hours of fruitlessly searching the bird strike zone, where Emma was certain Russell would have focused any cameras, she could hear nothing but the sheriff's voice in her mind, infuriatingly smug and condescending. *I'll tell you what. From here on in, why don't you leave the policin' work to me and just stick with all your nature nonsense. Because it's pretty clear you aren't cut out for sleuthin'.*

Leave it all to him, and go back home to teach Professor Paulsen's soul-killing classes. Maybe everyone was right and that was what she needed.

Or maybe I'm just scared out here, afraid of Jeremy lurking somewhere nearby, waiting for the moment I let my guard down.

Frowning, she shook off her fear, aggravated beyond

measure that he still held the power to shake her up with what she was almost certain had been nothing but a cruel bluff. After all, she'd been beyond careful to make certain that no one had followed her this evening. And Jeremy especially would've had no way to predict that she would have ventured here tonight.

It's only the exhaustion talking, that's all, she thought as she stumbled over a jutting tussock. She went down on one knee, only to feel sweet River pressing close beside her, reaching up to lick her face and whining softly.

"I know, girl," Emma said, smiling at the way the retriever, in her obvious confusion over their presence out here so late, kept attempting to lead her back to the vehicle that would get them to a cozy bed in a comfortable room, where the dog was certain they belonged. "I'm about ready to call it a night."

They might as well, since this was hopeless, continuing to search for the proverbial needle in the haystack in the darkness. Though Emma had a reasonable idea of the right area to look if Russell had wanted to capture any unscheduled bird collections, the little cameras would be all too easy to miss and were impossible to track electronically without specific tags keyed to her phone.

Lacking such guidance, the only things of interest she'd come across so far were a large band of feral hogs, which prompted her to leash River more for the dog's safety than her own, and enough scorpions to make her skin crawl.

With a defeated sigh, Emma stood again, coming to her feet more slowly than usual, since her body had stiffened up from the attack the night before. As she started toward the Jeep, out of the corner of her eye, she caught a flash of light. Pointing her beam in that direction, she cried out at the glint that reflected off a tiny lens.

"Finally!" She dug excitedly among the narrow-leafed branches of a tough and thorny shrub, beyond caring about the scratches when she uncovered the camouflage-patterned camera that had been secured there using zip ties. Unable to remove the camera without a sharp knife, she opened the front and popped out its memory card, which she zipped inside a pocket for safekeeping.

Excited to get back to her computer to review the images, she rearranged leaves to hide the camera again, grabbed River's leash and hurried back to her Jeep with a fresh energy hastening her steps.

Inside the Jeep, Emma's mood changed quickly when the engine wouldn't start. As she retried the ignition, her heart sank as the weak whirring died completely. "Oh, no," she said, unable to fathom why her normally reliable vehicle would do this here and now. While the issue might be minor, she had no way of dealing with it without assistance.

When she checked her phone, her heart fell further when she saw the battery had died—her own fault, since she'd forgotten to charge it after the sheriff had returned the missing cell. But with no way to call anyone, she had little choice but to hike out in order to get help. She blew out a breath, knowing it could take at least an hour to reach the gate on the rough road in the darkness. And she might wait outside it all night before anyone came by—if they even stopped to offer assistance.

"I'm afraid this is going to be one long night," she told River, wondering if the two of them would be better off sleeping in the Jeep until daylight. But even then, with the turbine shut down, there was no guarantee that help would come, and no one had any idea she was out here. Plus, once the late-August sun rose, temperatures would quickly grow unbearable.

As she sat considering, she recalled a Green Horizons engineer giving her a tour of the area before she'd embarked on her study. They'd been close to this spot when he'd waved to a dirt road leading westward. "If you or your assistant ever run into any issues," he'd said, "you'll find the main ranch headquarters about three miles up the way there. About a mile past the mansion, you'll see the barns and then a little office building, where you should ask for the ranch manager."

But she didn't know the ranch manager. The only person she knew, the only one she trusted to help her out of this jam, was the man living in the closer Kingston mansion—the same man who'd be furious to know she'd defied his order.

"Well, he's bound to find out anyway," she told River as she climbed out of the Jeep with her flashlight and the day pack containing drinking water and Russell's gun. "I might as well face him head-on."

Beau, too, would understand what her discovery at Turbine Number 43 might mean. And he seemed too reasonable a man to turn his back on a chance to get an actual look at Russell's killer.

As she walked, coyotes' yips and howls chorused in the distance. Pulling River closer, Emma ignored them and instead imagined herself bringing Beau around to her way of thinking. Imagined convincing him to help her ensure that any evidence turned over to the sheriff wouldn't simply disappear without another witness to corroborate its existence.

It was a good plan, she decided, using her flashlight's steady beam and the crescent moon above to guide her steps. A plan that eased some of the gnawing tension in her belly and warmed her with the faintest flickerings of hope.

Except it wasn't hope, but headlights, that unexpectedly crested the low hill about fifty yards ahead. Crested and accelerated when she waved her arms at the grill of a large vehicle barreling toward her.

A few minutes after reporting the abandoned Jeep, Beau received a call back from the sheriff himself.

"So I hear you want my help now," Wallace said, his voice rough as if he'd just been awakened. "Imagine that."

"You *are* the sheriff, aren't you?" Beau challenged, pushing past his anger over the alleged new will to focus on what most mattered at the moment. "Looks to me like there might've been a crime here. Trespassing, at the very least, since I warned Emma Copley to stay off my land, but I'm a hell of a lot more worried about her safety than I am about that right now. Looks like her vehicle's been intentionally disabled, out here by Turbine Number 43, and I found her dog, wandering alone. Shaking like a leaf, with blood on her fur."

"Dog injured? Shot or cut up?"

"Not that I can find," Beau said. "I'm worried the blood's not hers. And no one's responding when I call out."

"What makes you think Dr. Copley's car's been tampered with?"

"Hood was ajar and the drive belt looks like it's been sliced to me. No wear, no fraying."

"Sometimes they can go like that," Wallace said. "And maybe she raised the hood herself to see if she could figure out what was goin' on. Or she could've cut herself somehow tryin' To play mechanic."

Beau had to admit it was a possibility. The amount of blood on River had seemed fairly modest.

"You look for her along the road back to the gate?"

Wallace asked. "Maybe she's on foot, thinkin' she can thumb a ride back into town."

"Not yet. Thought I'd better call this in first, given the circumstances. But I did check out the turbine. Found it still locked up tight."

"Then I'm sure you and a couple of your kinfolk— I mean those overpaid vaqueros you've got working for you—can find her wanderin' around lost out there."

"Damn it, Wallace, can't you put aside your self-serving trash talk for thirty seconds and do your job? Or at least send out a couple of deputies who will?"

"You know what? The voters in this county think I do my job just fine, and I'm sick as hell of you and that woman goin' around sayin' otherwise. So go find her your own damned self if you can—if you aren't too busy running *my* ranch into the ground to bother."

Beau wasn't sure which of them hung up first, only that he'd never wanted to thrash a man so badly in his life. But with the dog shaking against his legs and dawn staining the horizon, he roughly thrust aside his anger, wanting only to find Emma. And when he did, he swore, if she was alive to do the telling, he would damned well listen to her this time—after giving her one hell of a hug, out of sheer relief.

The idea of touching her like that, of having an excuse to wrap her in his arms again, held a powerful appeal. One he shoved from his mind, focusing on the task at hand.

"Where is she, River?" he asked. "Where's Emma?"

The dog whined up at him, her dark brown eyes beseeching. But if she had any answers, she didn't volunteer them.

At least Wallace's suggestion about looking along the roadside leading toward the ranch gate made sense to Beau. Before calling Fernando to organize a search team, who might inadvertently destroy any evidence of foul play, however, Beau decided to drive the route on his own.

He took River to his truck, where he lifted her onto the passenger seat beside him. With his high-beam headlights turned on and his windows partly open, he headed for the ranch gate but spotted no sign of Emma. A few times, he paused to shout her name, honking his horn and bellowing that he was here to help her, but the only thing that gained him were a few moos from curious cattle, who lifted their heads to search his truck's bed for signs of hay.

Turning around, he headed back, and on a whim passed both her Jeep and the turbine, figuring she might've decided to risk his wrath by hiking toward ranch headquarters—and his home—in the hope of finding someone quickly.

He didn't get a third of a mile before River turned abruptly toward the window and barked several times, tail wagging. In her excited scrabbling, one of her paws landed on the toggle switch, lowering the glass completely.

"No, girl! Stay!" he said, hitting the brakes as the dog started through the open window. He reached too late to close it, seeing her leap down and scramble away. He cursed and put the truck in Park. Taking the lantern and the rifle, he followed the path River had taken, one leading roughly in the same direction from which he'd just come.

He lost sight of the dog a couple of times, but the dawn's pearly glow allowed him to safely jog in the general direction she had taken. He hoped like hell that he was right following his hunch that River had heard or smelled something that might lead them both to Emma instead of frightening an already-spooked dog into running wild to escape.

Trotting down into a deep draw, he caught sight again of the looming turbine—and a light-colored form sniffing at the ground not far ahead.

"Hey there, River." Breathing hard by now, he crept closer, edging toward where he saw that the end of her leash had snagged on a jutting stone. If she panicked, she'd most likely pull free, giving him no choice but to get out of this ravine to find enough of a cell signal to call Fernando. Certainly, an organized group could cover far more ground, more quickly, and the vaqueros knew this land better than anyone.

Finally in range, Beau crouched down, reaching ahead of him to free the leash—

And flinching at a crack like thunder and a spray of dirt erupting from the gravel a couple of feet to his right.

Military training kicking in, his body reacted even as his mind screamed *Gun!* He sprinted for the nearest outcrop, dragging the struggling dog toward cover before whoever was out here managed to kill them both.

No second shot followed, let alone the fusillade he more than half expected, but adrenaline had his heartbeat thundering in his ears. That and River's panicked yips and the scrabbling of her nails on gravel made it impossible to make out the shouted words—

But he still recognized the voice echoing through the tight draw.

It was Emma, yelling something, her words a desperate shriek. It took an additional split second for the anger in them to cut through his surprise, along with the suspicion that she had been the person who'd damned near shot him dead.

"Let go of her right now!" Emma shouted, shaking so hard she could barely aim the gun from where she lay propped up on her elbows, with her lower body hidden beneath the shelf of rock where she'd spent hours hiding.

Part of her problem was exhaustion, worsened by the discomfort of a long night spent wedged in a dampish space barely tall enough for her to crawl into. But terror was the biggest issue, along with the knowledge that she might actually have to shoot a living, breathing person as she'd feared.

Sure, she knew how to use a pistol. At her retired cop stepfather's insistence, she'd bought and learned to use one after filing for divorce last year, though she'd felt so uncomfortable with the idea that it had remained locked up untouched in her Austin condo ever since.

Yet here she was, blinking back tears with her body half outside her makeshift shelter, aiming at a man, not just a paper target. Because she couldn't let him hurt River—or use the dog to lure her out.

"Drop that leash, or I swear I'll blow your head off," Emma called, fatigue throbbing through a body scraped raw from last night's frantic escape of the truck that had sped toward her when she'd tried to flag down the driver. Engine roaring, it had left the road, racing after her as she'd swerved, desperate as a fleeing rabbit, into a ravine too narrow for the vehicle to follow.

Scrambling downhill, she'd fallen hard, her feet tangling in River's leash. The rocky ground had torn the skin off her hands and ripped out the knee of her pants. She'd apparently kicked the dog on her way down, too, for River had yelped and raced off, her tail tucked between her legs. Not daring to call after her, Emma had run farther between the steep walls, praying she wasn't trapping herself in a spot with no escape.

"What are you doing, Emma? It's me, Beau." He'd withdrawn behind a bank of loose rock, completely out of sight now, but from the way his voice echoed off the stone, he hadn't gone far. "I'm here to help you. Are you all right?"

She caught her breath, her gun hand shaking harder. Her mind lurched between the horror of knowing that she could've accidentally killed Beau Kingston and the worry that maybe, just maybe, that's what she should have done.

"I found your Jeep this morning," he continued when she didn't answer, "And then I found River, with blood on her."

"She's hurt? If you've hurt her—"

"Of course I didn't hurt her. I'm not hurting anyone. You know that. You know me." He sounded worried, though, uncertain she wouldn't pull the trigger once again.

"I—I *thought* I did. But you— You tried to—" Emma was weeping freely, vacillating in her certainty that it had been him last night. But it surely could have, coming from his house so late. The truck had looked like his, too, roughly the same size and age. "I couldn't see the truck's plates—or make out the color, dark as it was."

"What truck? What are you talking about? Come on, Emma. All I know is I was sleeping when I got a call saying your Jeep was spotted out this way. I was mad at first, I'll admit it, but mostly worried when I couldn't find you. And scared half out of my wits when I saw your engine's belt had been cut."

"*Cut?* You mean on purpose?" Her heart kicked in her chest.

It made sense, though, that the person who'd tried to run her over would have set her up to be walking along that roadway last night. The question was, was the same man trying to lure her out of hiding now? Her mind flew back to the look Sheriff Fleming had given his cousin when she'd mentioned that the wind farm might be shut down if there had been a cover-up.

Cost you a pretty penny, too, now wouldn't it, Wallace's words rang through her memory, *what with all that money you're about to rake in with that new turbine construction?*

Beau had acted as if nearly doubling the size of the wind farm meant little to him personally, seeming more upset about the loss of clean energy and much-needed local jobs. But hadn't he changed toward her abruptly following that conversation, banning her from the property soon afterward?

"You *know* me," Beau repeated, his voice steady, calming. The same reassuring voice of the man who'd helped her after Russell's death. The man who'd waited at the hospital with her the night before last, when he could have easily left her for someone else to deal with. Had it all been a show meant to find out how much of a risk she was to his new deal with Green Horizons—or how much she really knew about what her grad student had been up to?

"I've shown you who I am," he added. "And here I am, proving it again. Go on, River. Go to your mom."

"River!" Emma cried, her heart leaping as the big dog hurried in her direction, the leash trailing.

At the sight of her, River picked up speed, her thick tail wagging and her mouth curved in an expression of pure canine joy. Reaching her destination, River tried to cover her mistress's face and hands with kisses—and would have succeeded had Emma not pushed her away and ordered her to settle down.

"It's all right. We're all right," Emma told the friend she'd been so worried for, stroking the thick golden fur. And then, abruptly, her instincts kicked in, pushing past her fear and prompting her to call out. "I—I'm coming out now, Beau, if I can still move my legs. I'm kind of wedged in under the—"

She gasped and stiffened, a reaction prompted not by pain or stiffness, but by an unmistakable noise she heard coming from beneath the rocky ledge. A sound that had River, too, reacting, crouching down on her front legs and barking as she tried to thrust her head past Emma's hips.

"No!" Emma struggled to grab the dog's collar before she made a bad situation even worse. "No, girl! Stop it!"

"Emma, what's wrong?"

Still fighting to control River, Emma didn't answer.

Beau grabbed the dog's collar, dragging her back and ordering her to hush. When the dog finally fell quiet, Emma heard the buzzing again, now angrier and louder.

Only this time she felt the rattlesnake slithering along the length of her leg.

Chapter 8

Growing up on this ranch, Beau had heard the sound more than once. The shaking of a rattler's tail. Very big and very close, in this case, the nerves coiling in his gut told him. And judging from Emma's milk-pale face and widened eyes, she was as aware as he was of the danger it represented.

He raised the barrel of the rifle, taking aim at a threat that he knew from experience liked to hide out among these rocks. But the dog whose leash he held startled at his movement, making the barrel of the weapon wobble.

When Emma looked up to see the gun's muzzle drift past her face, she shrieked and tried to scramble out from beneath the ledge.

Beau warned, "Be still—don't move."

But as she pushed herself out, her sharp cry told him it was too late—as did the sight of the tan-and-brown rattlesnake—a fat diamondback over a yard long—dangling from her lower right leg.

Kicking at the thing, he convinced it to let go and try to strike at him. As Emma crawled free of the threat, Beau took aim and shot the serpent's head off with an echoing blast loud enough to make his ears ring.

Emma was sobbing, grabbing at her calf. "It got me. Latched right on. It's already throbbing."

"You need to try to calm down, slow your breathing." Beau tightened his grip on River's leash to keep the dog from the severed snake's head, which could still inflict a deadly bite on reflex. "We'll need to get you to a hospital, but for right now, keep as still as you can."

Emma dragged in an audible breath, her body racked with shaking. But the crying stopped, her voice steadying as she said, "Let me hold on to River. She'll be calmer with me."

"You'll be all right. Don't worry," he said, passing her the leash and trying not to think about an incident when he'd been fourteen, when one of the vaqueros had lost a leg—and nearly his life—to a bite from a far smaller diamondback than this one.

Emma draped her arms around the dog and leaned her head against River's shoulder. While she shushed the whining animal, Beau kicked the reptile out of the way.

Once he'd finished, he said, "Do you mind if I look at the bite? And are there any other injuries I need to know about? That blood I found on River—"

"Mine, I suppose. I tore up my knee when I was running from a man in a dark pickup." She shivered. "I thought—I thought it was you."

"That was why you shot at me?"

She shook her head. "The—the truck looked like yours—at least I thought it did. And it was coming from the right direction."

"From ranch headquarters?" He grimaced, thinking

how his father had purchased five dark gray, four-wheel-drive pickups last December on a year-end fleet deal for ranch work, along with the fully loaded blue model Beau had inherited from the old man. Could one of the ranch vehicles have been taken from the equipment shed, one she'd mistaken for his own truck? "I'll check," he promised. "If the truck was one of ours, there should be video."

"Okay," she said. "Sit, River."

When the dog settled, Emma began rolling up her pant leg.

"Here, let me," Beau said, laying down the rifle and pulling out a pocketknife.

When she flinched, he shook his head. "You're going to have to trust me. I need to cut through this material and get off that sock and hiking boot, too, before the leg swells too much."

Her body rigid, she held the dog close to her body.

"Listen," he told her, "I'm not the one who tried to run you down. And right now, you need to trust me if you want to get out of this situation in one piece."

Shoulders sagging, she nodded. "You're right. Just don't cut the wound to try to suck the poison out. That's an old wives' tale that does more harm than good."

"Way ahead of you there," he said, splitting the seam up to knee level. When she removed her boot and pulled down the sock, he gestured toward an already-purpling area on the meaty part of her calf, where blood dripped from a small puncture wound. "That's it, right? Only the one fang got you?"

"Looks that way to me," she agreed. "I'll bet the other one caught on the pant seam here."

"That's good news. Only half the venom."

"Still bad enough if I don't get to the hospital pretty quickly. I've seen rattlesnake bites up close before."

Seeing her light green eyes losing focus, he reached out and squeezed her forearm and felt that her skin was cool and clammy. "Look at me, Emma. I need you to stay with me." He couldn't have her going into shock.

Sucking in a breath, she straightened and nodded at him. "I—I'm sorry. I'm just— It's been a very long night, and that—I felt it crawling along my leg, where I couldn't even see it." She shuddered visibly.

"That snake's history, and we're getting you out of here," he reassured her, not liking her pallor. "Fastest way to get you help'll be for me to carry you out to my truck and call on the way to the hospital in Pinto Creek to make sure they're set up to treat you. If not, we'll ask them to have a chopper meet us and get you to the nearest trauma center that's properly equipped."

"You can't carry me and handle River on your own. And what if he comes back—the man who tried to kill me?"

"I'll keep my rifle handy. And as for carrying you and dealing with River, I can manage."

"Maybe you won't have to, not all on your own." Wiping away tears, she turned to glance in the direction of a lone emergency siren in the distance. A siren that was drawing nearer. Relief washing over her face, she confirmed, "I'm pretty sure that's the sound of the cavalry arriving."

"You are either the damned unluckiest or the luckiest woman in all of Texas," Sheriff Fleming told Emma as he strode into her room at the local hospital, where she'd spent the last two days undergoing treatment with the antivenin they kept on hand against occasional bites from the area's most common poisonous snake. With his gray-blond mustache neatly groomed, he wore a freshly pressed uniform, and his badge gleamed as it caught a ray of morning sunlight from the blinds. "I hear that rattler didn't get you with both barrels, or you might've been shoppin' for a peg leg this week—if you'd lived to shop at all."

She didn't feel so fortunate, with her lower leg still swollen and her head fuzzy from the painkillers she'd been given. She felt vulnerable here, too, uncertain who had tried to kill her and isolated from her family, her students and her colleagues, with the exception of a call from her department head, who'd gruffly offered to have someone fetch her back to Austin as soon as she was discharged.

The proposal had come on the heels of Dr. Lee's stern lecture about her "irresponsible" and "dangerous" behavior, returning to the turbines before the energy company had completed its safety review. Emma was still fuming over his attitude—and bewildered by the unmistakable impression that she was no longer the bright young star of the department, on track for an early tenure. Instead, when she'd asked about her new assignment, he'd abruptly cut her off and told her bluntly that if she wasn't back on campus for the start of the semester, she needn't bother coming back at all.

After waiting for a food service worker to remove her nearly untouched breakfast tray from the room, Emma told the sheriff nonetheless, "I do feel lucky to have made it through this past week. In spite of all the hospitality your county's offered."

"You are going to be okay, aren't you? No long-term issues with the...?" He gestured vaguely in the direction of her leg, which remained elevated on pillows beneath the bedsheet.

"I'll be on crutches for two or three weeks, but I may

be released tomorrow." She blinked at the bright wash of color he was holding. "Are those—you brought me flowers?"

Wallace held them up, his grin expanding, making him look like a different person than the angry and defensive lawman she'd dealt with up until now. "My wife picked them out. You like 'em?"

She blinked, her vision coming into focus. "You have a wife?"

He held up his left hand, flashing the gold band on his ring finger. "Don't sound so danged surprised. Rumor has it I can be quite charming."

As she struggled not to choke on that claim, he cleared his throat and added, "I figured you could use some cheerin' up, with everything that's happened…though I see I'm not the first to have that thought."

Ignoring his glance at the dozen yellow roses in the green vase sitting on the windowsill, she took the flowers he offered, a sunny mix of carnations, daisies and purple asters, neatly wrapped in plastic. "That's very kind. Please thank your wife for me," she said before adding, "and thank you for coming. You have news on the investigation?"

"No arrests yet, if that's what you're hopin', but we do have things to talk about." He wandered a few steps closer to the roses before plucking the attached card and frowning down at the get-well message from Beau Kingston. "I only hope I haven't come too late to sound the warning."

A note of fear pinged through her, a reminder of her panic when she'd seen that pickup hurtling toward her. But she'd been wrong about its driver, she was certain. Sure enough that she'd accepted Beau's generous offer to care for her dog at his home until she was released from the hospital.

Since the ambulance had taken her, however, she hadn't seen him again. Nor had she heard from him, other than the delivery of the flowers with their thoughtful but no-more-than-polite note.

"Warning about what?" she asked Wallace.

"Your vehicle really was intentionally disabled, according to the mechanic at the garage where I had it towed," the sheriff told her. "But the thing was, the only prints we found on the hood belonged to Kingston. So maybe it's not so surprising that he knew right off, even though it was dark when he called it in, that somebody sawed through your drive belt."

"So you're saying that—?"

"He could've done it himself. Could've considered you a danger to that big deal he's got pending, with all your talk of murder." A glint of malice lit the sheriff's blue eyes. "I know you figure him for the white knight, always comin' To your rescue, and I know the ladies around here have him pegged for the catch of the century, but if you knew the things about him I do... He's not even a real Kingston."

"What you're saying makes no sense at all." She shook her head as an image flooded her mind. "You should have seen him shoot that snake in two. That was a knee-jerk reaction, I can tell you—and it saved me from another bite. If he'd wanted me gone, he could've walked away, not killed the thing or flagged down help."

"Maybe he'd just as soon scare you off, if he didn't have to kill you."

She straightened in the bed. "And maybe this turf war, or whatever it is, that the two of you have going has clouded your presumptions, Sheriff. Doesn't it make more sense that whoever messed with my Jeep would wear gloves to disguise his identity? Or that he drove one of the hundreds of dark-colored pickups on the road around this county?"

Wallace's grimace dissolved into a shrug. "You could be right. If I was sure, I'd've damned well locked him up by now—"

"Right next to that registered sex offender you arrested—that's where you'd put your own cousin?"

Fleming huffed out a breath. "About that. Turns out ol' Jorge's not looking so good for your assault on the night of the memorial service. Looks like there was some big brouhaha with his common-law wife right around the time you got jumped—enough hollerin' and screechin' that the neighbors called in a noise complaint."

"Did this woman maybe scratch him?"

The sheriff shrugged. "Not that she's admitting, but they've mixed it up before on more than one occasion. And she's the one with the record for domestic battery."

"Sounds like a charming couple."

"Every county's got its share. The other thing is, we found a splotch of blood on your clothing from the night of the attack. It wasn't yours, but it didn't match his, either. So, considering the lack of evidence, I had to cut him loose."

"Well, at least you're not wasting any more time on the wrong man while my real attacker's walking free. Now if you'll quit wasting time worrying about Beau, who was still inside the community center when I was jumped, and maybe check out my ex-husband again—"

"First off, who's to say Beau didn't put someone up to helping him, what with all his money and those vaqueros—that's what they call those Spanish-speakin' cowboys on his place—dependent on him for their jobs. And secondly, your ex-husband—"

"Called and threatened to come after me that night because his uncle fired him."

"I read that in Deputy Kendall's report. You claimed Hansen told you his uncle was upset about having been put into a position to lie for a family member."

"That's right. And when Jeremy lost his temper, he ended up evicted, too."

Wallace pulled the face of a man who'd been expecting a drink of ice-cold sweet tea, only to swill a mouthful of cider vinegar. "Well, the uncle was singin' a different tune when I checked in with him again last night. He told me everything was right as rain between him and his nephew and he knows nothing about any landlord problem. Jeremy's just off fishing for a few days with a buddy at his cabin."

"So once more, you're buying into another of his uncle's lies on Jeremy's behalf." Emma sighed and shook her head. "And you *personally* spoke to my ex-husband?"

"I haven't been able to reach him so far," Wallace admitted. "And the uncle couldn't lay his hands on the friend's name or contact number. He's tryin' To track 'em down for me, though. Then I'll ask local law enforcement to check up on him, just to make sure he's where he claims."

"Jeremy is not out fishing somewhere." She crossed her arms over her chest, her nails digging into her own flesh in her frustration. "That much I can guarantee you."

"If I had to go with my gut, I'd say your ex has just been mouthing off again, trying to rattle your cage."

"I'm not sure I'm willing to gamble on your gut feeling, especially after two attempts on my life."

"I'll look into it," he promised, "but that doesn't mean I'm taking the heat off Kingston. Or that you should let your guard down around him, either. That gun you were carryin' when we found you—if you drop by the station, I could let you have it back, for personal protection."

Her stomach fluttered, and she knew that if she was going to tell him where the pistol had come from, now would be her last chance. But explaining why she hadn't reported it earlier would be difficult at this point. She might even be charged with interfering with an investigation.

Instead, she let the moment pass. "Before we go any further," she said, "there's something else I'll need you to consider."

"Something you forgot to mention to Deputy Kendall?"

"Actually, it's something I need to show you. Something I found the other night, out by the turbine." She laid the flowers on the bedside table, and then pointed toward a built-in cabinet. "Would you mind grabbing my purse out of the top drawer for me?"

"You *found* something?" Wallace frowned, his drooping mustache ruffling. "If you had any evidence, you should've immediately turned it over. If there's anything to it, to be usable in court, the chain of custody has to be clearly—"

"The afternoon Deputy Kendall came by, I was seriously hurting and sick from the medication. So the card I'd tucked inside my pants pocket wasn't something I was prepared to discuss." In truth, she'd forgotten all about it until the next day.

"Card?" he asked.

"My bag?" She gestured toward the drawer, which she couldn't reach without tugging her IV line and sending pain shooting through her leg.

"Oh, sure." He passed her the purse.

Unzipping a pocket, she pulled out a small blue memory card. "I removed this from a camera I found hidden near Turbine Number 43," she said. "I believe Russell placed a number in various locations to confirm his suspicions that more birds were dying than we were documenting. But it's very possible he could've recorded more than a conspiracy to beat us to the carcasses of protected species."

"You think he might've gotten a shot of somebody payin' a visit to the turbine around the time of his death, don't you?" asked Fleming, his brows rising. But before she could answer, he stuck his hand out. "Let me see that."

She released a long breath through her nostrils before dropping the card into his hand.

He turned it over to examine it, as if a visual inspection would reveal its digital secrets. "Have you opened up any of these pictures? Tampered with them in any way?"

"I wouldn't even know how." She felt heat creeping upward from the neckline of her hospital gown. "These cameras are motion-activated, so there are likely scores of shots. Probably hundreds, considering all the activity around the turbine after Russell's death."

"That's not what I asked you. I want to know if you've—"

"I didn't even try to look through them, not here, where anyone could walk in." Emma drew in a deep breath, gathering her nerve before continuing. "But along with my purse, your deputy brought me my laptop computer out of my Jeep, and I did use that to copy the whole file to the desktop and a cloud-based storage vault before I turned the memory card over to you today."

The sheriff's eyes narrowed a fraction, his color deepening as he began to piece together the possible implications. "And why exactly, Dr. Copley, would you feel the need to do that?"

"For safekeeping, for one thing, in case that memory card was somehow lost…or something," she said, not allowing her gaze to waver as she recalled the only item missing from her recovered purse. "And also, that way, it was a great deal easier to create a simple link for me to email to an investigator—Texas Ranger Lieutenant Cody Williams out of the Department of Public Safety. I thought you might appreciate the help."

Chapter 9

When Beau entered Emma's hospital room, he was surprised to find her up already. Dressed in a pair of light cotton pants and a turquoise scoop-neck T-shirt, she was balanced awkwardly on one crutch and one leg as she put the contents of a drawer into a white plastic bag with the hospital's logo printed on the front.

"You need some help with that?" he asked. "You look like you're teetering a bit there."

Turning, she lowered herself onto the edge of the bed. With her sun-streaked hair freshly combed and the color returned to her face, she looked flustered but far healthier than she had the last time he had seen her, with a small adhesive bandage replacing the larger gauze square on her forehead.

"I'm all finished, thanks," she said. "Can you believe they're springing me from here already? Maybe it was Sheriff Fleming's idea. As furious as he was with me this morning, he's probably planning to escort me to the edge of town like in one of those old Westerns."

Beau felt his jaw tighten at the mention of his cousin. According to Beau's lawyer, this damned *convenient* will Wallace had come up with could actually be accepted by the court as legal, since it had turned up such a short time after the original was filed. But until the document was properly authenticated, there was nothing for Beau to do but wait, work and go through the motions of a life that could be snatched out from under him at any moment.

"So what's Wallace's problem with you this time?" he asked.

Crossing her arms, she slanted a look his way. "I took the ball out of his court, or partly, by turning over what might be evidence in Russell Jorgenson's murder case to the Texas Rangers."

Beau fought back a grin at the thought of the insult to the jackass's ego, to say nothing of the threat, since the Rangers routinely investigated officials within the state who were suspected of malfeasance. "I'm surprised he didn't go completely nuclear on you."

She winced. "Close enough. Let's just say the nurses were once more unhappy with his volume."

"So you've told the Rangers everything that's been going on here?"

"I had a conversation with one of the lieutenants. Afterward, I emailed him a link to the photos I found by the turbine where Russell died. I haven't checked out the pictures yet myself, but—"

"Wait. You mean you actually found them? The game cameras you thought might be there? You didn't tell me before."

"One of them, anyway, and, um, no, I didn't mention it." Her gaze avoided his.

"Come to think of it," he recalled, "you were a little busy back then, trying to decide whether to blow my head off or to trust me."

"If you'd been where I was, forced to run for your life in the darkness—"

"But we established that that wasn't me, *right*?"

She hesitated a beat before answering, with a smile that didn't touch her eyes. "Are you kidding? I let you take my prized possession. How is River doing?"

He pulled out his cell phone and showed her a picture of her dog sprawled on a mahogany-colored leather sofa, her tongue lolling as she enjoyed a belly rub from his boys. "Hating ranch life. Clearly."

"She'll never want to come home. They're adorable together." A smile warmed her expression, lighting her face like a shaft of sunshine.

Beautiful, he thought, the surprise hitting him a fraction of a second later, along with the pleasant punch of the confirmation that he still had it in him to appreciate an attractive woman, even one he ought to have the good sense to stay miles away from. Yet here he was again, unable to keep from worrying about how she was doing or if she was all alone.

"The boys love River," he said, "and she's welcome to stay as long as you need. If I'm lucky, her good manners will rub off on our big galoot of a puppy."

"I appreciate the offer, but I should pick her up today."

"Because you don't fully trust me." The thought bugged him way more than it should have.

She answered carefully, "The sheriff did give me several reasons why I shouldn't."

Beau made a scoffing sound, recalling his brief phone conversation with the jackass earlier. "Those *incriminating prints* on the Jeep, right? The ones I told him he'd find since I'd checked out your engine after finding the hood ajar."

"That part didn't make a whole lot of sense to me, either," she admitted. "And I also find it hard to believe that you'd try so hard to scare me off one night, only to come to my rescue the next morning."

"Yet here you are, still nervous..." He took two steps closer and made note of the slight flinch, the way her muscles tensed. Did she really still imagine he would hurt her, or was she this jittery around all men? He thought about his earlier suspicion that she'd suffered more than emotional abuse at the hands of her ex-husband.

"Come on, Emma," he urged. "Seems like these harebrained accusations are nothing but one more desperate strategy to try to pull the rug—and the ranch—out from under me so he can claim it."

"Claim it? He can—what do you mean?"

"Never mind about the whys and wherefores. Just tell me you don't buy into his self-serving garbage and I'll take you to your Jeep."

"My Jeep? I thought—wasn't it impounded for the investigation?"

Beau shook his head. "All Wallace did was have it towed over to Marco Adams's garage, where an evidence guy searched it and dusted it for prints. As soon as they released it, I took the liberty—I hope you don't mind—of asking Marco to replace that drive belt and give it a good going-over to make sure it's roadworthy."

Surprise splashed across her face. "You did what? Why?"

Because I couldn't stop thinking of you, cowering under that rock ledge all night with only a rattlesnake for a companion. Because I can't stop thinking of you period just lately.

But Beau couldn't let himself admit that, so instead he shrugged. "I figured you had enough to worry about without sweating that kind of detail. The bill's all taken care of, and Marco said the Jeep's running good as new now." With a teasing smile, he added, "Although you're free to check with him to make sure I didn't tamper with your brake line."

Emma's jaw dropped before she recovered. "Thank you so much. I don't know what to say."

"Your thanks is more than enough." He felt the uptick in his own pulse as he added, "But that's not why I did it."

"Why, then?"

"Truth is, I feel a little guilty about banning you from the ranch," he admitted, wondering when the last time he'd let down his guard enough to be so honest with woman. It didn't come easily to him now—he'd been raised to believe that real men blustered through their blunders rather than admitting them. But all that baggage he'd been toting got awfully heavy after a while. "I should've listened when you tried to tell me there might be proof there that Russell had been murdered. If I hadn't been so damned high-handed, you wouldn't be here now, hurt."

She searched his face before saying, "What happened to me wasn't your fault. Whatever the sheriff thinks about it, I'm certain of that much."

Hearing her say that, he decided, was worth the price of the repair bill and then some. But instead of telling her, he changed the subject. "I wanted to let you know that our security cameras seem to be on the fritz, but I checked to see if there was any record of someone taking one of our vehicles from our equipment shed prior to the time that vehicle came after you."

She perked up, pushing herself more upright. "Oh?"

He shook his head, aggravated as hell to think about

their so-called inventory control system. "I can't rule out that the truck that came after you was one of ours. A couple of the pickups weren't where there were supposed to be that night and hadn't been in days. Trouble is, it turns out our guys have been pretty lax about signing them out the way they're supposed to. And lots of times, they just toss the keys to the next hand who needs to use one instead of returning it the way they should."

"So you're telling me you don't know where the truck that tried to hit me came from?"

"Fernando, my ranch manager, is trying to track down the whereabouts of all the vehicles missing from the shed." He'd be seeing to the flaws in their security system as well. "But, yes, you're right. There's no guarantee that some complete stranger didn't manage to steal one of our pickups or drive his own through an unlocked gate or cut fence we haven't found yet."

"It could have been anyone who jumped me after the memorial service, too," Emma said. "The sheriff told me they've definitely excluded that sex offender he arrested, so he had to turn the guy loose."

Beau clenched his jaw, frustrated as the one piece of the puzzle that had made sense slipped out of his grasp. "So it's likely the same person came after you both times."

"Unless this time, it was my ex-husband—not long before that truck showed up, Jeremy threatened me again. He blames me for being fired after the sheriff called to question his boss about harassing me before."

Back in his MP days, Beau had arrested men like that, pathetic losers whose refusal to take the blame for the problems they themselves had caused boiled over into a rage they directed at their women or kids. The worst lashed out with fists or weapons, while others used words to inflict the kinds of wounds that left less visible, but sometimes even crueler, marks. "You think he's really got it in him to drive down here to hurt you?"

She shook her head. "I already know he's left his place in Waco, but it's hard to say how far he'd go. Or if he even knows where I am. For all I know, he's skulking around Austin somewhere, trying to get my friends to tell him where I moved after our split."

"They wouldn't tell him, would they?"

"Not on purpose, but he's really clever about spoofing calls and conning people with stories about a family member's accident or—" She spanned her temples with the fingers of one hand as if to ward off a headache. "If you'd only known the man he was before—I still can't believe what he's turned into."

"Sorry to hear it." Remembering the helplessness he'd felt watching his own wife changing and all the pain that it had led to, Beau reached out and touched Emma's arm. "Sorry about all this."

"There's no reason to apologize." Emma's green eyes sparkled. "Not unless you were somehow in league with that rattlesnake."

"If so, he definitely got the bad end of that deal," Beau said drily. "But speaking of partners, one of my security business cohorts back in Colorado is a licensed private investigator. He's currently in Texas on business, so why don't I put in a call to see if he can lend a hand?"

"How?"

"I'll ask him to track down your ex's movements and try to figure out what he's been up to. Unless you'd rather wait for the authorities to do it."

"I don't think it's a priority for the sheriff. Especially now that I've reached out to the Rangers," she said.

"I'll call him this afternoon, then. I'll just need you

to write down as much identifying information as you can. Full name, previous addresses, birth date and his Social if you know it."

"I can do that," she agreed, "but I'm paying for this detective's time myself. I insist on it."

He started to argue, but the look she pinned him with said that she was serious. And would refuse to cooperate if he didn't agree.

"I'll tell you what," he said. "I'll ask Ty—his name is Tyler Phelps—to invoice you, so I'll need your mailing address, too." Most likely, Ty would never send the bill, considering whatever time he spent a down payment on Beau's helping him out of a sticky situation last year. But there was no reason to get into any of that now.

"All right, then. Thanks," Emma said as a petite blonde nurse whose pink scrubs were stretched over her midsection arrived with discharge papers.

Giving Beau a speculative look, she asked, "You're her ride?"

"Sure, I could be." Beau looked to Emma for confirmation. "Let me drive you over to check on your Jeep and collect River. Then we'll figure out where to go from there."

"Wherever it is, I won't be driving." She gestured toward her lower right leg. "I'm still so sore, there's no way I could manage. I doubt I could even tolerate the ride back to Austin."

The nurse ran through the doctor's orders, which included a schedule for Emma's medications, the elevation of her injured leg and instructions to return if signs of infection appeared. Once she'd finished, she said, "I have the wheelchair in the hallway for your discharge, but it might be a little while before I can round up an orderly to push it." Her face colored as she laid a hand on what was certainly a baby bump. "Right now, I'm afraid, I'm restricted from lifting or pushing anything heavier than—"

"Don't trouble yourself about it," Beau said. "I'll push the wheelchair."

"And congratulations to you," Emma added.

"Thank you." The nurse flushed, and her nose crinkled. "My husband and I are so excited. We just found out that it's a little girl."

"H-how wonderful for you."

As Emma turned away to pick up the bag she'd packed, Beau caught the sadness flickering across her features. Maybe once she had dreamed, too, of a loving marriage and a future that included motherhood. A future that had given way to a present filled with pain and fear...and loneliness, he suspected, for other than her students and employers, whom did she have in her life? The friends she'd mentioned, sure, but no one who'd appeared this past hellish week to help her.

But isolation could be a choice, he knew. After the rollover in Colorado, his grief, guilt and self-loathing had gradually driven away everyone, from his partners in the firm he and two marine corps buddies had started, which offered private security in an upscale ski resort town, to Melissa's sisters, who had put their own grief and their lives on hold to tend to his boys until Beau was well enough to leave with them for Texas. It had taken far longer, and an extremely tough talk from Aunt Alicia about what his behavior was doing to his sons, before he'd taken his first tentative steps toward normalcy...

Or at least to faking it, as best he could, one day at a time.

With this in mind, he loaded Emma's few items in the rear seat of his truck at the passenger pickup area a few minutes later.

"Do you want to sit back here and try to prop your leg up?" he offered, thinking he could move the booster seats.

"Thanks, but I should be fine up front." She smiled and gave a small shrug. "That pain pill they gave me right before you came in is pretty good stuff."

"I thought you were starting to droop a little."

"I'll be fine," she insisted, but he couldn't help noticing, once they both were situated in the front seat, how she hid a yawn behind her hand.

He left the hospital's loading area and pulled into a nearby parking lot. "Why don't we skip the shop, and I'll just have one of my guys pick up your Jeep for you?"

"That would be great," she said. "They can drop it by the motel and leave the keys for me at the front desk."

"You're sure that's a good idea? Going back to the same spot where you've been staying all along?"

"It's the only dog-friendly place in town."

Beau shook his head, mentally reviewing the aging structure, a one-story horseshoe-shaped bank of connected rooms. "I don't like it. Exterior entrances and exits, impossible to secure, and worst of all, whoever's out to harm you will be able to track you down in no time flat."

"River'll sound the alarm if there's a problem," she ventured.

"I remember she barked at Wallace, but we both know that dog's more likely to lick a man to death than bite him. You need to hightail it back to Austin instead of tempting fate again."

"So I've been told, repeatedly, by many people. Some of them even using the same words." Brittle as glass, her voice was sharp with anger. "They keep saying I need to leave immediately. Forget Russell and the study. Forget everything and go back to what's left of my life. Well, maybe I don't want the life they're offering. Maybe I don't want to tuck my tail and turn my back on murder."

"What are you talking about?" he asked, certain he had to be missing something. What the hell had he said to set her off like this? "You can tell me."

"Can I? Because you're doing it again. Ordering me to behave myself and leave town—"

"Nobody's ordering you to do anyth—"

"Next thing I know you'll be saying it's for my own 'mental and physical health and safety,' just like the others did."

Shaking his head, he put the truck into Park and looked at her. "You're not making sense. What others? I can't help you, Emma, if you don't help me understand."

She shook her head. "Mrs. Reddy, with the university, for starters." Her hands clenched, she told Beau about a call regarding the cancellation of another research project, followed by a demand that she return to teaching for her own "mental and physical health and safety."

Nothing about that seemed particularly odd to Beau, until she explained how the sheriff had, only hours later, tried to convince her to leave town using those exact words.

"I get it now," Beau said, "why you went to the Texas Rangers. But that doesn't mean I want them to end up coming to look into *your* death." The thought of sitting through a memorial service with Emma's photo on a placard hit him like a gut punch. He couldn't let it happen. Couldn't let her take the risk.

"I don't want that, either," she said. "But do you know what else I don't want? To be intimidated any longer by a man telling me if I do this or don't do that, or don't keep my mouth shut about what he's done already, he's going to make me pay. Because I've already paid—and dearly—and poor Russell... I'm afraid he's paid a price on my behalf, too."

"So what do you intend to do then?" Beau asked.

"To find the truth and see whoever's behind this brought to justice. And to prove to my ex-husband that I'm through living in fear of his intimidation. Even with only one good leg under me, I'm more than strong enough to stand my ground."

"And probably to kick his ass, too, if guts were all it took," Beau said, wondering if he'd ever met a braver, more determined woman. But as much as her attitude impressed him, he also wondered how much of it was a facade covering the cracks in her foundation. "You've already proven to me—to anyone with eyes to see—that you're no shrinking violet. But during my years with the marines, I saw a lot of tough guys learn even tougher lessons. One of them was that all the bluster in the world won't stop a blade or bullet."

She frowned, her forehead creasing. "So I'll start checking around after we get River, try to find another place where we can stay. Maybe on one of these online vacation rental websites, where people rent out little guest houses or rooms in their own homes."

Beau was familiar with the concept, which was popular in the mountain town where he and his wife had lived in Colorado. "This isn't exactly vacation country, so I doubt you'd find much like that close by."

"I'll check the web anyway, and ask the manager at the motel if she has any better ideas. Nadine's been so helpful, especially since Russell..."

"I can almost guarantee you Nadine'll have some good ideas." Back in their school days, she'd always been the type to walk a kid with a stomachache to the nurse or whisper a quiet word to the teacher if she noticed a classmate was coming to school without lunch, and he knew she'd been involved for years in raising funds to support the community food bank and purchase school supplies for foster kids. Beau felt certain she'd step up and make sure Emma found a safe place, where no one would ever find her.

Which meant she would no longer be his problem, or his responsibility...

No matter how the pressure in his chest tried to tell him otherwise.

As they headed toward the ranch to collect River, Emma couldn't help but notice how quiet Beau had fallen, his profile seemingly carved of granite, the hands that gripped the wheel chiseled out of some even more unyielding stone.

Distancing himself from the mistakes he's sure I'm making. Or maybe he was simmering beneath the surface, angry that he couldn't control her. *Why should he be different from every other man on earth?*

If she'd come to feel anything else toward him, from the warmth that had blossomed in her cheeks when the older woman who'd delivered the yellow roses had peeked at the tag and said, "From Mr. Kingston himself—you lucky girl!" To the fresh fizz of pleasure that had caught her unaware when he'd reappeared this afternoon, Emma needed to remember that it wasn't safe to trust him. No matter how many kindnesses he offered, she'd be a fool to drop her guard. Instead, she told herself that any man who'd spent the time and, with the repair of her Jeep, money that he had on her had to have his motives. Motives he hadn't seen fit to explain.

As the miles passed, however, she found herself relaxing in his silent presence. She watched puffy white clouds blossom in an otherwise blue sky until her worries drifted away.

Sometime later, she woke to the bumping of the truck's tires over the cattle guard.

"Sorry about the jostling," Beau said. "Having a nice sleep?"

"Mmm." She rubbed her neck, kinked from the way she had been leaning. "I'm afraid that pain pill had a little more kick to it than I expected. But at least the leg's not hurting."

She felt oddly disconnected from her body. Except for the weight of her eyelids, which she could scarcely keep open.

Glancing over at her, Beau frowned. "If I'd been halfway thinking earlier, I would've taken you straight to Nadine's so you could put your leg up. I could've brought River to you instead of dragging you all the way out here. You're obviously in no condition to—"

"It's fine," Emma said, raising one anchor-heavy hand to rub her eyes. "Just a little…"

The world dimmed once again, until she awakened to a dream. It had to be a dream, with Beau standing outside the passenger door of the parked pickup, opening it and smiling at her.

"We're here," he said, offering his hand. "My home."

Except this couldn't be his home. Or any house at all. In Emma's sleep-hazed vision, the massive, two-story structure, with its gleaming white stucco walls, its flat red-tile roof and the high castle-like crenellations, looked like a spa for billionaires or an exclusive boutique hotel somewhere on the Mediterranean. She squinted in the light, struggling to take it all in, from the lush plantings, an oasis of graceful palms, tropical flowers and citrus trees, to the fountains—she counted three—along the front to the red steps leading up beneath an arch-covered portico several times her height. Beside that doorway hung a placard, engraved with the ranch's distinctive running-K brand and a year more than a century in the past.

"*This* is where you grew up?"

"Not exactly," he admitted. "But it's the place I'm calling home now, with my sons and my aunt Alicia."

"I don't understand," she said, thinking that she'd known, at least on some level, that the Kingston name meant wealth. But wealth on this scale, with this kind of history behind it, was more than she'd ever imagined.

"My great-grandfather built this place after the original homestead burned down." Beau handed her her crutches and then retrieved her bags and the flowers from the rear seat. "It was used mostly to entertain dignitaries, and later for family gatherings before most of the relations sold their stakes. My father decided to move in after he inherited. He believed that whoever headed the ranch should always be in residence."

"You didn't live with him?"

"After my mother passed away when I was little, my father thought—he thought I'd be better off living in one of the property's smaller residences with my widowed aunt."

"Was he right?" she blurted before she could stop herself, prompted by the shadow she saw pass over his face. A flush of heat had her shaking her head. "I'm sorry. That's none of my business. I must still be half-asleep, to pry into your—"

From somewhere nearby, she heard barking. A familiar, joyful sound that echoed along the portico, followed by the scrabbling of toenails against tile.

"River!" she cried as her dog raced down the brick

staircase and ran to her, wagging, crying and rolling over to paw the air as Emma squatted awkwardly to greet her. "Where did you come from, girl?"

Emma hadn't long to wonder, as the two small dark-haired boys she'd seen with Beau at the memorial service came tearing outside, both in shorts and T-shirts, frantically calling after her dog. At the sight of their father, the taller, freckled boy stopped short and grabbed his little brother's hand to explain.

"I didn't mean to let her out. I promise! She heard a noise and got excited, and when I went to check the door, she pushed right past me and went flying."

"We tried to catch her so she wouldn't get lost," the little one piped up, giving Emma a glimpse of a missing front top tooth. "But she was too fast."

"It's fine, boys. She's right here," their father reassured them as River wriggled insistently nearby, angling for a belly rub. "And it doesn't look as if she's going anywhere."

"She must've heard my voice." Emma gave the dog another pat before using the crutches to lever back to her feet. "I'm just glad I had such responsible young men looking after her."

"Did you know she likes marshmallows?" asked the smaller boy, looking so serious that Emma had to bite back a laugh. "The little ones. Aunt 'Licia told me not to, but I sneaked her two of mine."

"It was three. I saw you!" his older brother insisted.

"The marshmallow fiend's Leland," Beau said. "And the marshmallow transgression authority is my big guy, Cort."

Emma couldn't help but smile. Did he have any concept of how adorable the three of them were together?

"I'm going into third grade," Cort boasted.

"And Aunt Alicia says he's out to read a whole book for every freckle," Leland told her.

"*Two* books, and chapter books, too. I'm not any little first-grade baby."

When Leland opened his mouth to argue, Beau said, "That's enough of that, you two. How about you carry inside Miss Emma's flowers, Leland, and Cort can open that door like a young gentleman."

As the boys squabbled over which was the more prestigious task, Emma told Beau, "I really didn't come to visit, just to get my dog."

His brilliant smile showcased a set of dimples that she hadn't noticed. The same dimples evident in both of his sons. "Are you trying to get me horsewhipped, Dr. Copley?"

"It's Emma, please," she reminded him, wanting to look over those photos before she could be charmed into forgetting her vow to remain cautious when it came to this man, "and I don't know what you mean by—"

"Because if I don't bring you in and introduce you to my aunt, you have no idea the tongue-lashing I'm in for."

"Really, Beau," scolded a petite blonde older woman Emma hadn't heard approaching. She wore an ivory linen pantsuit perfectly complemented by her coral-colored lips and nails. "You'll have our guest believing I'm a dreadful shrew. I'm Alicia Kingston Parker, dear. Welcome to the ranch. And please don't judge us by my nephew's latest project here."

Shifting her cane, the woman nodded toward the leggy, flop-eared pup who was now play-bowing before River in an attempt to entice the retriever into a game of chase.

Emma accepted the woman's right hand gently, mindful of the swollen knuckles. "Thank you so much," she said. "I'm—"

"This is Dr. Emma Copley, Aunt Alicia," Beau said before nodding toward the young dog. "And that hot mess is Maverick."

Annoyed when River ignored his antics, Maverick boomed a thunderous woof that echoed beneath the archway.

"Let me take him out to his run," Beau said, "before he deafens us all and knocks you off your crutches."

Snagging the young dog by the collar, Beau enlisted his sons' help to lead Maverick around the side of the house.

Left alone with Mrs. Parker, Emma repeated her request to be called by her first name before adding, "And thank you for allowing River to spend a few days in your lovely home. I'd heard that it was something special, but words don't do it justice."

"River has been a first-class guest," the older woman said. "But let's not keep you on your feet in this heat. Come in, where you can sit and rest your poor leg. Beau told me about your unfortunate encounter with the snake."

Emma wondered if he'd shared anything about her run-in with the man behind the wheel of the truck, or if he'd kept that detail to himself to avoid frightening the older woman. Either way, there was no way to politely avoid Mrs. Parker's invitation to come inside the entryway, an airy space whose tall white walls were lined with large paintings featuring beefy red-brown bulls, a sleek, dark racehorse garlanded in roses and numerous framed photos. Many were black-and-white prints of what Emma took to be Kingston ancestors standing with various well-dressed men and women, including one she recognized as a former US president.

Beau's aunt led her through a doorway into a high-ceilinged room whose furnishings tended toward dark woods and rich, soft fabrics. Noticing the room's formality, Emma felt as if she'd entered a museum.

"Are you sure I shouldn't leave my dog outside, too? Her hair—and he looks disapproving." Emma nodded toward the bearded man standing stiffly in a full-length portrait above the fireplace, his hawklike gaze regarding her severely.

Mrs. Parker's blue eyes danced. "Captain Kingston? I think not," she said before sharing several entertaining tales about her ancestor, a hard-drinking Civil War blockade runner who'd stolen wives, been arrested for brawling, and famously ridden a horse into a hotel lobby to challenge a rival to a duel before founding the ranch that eventually catapulted him to respectability. Or as much respectability as land and cattle could buy.

Emma laughed, liking the woman more with every moment. So it was that by the time Beau came back with the boys, his aunt had persuaded her to stay for what she insisted would be a light, informal lunch.

"You're sure you want to?" Beau pulled Emma aside as the boys were washing up and his aunt was making some arrangement with the cooks. "You're certainly welcome to. I mean, you have to eat, but I'm sure, just getting out of the hospital… My family can be a little—"

Leland popped his head into the doorway and grinned in their direction before abruptly racing away after Beau pointed him back out with a stern look that had Emma fighting laughter.

"—*overly enthusiastic,*" Beau finished, reddening a little when his gaze connected with hers. "And, um, *under*-subtle, I'm afraid, about their excitement over my bringing an actual human female to the house for the first time since Melissa…"

"Melissa was your...?" Emma asked, lowering her voice to make certain she wasn't overhead.

"My wife, yes," Beau said, the pain in his eyes like a shaft of moonlight falling on dark water. "I don't— Not that you've asked, of course, but I'm not looking to replace her."

"And I'm not looking to—" Emma blurted, holding up her hands as a nervous chuckle broke through. "I already have one husband I can't get rid of. Not that you're a Jeremy. I don't want you to think I've been comparing—"

She groaned and shook her head, heat suffusing her face. "Maybe I'd better make my apologies and leave now, before I have to go back to the hospital and have my foot surgically extracted from my mouth."

Beau laughed. "Maybe you *should* stick around. I haven't had this much fun with a woman since you tried to shoot me."

"You're never going to let me live that down, are you?" She stroked the top of River's head.

He grinned in response. "Not until you learn to aim better, anyway."

"You'd better watch it, then, in that case. My cop stepfather told me when he took me to the range that I'm pretty much a deadeye," she said. "I only missed the other day because I had such a bad angle."

"Must've been that that rattler you were snuggling threw you off."

She grunted as the memory stabbed at her injured leg. "Ugh. Don't remind me. Makes my skin crawl every time I think about those slithering scales."

Mrs. Parker interrupted, calling the two of them to wash up and come to the breakfast room, which she explained the family preferred to the formal dining room. Soon, they were seated around a long plank farmhouse table, where a pair of plump women wearing thick silver braids and colorfully embroidered dresses chatted amiably as they carried in trays with bowls of rice and beans along with the makings of beef and chicken tacos.

"If you like yours blistering, try the green sauce," Beau advised, passing two small bowls of fresh salsa, along with avocado. "Semi-spicy, go for red—"

"Or Yankee-style, go bare naked," little Leland blurted, earning a scolding about "company manners" from his great-aunt and a stern look from his dad.

But Beau's wink in Emma's direction had her tamping down another smile, and the meal, with its delicious flavors, flow of conversation on topics ranging from hopes for a drought-busting rainstorm in the near future to the fat bullfrogs the boys had recently discovered at a nearby water hole, and childish laughter warmed her heart.

It also reminded her painfully of a time she'd hoped to have this. Not the grand house, the sprawling ranch or servants, but she ached for the loss of her own, more modest version of this table, with her mother fawning over her first grandchild, her husband behaving himself—his hostility kept in check by the presence of Emma's protective stepfather—or who knew? Maybe fatherhood would've restored the loving man she'd married.

After the lunch plates were cleared away, Beau excused himself to take a call that came in on his cell, leaving her to chat with his aunt and answer rapid-fire questions from his sons, who'd been awestruck when she'd told them that the frogs had gotten their names because their loud croaks sounded like cattle mooing and that the lady frogs ("Are the girls called cow frogs?" Leland had asked earnestly) were actually the biggest.

After about ten minutes, Mrs. Parker frowned and

said, "If you don't mind, I'll go check on my nephew… and remind him not to neglect his guest. I do apologize."

"Please don't," Emma said. "It's always a pleasure talking with two bright, young nature lovers."

As the boys' questions shifted from the ranch's slimier inhabitants to what it had felt like getting bitten by a rattlesnake, she resisted the temptation to sneak a glance at her watch. As pleasant as she'd found this visit, and as much as River seemed to be enjoying the attention she was getting from her new admirers, who'd joined her down on the rug, Emma was growing restless. With every minute that ticked by, she could feel her leg swelling more, a reminder of her need to elevate it and maybe even grab a nap at the motel before she began her search for another place to stay. And she really needed to go through those photos from the turbine as soon as possible.

"Sorry for the delay," Beau said, reappearing in the doorway. "I've found that lawyers are harder to get off the phone than telemarketers."

In spite of his jest, the tension in his face gave Emma the distinct impression that his call hadn't been good news.

But Leland abruptly pointed at the folding wheelchair his father was pushing and announced, "Hey, that's Grandpa's."

"Yes, it was." Beau's tone was patient as he explained to his sons. "But since he's not using it any longer, I thought Dr. Emma here might be more comfortable getting the grand tour of the place on wheels than she would be struggling on those crutches."

"As much as I'd love the chance to look around, I'll have to take a rain check." Emma used the table to push herself up onto one foot. "I really need to be getting back to town now."

"I was telling my aunt the same thing," he said, "but she had another idea. A better idea, now that I think on it. Why don't you stay here instead? We have plenty of extra space and as much privacy as you could want, in one of the guest suites, and the place is far more secure than anything you'll find in town."

His offer sounded sincere enough, but Emma noted the guarded look in his eyes. Or maybe he was just distracted, troubled by whatever his attorney had said.

"I really appreciate the offer," she said, "but I wouldn't want to put you out."

His aunt came up behind him. "I'm only 'put out,'" she told Emma as her painted nails sketched air quotes around the two words, "that the same nephew I was responsible for teaching manners didn't invite you to stay from the first. After all, you were hurt right here on Kingston property."

"Stay, please! And then maybe you'll even have time to show us where that nasty old snake bit you," piped up Leland, who'd been disappointed earlier when Emma had turned down his request to peek beneath the bandage on her leg.

"I hope they haven't been driving you too crazy. Or that you didn't feel too pressured, with everyone after you to stay," Beau said after his aunt herded the boys upstairs to get ready for a birthday party she was taking them to shortly. Beau wheeled Emma through the mansion's ground floor, a series of rooms whose heavy ranch-style furnishings were offset with glass mosaic accent windows as brilliant as the plumage of tropical birds, while River trotted just ahead, parading through the grandeur as if she'd lived here all her life.

"This is amazing," Emma said, pointing out a large fountain built up against a foyer wall before looking up to see him watching her expectantly, waiting for her answer. "The colors, the patterns, the history running though it. And I've enjoyed getting to know Cort and Leland and your aunt, too. You have a lovely family, even if they did con you into extending this invitation."

He moved out from behind her. "*I'm* the one who invited you."

"But you didn't mean to, did you? You're obviously very busy with—is everything all right, Beau? The look on your face after you took that call…"

He grimaced before shaking it off. "It's just ranch business, that's all. Nothing for you to worry over."

"But you're worried, aren't you? Really worried about something?" When he didn't deny it, she continued, "And I know you wouldn't have asked me here without your aunt insisting, and the boys chiming in with their—"

He silenced her with a smile, his deep brown eyes lingering on hers as he reached down and ruffled the silkier fur behind River's ears. "Maybe that's so, Emma. But there's no maybe about the fact that I'm very glad they did."

Emma felt that tingling rush again, her own blood, warm and alive as it hurried through her body. For a moment, the years fell away, and she was sixteen again, not thirty-three, feeling herself unfurling like a seedling in the sunlight of another's interest.

"I'm glad, too," she said quietly, sounding almost as shy as that girl had been. *Just don't be as stupid*, she warned herself, her hand drifting to cup the emptiness of her lower abdomen.

After getting Emma to write out the information about her ex to give to the PI and helping her settle into one of the guest suites in the mansion's one-story south wing, Beau left her to elevate her leg and rest for a while. Though he was a little concerned about his aunt and especially his boys reading more into this visit than was good for any of them, it was worth it knowing he wouldn't have to worry about Emma, alone and vulnerable in some rented room. She'd be comfortable here, too, since he'd discreetly asked Sarita and Consuelo, the sisters who'd worked for decades organizing his father's kitchen and welcoming the ranch's guests, to see that Emma's bed was turned down and the mini-fridge stocked with beverages and light snacks. Beside each in-house phone extension, Emma also had a list of numbers to call if she needed anything else—a list to which he'd added his own cell number.

But he didn't have the time to dwell on why it felt so damned good taking care of her and watching her interacting with his aunt and the boys—not after finding a half dozen messages stacked up on his cell phone, which he'd left to charge following his conversation with his attorney, from the normally unflappable Fernando. Though he'd given no specifics, the ranch manager had asked—increasingly insistently—for Beau to please come by ranch headquarters as soon as he could make it.

Had Fernando learned something about one of the trucks missing from the equipment shed the night of Emma's attack—possibly something that would implicate one of his own men? Or had there been some kind of emergency, perhaps an accident that had left a valuable ranch animal or, heaven forbid, one of the vaqueros seriously injured?

As Beau jumped into his truck to make the short drive, he breathed a silent prayer for his workers' safety. And for the ranch itself, which was teetering on a series of loans and strung-out promises until the first of the new Green

Horizons payments happened. *If they happen*, he thought, his gut clenching with worry over what the government would make of a possible murder investigation related to the endangered bird study it had ordered. Would they really shut the wind farm down, or freeze the permits the company needed to begin its new construction?

And would he still be around to worry over any of it— and all those depending on him for their livings?

As he rounded a bend, a cluster of corrals, barns and other outbuildings—the beating heart of the ranch operation—came into view. Alongside his truck, a small herd of quarter horses galloped along the fence line, their stocky black, dun and rust-colored backs gleaming in the sunlight, and a lump swelled in Beau's throat at the thought of the call from his attorney, of the possibility of laying down his worries—of handing off the lead-heavy baton to Wallace Freaking Fleming, a man he didn't believe for a moment his father had thought fit to run the operation.

Beau swallowed back a surge of dread, wondering how the ranch that had once seemed more like a sentence than a legacy, a place that he'd once run from to escape his history, his heritage and the questions that hung over both, could have possibly come to mean so much to him. After parking in his usual reserved spot beside the half dozen vehicles of various payroll, invoice and other employees who worked in the long white stucco building housing the ranch's central offices, he was surprised to encounter Fernando in the shade of the building's cedar-posted porch. Seated in one of the massive carved rockers, the ranch manager, always so capable and fit that he seemed nearly ageless, was bent forward, his graying head supported by his hands as if it were too heavy to hold up. The cup holder built into the chair's armrest held, not the water or iced tea he normally stuck to, but one of the pint-plus beers many of the hands favored, with several of the large cans crumpled up beside him.

He's plastered. The realization was a shock, since Beau had never seen him touch a drop of alcohol before. Not in celebration or commiseration. Not so much as a single cold beer with Beau's father or the vaqueros at the end of a long day.

"Is it—is it your wife?" Beau asked, lowering himself into the other chair. He didn't want to sit, not really, but whatever this was, if felt important enough to deal with face-to-face, on the same level.

"No, jefe. Esmeralda is—with these new treatments, she does better. The doctors give us hope, and my sons and their children—they give her much to live for. At least those who are *loyal*."

"Then it's Antonio? Has something happened between you?" Beau was uncomfortably aware of the growing friction between Fernando and his youngest, whom he'd been carefully grooming to one day replace him, over Tony's recent trips to distant cities to interview for highly competitive paid positions in large metropolitan fire departments.

Beau, who had secretly lent the kid a little money to assist with this endeavor, hoped like hell Fernando hadn't caught wind of an act he'd surely see as a betrayal.

Fernando sloppily waved off the question. "Antonio— bah! He is always at that station. Or off running after some girlfriend or another."

"Then why this?" Beau gestured toward Fernando's drink. "And why all the messages blowing up my phone? Did you find proof that one of our men tried to run down Emma Copley?"

Fernando hesitated, scowling, before shaking his head

emphatically. "I believe no such thing. Our vaqueros are still honest, hardworking men, not thieves and killers, the sun still burns in the sky, watching over this ranch and this life, the life I tell all my sons is a good and honest life, a future they can hold their heads high and be proud to pass on to their families—if they are allowed."

"What have you heard?" Beau demanded, thinking of his lawyer's phone call. "Who have you been talking to?"

This morning, Fernando had planned to run several errands in town. He'd have known people at every stop, any one of whom could have heard some rumor. Any one of whom could have decided it was only fair to warn their respected friend that the winds were shifting.

Fernando straightened, scowling and shaking his head. "This does not matter so much, I think, especially since I heard it here and there and—*hijole*, Señor Kingston. All the town buzzes like a hive of killer bees."

"Buzzes about what?" Beau damned well needed to know how much damage control he was looking at—if this damage could be controlled at all.

"This news that soon, there will soon be another jefe running this ranch. And that your cousin Sheriff Fleming is no friend of the vaquero."

Beau swore under his breath, furious that word had already gotten out—probably leaked by Wallace himself even before Beau had gotten the call at lunch letting him know that the second, more recent will had been authenticated. Whether or not that meant the probate judge would rule to reverse the prior will was still in question. But the fact that his own lawyer had suggested discussing a financial settlement to make the issue go away worried the hell out of Beau, who'd angrily refused the suggestion.

"I can't believe the old man could've done this." Gritting his teeth, Beau shook his head in exasperation. "He told me himself that Wallace oughta stick to law and order."

Damn fool may think he's got all the answers, Beau could hear his father saying one afternoon after his cousin had apparently worn out his welcome, *but he hardly knows a bull calf from a heifer or has the business sense of either.* Turning toward Beau, the senior Kingston had looked him in the eye and said, *When I'm gone, in the name of family loyalty, I hope that you'll continue supporting that boy's reelection campaigns, but promise me, you'll never invest a dime of the ranch's money into any of his harebrained schemes.*

"He believes that we are all the same," Fernando went on, gesturing broadly so that beer sloshed out over his work-roughened hand. "Thinks that the men who have worked this land for generations and know how to bring the best feed and the finest horses and cattle from it are worth no more than any hungry, sunburned farm laborer or a gang member from some city."

Beau scoffed at that. "So one Mexican's as good as the next, I take it? And never mind the legalities of hiring noncitizens, as long as he can save a buck."

"And take the health care from dependents, like my wife, and the retirement from men who've served this family their whole lives. He has been talking of big changes, of a return to the days when men shook when a Kingston's boot heels were heard clicking on the tiles."

"You mean the days when we walked over our employees and ran roughshod over the wishes of everybody in these parts?" Beau snorted. "That isn't what my father wanted, and I'm not about to let it stand. The ranch's people, more than its cattle, its horses and its dogs or even the land itself, are its heart. And the vaqueros especially. I've worked at their sides, at your side, and I swear to you, no matter what it takes, you'll be taken care of. All your people. *Our* people."

Fernando gaped at him, his unguarded reaction striking horror as Beau realized what he'd just said. And that Wallace had rekindled other rumors. Rumors involving Beau's own heritage.

"Whatever you think I meant…" Beau shook his head. "I didn't. I'm not, whatever people say about me, about my mother and—"

"You do not remember her, no?"

"Not really, no," Beau said, taken aback by the sadness in Fernando's eyes, along with his bringing up a subject that had never been discussed. "I was only three when she died." It had been a brief illness, a seemingly minor infection that spiraled into organ failure before the doctors could find the right antibiotics. A death that had sent shock waves through the ranch and had his father, already once divorced, swear that he was through with marriage forever.

"She took you everywhere, your mother." A wistful smile stretched out Fernando's thick gray mustache. "So proud of you, she was. So eager to show off to everyone the newest little Kingston, to make your father see that you were every bit as special as his firstborn."

Beau tried to picture it, to imagine himself in those days before his father had hidden him away as if he were something tainted. Spoiled forever. To imagine the beautiful blonde he recalled only from a handful of surviving photos—preserved in a small album that included the faded image of Beau's Sicilian great-grandfather—smiling over his small accomplishments, demanding that they be acknowledged.

"She was a good woman and a loyal wife," Fernando asserted, pushing himself up from the rocking chair and onto his unsteady feet. "And I swear to you, I will not work a day—not a single minute—for the man who has slandered her good name by painting her the harlot. And slandered every man whose sweat and blood has watered this soil and enriched men less de—"

Abruptly cutting himself off, the older man turned away and raked a hand through his short, thick hair. "I should not say such things. This cerveza turns me foolish." He kicked at one of the empty cans at his feet.

"You've been here most of your life. You could run this operation on your own and blindfolded, if it came down to it," Beau said, knowing that Fernando had meant to say *deserving.* And certain that, without the heady combination of today's emotional upset and the unfamiliar alcohol, he would never have dared come anywhere close to voicing such blunt criticism of any of the Kingston clan. "You've more than earned the right to speak your mind. And to keep your job and take care of your wife and family no matter who is at the helm."

Fernando waved off the consolation. "Any fool may drink and cry about the unfairness of the world, of the way things were or will be. But when has that changed anything—or made not knowing what will come next any easier to bear?"

Chapter 10

Emma could have kicked herself, if she'd had two good legs to do it.

She'd meant to immediately pull out her laptop, to review the data she had transferred from the memory card she had recovered, but one look at the guest suite's plush king-size bed, with its fluffy white comforter and an inviting mound of pillows, had fatigue rising like a tide around her and her leg throbbing anew. Feeling safe here after Beau had pointed out the sturdy locks and glass breakage sensors on the windows, and in possession of a temporary access code that would let her in and out of both her room and the mansion's digitally secured exterior doors, she arranged herself into a comfortable position, meaning only to take a short nap. Instead, she'd ended up sleeping through the remainder of the afternoon and evening. Sleeping hard enough that she must not have heard the bedside phone, whose flashing light prompted her to pick up a recorded message.

Pushing the button to retrieve it, Emma couldn't help but smile at the warmth she heard in Beau's voice on the recording. "Hey, there, sleepy lady. Hope you're feeling better. I stopped by earlier to see if you were up for dinner, but you were out cold. Hope you don't mind, but when River started scratching at the door, I fed her and took her out for a little romp with Maverick before I brought her back inside."

As grateful as she was for his consideration, it hit her that if he could let himself inside her room to take the dog out, he could have just as easily done anything else while she was sleeping. Anxiety buzzing her pulse, she threw back the covers and hobbled to her laptop, hands shaking until she saw it remained closed where she had left it, with the files from the memory card safely copied to her password-protected hard drive. Her phone, too, remained charging nearby, also apparently untouched.

"He's no Jeremy. He's not." The Beau who'd helped her in her time of need, who'd been so generous toward her, would no more tamper with her belongings than he would lay a hand on her in anger.

And yet her heart still beat hard as the memory of Sheriff Fleming's warnings floated to the surface, along with the thought of how Jeremy had won her over at first, too, with his kindness, the sort of declarations and grand gestures that had once made her girlfriends sigh with envy and breathlessly urge her, *If you don't hurry up and marry that man, I've already got my gown picked.*

Emma shuddered, remembered herself in lace and white silk, the unspoiled sweetness of her expectations. Of a love untainted by life's disappointments, and a man who'd snapped instead of bending after things began to go wrong. A man who'd shoved her on the first occasion when, around the same time, a drinking buddy of his had joked about Jeremy having to call her *Doctor* whenever he came to her in bed.

As remorseful as he'd been, as tearful when he'd begged forgiveness, the brief calm that had followed that storm hadn't lasted. Instead, he'd gotten into her phone and computer files repeatedly, as delusions of her affairs chewed through his trust like a plague of black moths.

Easing herself through a series of deep breaths, she returned to bed, where she accessed her laptop's hard drive and opened the folder she had previously copied to the desktop before sending a second copy to safekeeping to the online cloud. There, a series of tiny thumbnail images filled the screen—hundreds of them, at least.

"Oh, boy," she murmured, realizing that it could take her all night to go through every photo chronologically, beginning from the first, which had been shot a week prior to her assistant's death, and moving to the last, taken the night she'd removed the card from the camera.

But no matter how long it took, she had to know what was there and if there was anything that might convince the authorities that Russell's death had been a murder.

"Don't get your hopes up too high," she warned herself, recalling that the camera she'd found hadn't been directed toward the turbine's base. It was entirely possible that whoever had forced Russell through the access door and up the ladders could have remained entirely outside the device's range.

She settled into the work anyway, beginning with midnight on the date of her student's death. The first images she opened were in black and white, since they had been taken in the hours before sunrise. In several, whitetail deer browsed; in another, a jackrabbit nibbled.

But one shot, taken at 3:24 that morning, had her gasping, for it captured the partial image of a person, so close to the camera that only a sliver of the head, turned from the camera, the grainy, overexposed arm and shoulder, and part of the lower leg were showing...

Along with the pistol that he—she thought it was a male—held. The gun he must have used a short time later to force Russell to his death.

She searched further, praying she'd find a better shot, one that would offer a better chance to identify the culprit...and choking back a sob when she came to a partial image—the last photo of a living Russell—taken the morning of his death, walking toward the turbine. He'd been caught in midstride, his hand reaching forward and his mouth partly open as if he'd been captured calling out to someone. Or maybe he'd been belting out one of those horrible headbanger anthems he loved so much. She wiped her eyes, longing to hear him sing again. Or to have the chance to demand to know what he'd been thinking, setting up those cameras without a word to her about them, or whom he might've told about the data he'd collected.

The next image she came across showed River, and then Emma herself, taken after they'd arrived to look for Russell. Everything else before had clearly happened out of range of the camera she'd discovered. Could there still be more out there, waiting to be found and turned over to the Rangers?

Forcing herself to move on, she continued going through those images she did have, focusing now on shots taken after the arrival of emergency workers, Green Horizons technicians, and she even caught a glimpse of Beau Kingston amid the photos captured that day. But none of the images jumped out as a match to that first bad shot of the armed individual from 3:24 a.m. None of them would help identify the man she felt certain had ended Russell's life.

As she continued poring over photos, her burning eyes eventually grew bleary. Her mind started playing tricks on her, assembling human faces out of blobs of light and shadow and possibly missing things as well. It was time to call it a night, she knew, glancing over at the clock on the night table and seeing that it was after four.

But her gaze lingered on Beau's number on the bed-side table, and she remembered his invitation to call him day or night. She was tempted to reach out, to show him that single relevant partial image that she *had* found. To prove to him she was more than a paranoid troublemaker with a penchant for wandering into danger.

Why does it matter so much what Beau thinks about you? Why does he?

She tried to shake off the idea, telling herself she needed nothing more from the rancher than his help. Besides, he'd surely be asleep now. There was no reason to wake him.

Unless you're looking for an excuse to get the man alone here, in this private suite? A man whose gaze she'd felt roaming her body when he'd thought she wasn't looking.

Ridiculous, she told herself, her face heating with the thought. It was only her loneliness, her isolation from everyone and everything she knew, making her vulnerable to a handsome man's attention.

Eager to prove she was smarter than she'd been at sixteen, she flipped over the card with his phone number, determined to grab a few hours of shut-eye. She'd see him in the morning, she promised herself. In a room without a bed.

* * *

Beau was still in bed when he received a call a little after seven the next morning.

"You sound like hell," his former partner Tyler Phelps said, the distinctive rasp of his voice as good as any caller ID. "Hope I didn't wake you."

"If I'd slept worth half a damn last night, I would've been up for hours already, tackling the backlog of work I've got piled up." Instead, Beau had wasted hours worrying about the ranch's future and the woman staying under his roof. Whenever he had dozed off, he was soon jerked awake by nightmares where Emma went missing from her bed and Wallace only laughed at him when he called 911 for help.

"Remind me to steer clear of the farming life," Ty said. "It's too damned early as it is for my taste."

"*Ranching* life. I've told you a dozen times before I'm not a farmer." Beau snarled at the phone before Ty's laughter made him realize that his old friend was jerking his chain for pure entertainment value. Which, ever since they'd suffered through boot camp together back on Parris Island, had practically been an Olympics-level competition between the two of them.

"Maybe you should go back to bed. Your sense of humor's still asleep, Farmer Beau."

"You ever come up with something funny, I'll go ahead and wake it on up, Pirate." Crossing his bedroom, Beau smirked as he reached for a pair of jeans to pull on over his boxers. But considering everything Ty had gone through this past year—hell, in all the years since an IED had scarred his right side, damaged his voice and forced him to wear an eye patch—it was a relief to hear him dealing grief instead of stewing in it.

"You might want to wake up yourself," Ty said, sobering. "We really need to talk."

"About Jeremy Hansen? Have you found him?" Fully awake now, Beau raked his fingers through his hair.

"I don't know where he is, exactly, but I've got some information you need, and it isn't just on him."

Fully awake now, he stopped halfway through the act of pulling a shirt off a hanger from the walk-in closet. "You dug into her, too, didn't you?" He'd given Ty Emma's name and address, after all, and his friend wasn't the sort to allow such an opportunity to pass. Was there something she'd been hiding from him, or had Ty gleaned enough from hints he'd dropped during several recent check-ins—calls Beau made to help ensure that the black dog of his friend's depression wasn't back to nipping at his heels—to start investigating issues surrounding the inheritance and ranch finances?

"Oh, I've looked into a lot of things," Ty said, "so why don't you meet me today in San Antonio if you can swing it? I'd come to you, but I'm afraid I've got a couple of obligations at this conference that I can't get out of. Besides, it might be better," he added darkly, "if we aren't seen together."

"Come on, Ty. Don't leave me hanging," Beau said, feeling the coarse hairs along his arms rise. And feeling frustrated, too, to be asked to drop everything, to travel for hours, without even knowing the subject. "What do you have?"

"I can't get into it on the phone, but you've got trouble brewing on more than one front, brother, and it's getting mighty tough to swallow that they're all unrelated."

When Emma finally woke and got up to take the dog out, it was already past noon and there was a note waiting for her. A note explaining that Beau had been abruptly called out of town to deal with "unavoidable ranch business."

After vowing to be back tomorrow, he'd urged her to use the time to concentrate on resting up and getting better. *And whatever you do, promise me, you'll still be here when I get back.*

"Where else would I go, with no way to drive and nowhere else to stay?" she grumbled, after pulling on a pair of lightweight khaki slacks to go with the navy tee she had chosen.

But despite the kindness of Beau's aunt, who personally brought her lunch after Emma politely declined her invitation to join the family, and his two boys, who sneaked down the hall later to gift her with the choicest shells and feathers from their personal collections, she couldn't relax in her comfortable surroundings. Not with the urgency she felt to find something concrete, some proof that would convince the Texas Rangers to come investigate in person. And not with her growing suspicion that every moment she wasted napping, eating or waiting around idly for Beau was time she couldn't spare.

After leaving another message for Lieutenant Williams of the Texas Rangers and completing her review of the images that afternoon, Emma took River out through the guest wing's side entrance. It was slow going on her crutches and hot as well, the air heavy with Gulf moisture, but by choosing a path close to the lushly landscaped area along the fountains bordering the mansion's facade, with the butterflies and hummingbirds fluttering among bright, tropical blooms, Emma could at least cling to the illusion of refreshment. River, however, had been cooped up too long to be content with her clumsy amble, so Emma unclipped her leash, allowing the big dog to work off some energy jumping at some darting lizards and bounding after a roadrunner.

"Stay close, girl," Emma warned, shuddering at the terrifying memory of losing her that night when the pickup had come roaring at them.

"It's over now. We're safe here," she whispered, as a shift in the warm breeze brought her the sounds of the two boys' voices, along with a distant splashing that brought to mind the pool she'd glimpsed through a window yesterday during her brief tour after lunch with Beau. Attentive as their aunt was, Emma would be willing to bet the older woman was personally supervising the pair, most likely from a comfortable lounge chair in the shade. And if Emma herself spotted any trouble—if any attacker dared to show his face around here—she had faith that any cry she raised would be heard and quickly heeded.

Still, she felt unsettled with Beau away and with Lieutenant Williams failing to return her calls. Her anxiety only deepened at the sight of a big sedan, black-and-white beneath its film of road grime, pulling into the long semicircular driveway, its brakes squealing as it stopped beside her.

"River," Emma called, unable to see the driver with the sun's glare on the windshield. The thrumming of her pulse sped as she thought of how angry Wallace Fleming had been after she'd informed him she had passed along evidence to the Texas Ranger. He certainly wouldn't be bringing her any flowers this time.

It wasn't the sheriff, however, but instead Deputy Jim Kendall who unfolded himself from behind the wheel and removed a paired of mirrored sunglasses to regard her with equally unreadable gray eyes.

"What brings you all the way out here, Deputy?" she

asked as River returned to stand in front of her. "Somebody report a rabid skunk that needed shooting?"

He shook his head, a smile ghosting over his thin lips. "No, ma'am. But the sheriff's asked that I deliver something."

"Beau's not here at the moment," she said, "so if there's an olive branch in your trunk…"

Kendall seemed to choke on air. "An olive branch… from Wallace…" He gave his head a shake, his short silver hair unmoving. "No, ma'am. This delivery's for you alone. Is there someplace—some private place inside where I can give it to you?"

She narrowed her eyes, regarding the tall, powerfully built man. An armed man who could either invent some reason to arrest her or snap her in two without trying. Though he'd seemed professional enough during their past dealings and even human, almost laughing at her lame joke, she couldn't forget who Kendall worked for, or stop herself from imagining how upset his boss must have been when he had somehow figured out where she was staying.

"Here would be just fine." Swatting at a troublesome mosquito, she spotted a pair of groundskeepers working near one of the fountains. Having witnesses around was good.

A look of concern softened Kendall's steely gaze. "You aren't—you aren't feeling nervous, are you, Dr. Copley? Because if you're uncomfortable here for any reason, I'm happy to wait for you to gather your things and give you a ride back into town."

"No, it isn't that," said Emma. "Everyone's been kind. Beau's aunt, Mrs. Parker, is so gracious, and those boys are sweet as can be." She smiled at the thought of the offerings they'd brought her, so achingly innocent that she yearned to get the chance to know the children better, though part of her already knew it was a bad idea to encourage any attachment.

"What about with *him*? Do you feel safe with Mr. Kingston?"

"Of course, and anyway, he's not here now. And I'm not a prisoner," she insisted. "You tell your boss that, will you?"

"I'll be sure and let him know you said so." The deputy went around to the trunk, which he opened to retrieve a small insulated case.

"What's this?" she asked as he handed it over to her.

"The handgun you had with you when you were bitten."

She peeked inside the zippered case before looking up. "I thought I had to go back to the office to pick this up. Sign some paperwork and—"

"Sheriff wanted to be sure you had this with you, since you've made the choice to stay here." Kendall schooled his voice to the same careful neutrality as his face.

"He did, did he?" she asked, the fine hairs behind her neck rising as she noticed that the gray eyes did not quite meet her gaze.

"And he asked me to remind you that in this state, a woman's got the right to defend herself against a threat. Any threat of mortal danger…whether it's from a snake in the grass or the kind that goes around masquerading as a pillar of this community."

The words hung between them, heavy as the heated air. Or maybe that was fury, burning through Emma as it hit her what this man was saying.

"Are you—are you honestly *suggesting*," she asked, balling her fists until her nails dug into her palms, "that I *shoot* your boss's rival? So that's why Fleming didn't come himself. He's using you. Don't you see that? Giving himself a layer of plausible deniability if something happens to his cousin. Only I'm sure the sheriff will disavow all knowledge when the Texas Rangers come to question him about this—"

"No!" Kendall's denial was a short, sharp sound that had River giving a single, protective *woof* and plunking herself down directly in front of her mistress. Ignoring the dog, he continued, "You misunderstand me. I never meant to imply that you should shoot anybody—"

"Have you met his little sons? You know they've lost their mom, right? You should see him with them, the only parent they have left."

"—only that you should protect yourself from danger, in any form it comes in." Kendall's face had drained of color, and he looked around nervously, as if he feared someone listening.

"What about the form of my ex-husband? Are any of you in that office as worried about the man I have to keep reminding you has threatened me on multiple occasions and was arrested for assaulting me?" Her stomach flipped at the thought of the incident in her dean's office, with its devastating fallout. "Do you even have any idea where Jeremy is now?"

"We—we have someone following up on that," Kendall sputtered. "I—I believe the sheriff did reach out again to Mr. Hansen's former employer—"

"Former? Then he really was fired?"

"The uncle did confirm that they agreed to part ways, but as for your ex-husband's current location, we're working with the Waco PD to see if they can bring him in for questioning."

"In *Waco*?" she asked. "But I told you days ago that Jeremy was on his way here—if he's not here already. I told the sheriff the same thing, too, if only his tunnel vision allowed him to focus on anybody but the man he'd evidently give me a medal for knocking off."

Kendall huffed out an exasperated sigh. "You're being obstinate. And hostile. The sheriff's right about you."

"You misunderstand. I'm *desperate* for help in ending the threat to my life before whoever's behind it is successful. And to get real answers about what happened to my student." Though she hoped that Beau's PI friend would soon successfully track down Jeremy, she needed law enforcement if she wanted him questioned—or held accountable for anything he may have done.

Not murder. Please, not that, she prayed, hoping for the sake of the boy she'd fallen for so many years ago that he hadn't gone so far.

"We're looking into all that. You just have to trust us."

"Trust you? After you show up here with that pistol and your broad hints about self-defense?"

"You know what, woman?" Kendall said. "Give me back the damned gun. You're right. There *are* forms you have to sign before I can let you have custody of this weapon again. Forms it seems I've forgotten to bring out here with me. So let me take the thing back, along with your ridiculous and totally unfounded misinterpretations."

"Fine," she said, thrusting the case back at him. And relieved beyond measure to have its weight lifted from her.

"I only hope you don't come to regret this," Deputy Kendall told her as he dropped it back into his trunk and slammed the lid down with enough force to make her flinch. "Because if you happen to need help, all the way out here, if could be a while arriving."

When his cold gaze locked with hers, it sent a chill

clean through her. The implied threat made her worried that the landscapers had disappeared. But relief came in the low rumble of an approaching vehicle. Though still in the distance, her heart leaped to see that it was Beau coming home.

Holding back River by the collar to keep the wagging, wriggling dog from running out to greet him, Emma returned her attention to the deputy. "The only thing I'm regretting," she told Kendall, "is having ever set foot is a county ruled by some ridiculous family feud instead of law and order."

"It's a hell of a long way from ridiculous when you're talking about a legacy like this one," Kendall fired back, gesturing toward the mansion. "A fortune in assets, built on the backs of generations, only to be *stolen* by a man everybody in this county knows is nothing but a two-bit bastard. You only have to open your eyes to see the rumor's true—his mama was keeping company with one of those hired Mexicans."

"Gee, I wonder who could be spreading that self-serving gossip." She glared at the deputy. "And what Sheriff Fleming could've promised you to buy himself such a loyal lap dog."

Chapter 11

"What was all that about?" Beau asked, watching the receding cloud of dust raised by the patrol vehicle as it headed back out the dirt road. On seeing the black-and-white sheriff's department markings, he'd mashed down the accelerator, itching to confront Wallace about what he'd learned from Ty.

Instead of the sheriff, however, Beau recognized Deputy Jim Kendall behind the sedan's wheel, but the man hadn't made eye contact as the two had passed, though they'd gotten to know each other well last spring when Jim's daughter played T-ball on Leland's team. More distracting still was the sight of Emma, red-faced and unsteady on her crutches, her lips parted as she stared down at the dirt.

"Everything okay here?" he asked. "You're shaking. Are Aunt Alicia and the boys—"

"They—they're f-fine. I—I think they're back at the pool playing." Emma turned in that direction.

Sure enough, Beau heard Maverick barking from back behind the privacy fencing that screened the area. A loud splash followed, and then the sounds of Cort's and Leland's laughter and his aunt shouting something. Probably her usual admonition to get that dirty dog out of the clean water.

"Best place for man or beast on a day like this one." Smiling at the thought, he grabbed his overnight bag from inside the truck's cab. "One thing for sure, it's too blasted hot to be standing out here. You look a little flushed yourself. Have you gotten yourself overheated or— The deputy didn't bring you bad news, did he? Anything on your ex yet?"

Though Ty had convinced a friend from the Texas Department of Public Safety there was sufficient reason to suspect that Jeremy might be behind the attacks against his former wife, the evidence was far too thin to get a warrant for cell phone and credit card information tracking. Instead, they'd have to rely on questioning his friends and former associates to narrow the search for a man who appeared to have deliberately dropped off the radar.

Shaking her head, she glanced back in his direction long enough for him to notice the dampness at her hairline and the tracks of tears under her green eyes.

"Are you—are you crying, Emma?" he asked as her dog nosed closer to her.

"I do that sometimes, when I'm mad enough." She gave her face a quick, defiant swipe, making him wish he'd tucked a handkerchief into the pocket of his pants.

Shelving his plan to try to talk her into joining him on the lanai or perhaps to soak in the pool if her leg was ready for it, he asked, "Mad about what? Did the deputy say something to upset you? What's happened?"

"Actually, he called me a—a lying bitch, just before he stormed back to his car."

"Jim Kendall? Seriously?" It was hard for Beau to reconcile his memories of the dad who'd rooted for the kids, bandaged skinned knees and passed out juice boxes with what Emma was describing. "What happened?"

"I provoked him, to be certain, calling him on what the sheriff put him up to," she explained, trembling with emotion. "But there was no way—it was outrageous."

Wallace, again. Beau should've known that the SOB was at the root of whatever trouble had come calling in his absence. "Come inside and we'll talk. I have just the place where we won't be disturbed, and we'll be comfortable in the AC."

Inside the shelter of thick white walls, it felt blessedly cool, with the tile and the trickling of the interior fountain adding to the relief. After dropping off his overnight bag beside the staircase where he could grab it later, Beau waited for Emma to catch up on her crutches before leading her down the hall to the den, the domain of so many past male Kingstons. Unlike the light, bright look that dominated the rest of the mansion, this retreat was paneled and furnished in dark, exotic woods. On one end, floor-to-ceiling bookcases formed the backdrop to a massive desk, while on the other, the mounted head of a massive black bull presided over a stone fireplace, several plush armchairs and a huge tooled-leather sofa.

"You should dispense gas masks to female visitors to this room—" Emma put down her crutches and heeded his gesture, settling on the sofa's edge while the dog lay on the thick rug at her feet "—to protect us from all the testosterone in the air."

Smiling, he pushed aside a letter tray stacked with papers before offering her a clean handkerchief from his desk drawer. "You should have seen it *before* I had the hunting trophies taken down and donated to a natural science museum. They loved their safaris, those old-time Kingstons. The ones packing a Y-chromosome anyway," he added, recalling his aunt's vocal disapproval of the practice.

"You're not like them?" Emma asked, dabbing at her eyes.

It was a question he'd heard—all too often dripping with snide innuendo—all his life. But in her lovely face, he saw not a trace of judgment. Only curiosity, a need to understand.

"When I was a boy," he explained, rolling up the sleeves of his linen shirt, "I felt left out, like I'd missed a rite of passage because my father never took me, not even for deer or doves or wild hogs like most all the guys around here grow up shooting." He remembered his brother and his older cousins, all laughing heartily over some incident or other that had gone down out at deer camp. Remembered aching for the day that he, too, would find his first .22 under the tree or—better yet— his dad would take the time to teach him how to use one of his many weapons. Or even have Fernando do it. That would've been all right, too—and for damned sure, less stressful. Beau hadn't realized that it was never going to happen until the day that a younger male cousin was invited and he was left back home with Aunt Alicia once again.

"But I had chance enough to work with guns after I enlisted," he continued. "And more than enough opportunity to get acquainted with the horrendous damage they can do."

"Why join the military anyway? A guy from a family like yours, a place like this—I can only imagine the opportunities you must have had available."

It wasn't the first time he'd been asked, especially since he hadn't taken the route most privileged sons did and gone in as an officer after college, instead choosing to do the toughest basic training alongside recruits of every background. "First off, serving in our country's armed forces *is* an opportunity, one I've never regretted for a single second."

"I'm sorry. I didn't mean to come off as if I thought there was no value. My late dad served, too, as a young man, and he always swore it was the making of him."

"It's fine." Beau nodded his understanding. "The truth is, I had something to prove back then—that I didn't need the Kingston name and money, or a damned thing from the father who never had much use for me, to make something of myself."

"Your father…" she echoed, a question in her eyes.

Uncomfortable with the subject, he cleared his throat and offered her a choice of water, iced tea or mineral water. "Unless you'd prefer something harder." Heaven only knew that he could use a stiff drink, if this conversation was going to move in *that* direction. "I know it's a little early, but you look like a woman who might appreciate a beer on a hot afternoon. Or maybe a whiskey—and there's a fully stocked bar hidden in that console, alongside the mini-fridge."

"I'd love that iced tea," she said, "unsweetened if you have it, but go ahead and have that drink, if you'd like."

"Tea's good for me, too," he said, figuring he'd better keep his wits about him.

"Great, and don't worry about a glass. I'm more than happy with the bottle."

"You've got it." He brought over two chilled bottles

and sat down on the sofa, his knees slanting toward her. After passing her the first, he took a long pull from his own and waited for her to do the same before saying, "My father, *yes*... So I take it Wallace has made sure you've heard the rumors."

"Just when I start to think the man's got an ounce of integrity—"

"Up until yesterday afternoon, I liked to imagine he might. Or that he was at least trying to do what he thought his favorite uncle wanted—hell, what my father probably *did* want at one time, considering the way he treated me when I was younger."

She shook her head. "That sounds awful, Beau. I'm sorry. But I'm confused. What's Wallace been up to, other than spreading ugly gossip?"

"Lying," Beau corrected, his confidence bolstered by Fernando's furious defense of his mother's honor, along with his own perusal of the photo of his great-grandfather. "But Wallace's filed a lawsuit insinuating that I've committed fraud by passing myself off as a *real* Kingston."

Fury flashed in her eyes. "How could you have possibly—? That's ridiculous."

"You're right. It won't hold water, legally, so now he's suddenly come up with a mysterious second will naming him my dad's sole heir—a will written during the years we were estranged."

"That sounds like a nightmare."

"It could be. Or worse. And there's even more, I'm afraid."

She leaned toward him, her expression as intent as it was sympathetic. "As bad as all that sounds, I'm almost afraid to ask."

"I met up with Tyler, my ex-partner. He had some news we needed to talk about in person."

"About Jeremy?"

"He's still working on that," Beau said. "But in the meantime, he's found out something surprising about Wallace and his reelection campaign last fall."

She drew back. "What would Wallace's election have to do with any of this?"

"He seemed to have an unusual number of cash donations, all of them right at the legal limit, a lot of them from names I didn't recognize. He also received several good-sized checks from what appears to be a shell corporation… only Ty's traced its domain name to an employee of Green Horizons."

"Why wouldn't they just donate openly to his reelection," she said. "It's not illegal, is it?"

"Not here, no. And it's not an outrageous amount of money, considering that it's such a rural county and Wallace didn't have much in the way of competition…which is why it's so surprising that someone's gone to that much trouble to try to blur the trail."

"It makes you wonder, doesn't it," asked Emma, "if they already knew they might have reason to keep their connection with local law enforcement on the down low?"

Beau nodded. "Just like it makes me wonder where my cousin, who I happen to know has been really struggling with two daughters in college and a string of business ventures that didn't pan out, all of a sudden got the money to start siccing lawyers on me."

"No wonder Wallace wasn't eager to climb up himself to see Russell's body…" she mused before turning a dark look on Beau. "Unless he'd already made the trip up earlier that morning."

Beau shook his head. "You know how I feel about my cousin. He's a schemer and a bully and as prejudiced as hell—"

"And don't forget sexist," she added with the barest hint of a smile.

Beau nodded. "Among his other charms, but I don't see him as a killer. Maybe look the other way or drag his heels on an investigation that he thought might cause trouble for his corporate buddies, but there's no way he'd willingly scale a height like that or risk being overpowered by a younger, stronger climber, when he could just shoot someone on the ground."

She frowned and then made a broad gesture that took in the room, the window and, presumably, what lay beyond it. "Not even to get his hands on all this? Because it seems to me a lot of people end up getting killed for less."

"And Wallace'll damned well have it over my dead body." A rush of emotion had him grinding out the words through clenched jaws. "Because I can't let him win. I won't, and not just for myself and my boys, either. I've provided for us before just fine—more than fine—on my own, and I'm more than ready to get back to doing it again. But I'll be damned if I watch him put out the men and women who've worked this land for generations like last week's garbage so he can try to scrape by with cheaper labor. And I won't watch the sweat and blood and know-how that've bound this soil and grass into an empire blown away like dust with his idiotic schemes."

"Don't say that," Emma whispered, her green eyes shining as she reached out and laid her free hand on his forearm. "Please don't say 'over my dead body.' Because the way I understand it, that's exactly what the sheriff's hoping to achieve."

"What?" he said, wondering if he'd missed something

in that moment because the shock of her touch, combined with the intensity of her gaze, had him all too aware of the den's heavy, closed door, of the fact that neither his aunt nor his sons knew yet that he'd come home.

He tried to push back the thought, along with the power of his attraction. And the shock that he could be drawn to a woman so fiercely committed to her own priorities, so willing to risk everything for what she thought was right. He was lonely, that was all, worn down by years of struggle without a woman to confide in—and the guilt that still weighed on him for his role in Melissa's death. His body, too, had an agenda, needs whose ever-present background thrum had slowly grown, since the day he'd first met Emma, into an insistent drumbeat.

The thump of it diminished, allowing him to think again, when she shifted her hand back to her lap and told him, hesitantly at first and then with an increasing tone of outrage, about her conversation with Jim Kendall. "I guess your cousin figured that, fancy lawyer aside, encouraging your shooting was an even surer method to getting you out of his way."

"But in the end, Kendall didn't give you the gun?" Beau asked.

"After I lit into him, I think he was afraid to. Afraid how it was going to look when the Rangers finally come calling."

"I guess this means," he finally managed, feeling the tug of a smile at one side of his mouth, "that you're finally done taking potshots at me?"

She snorted, nearly choking on a sip of her iced tea. After coughing to clear her throat, she said, "I'd say we both have bigger problems. And only some of them wear a badge."

He set his drink down and wiped off the condensation

on his pant leg before placing his hand on her shoulder. "Well, whoever it is we're up against, I'm glad as hell to be on the same side as a woman as brave and beautiful as you."

The sheer relief of knowing he was with her washed over her, rippling over her nerve endings like a warm breeze riffling a field of golden wheat. The sensation shifted direction, turning into a frisson of pleasure as the pad of his thumb glided along her shoulder.

Her gaze snapped up to meet his, but the rest of her went still as a rabbit flattening itself among the grasses as the coyote passed close by. Her heart thudding, she didn't realize she'd stopped breathing until he murmured, "You aren't afraid here, are you? You aren't afraid of me?"

"I'm not afraid of you, of course," she told him, angry with herself for the way her voice was shaking. "I'm a little scared, though, of myself now. Of what I—what we're—"

Without conscious thought, she reached up to brush back that thick sweep of jet hair that had drooped across his forehead in the heat. He caught her hand up in his and laced his fingers through hers, sliding their hands together.

"—of what we're doing here, I think," she forced herself to finish, pulled headlong into his eyes and the light friction of his work-roughened skin against the pulsing heat that threatened to erupt from hers. Fumbling to find the side table beside the sofa, she put down her drink as well. Then, carefully and deliberately, she raised a palm to caress the firm angle of his jawline, where her body thrilled to feel the masculine solidity of bone and muscle, the roughness of the faint suggestion of beard stubble. The intoxicating scents of man, wood oil and saddle leather in the room, too, crowded into her awareness. "I think that maybe…"

"Maybe what?" he asked, partly withdrawing and then meshing his fingers with hers in a rhythm that quieted the clamor of reasons she should beware.

"Maybe you should quit playing with my hand," she suggested, faltering through a smile to hide her nervousness, the flutter in her stomach, "and just go ahead and kiss me."

"I thought you'd never ask." With that, he pulled her close, his mouth slanting over hers with a heat and intensity that had her wondering how she'd ever imagined she could live in a locked closet of denial for the rest of her days. How she could survive the stresses of this week, this month—this life—without periodically shutting down her teeming thoughts and burning off her tension. *Like this*…

The kiss caught flame in an instant, as if both of them sensed the need to grasp this opportunity before they came to their senses. Or as if Beau were as starved for human contact as she herself had been. Lips parting and tongues swirling, she fitted her hands to skim the hard muscles of his pectorals, his biceps, her eyes closed against the onslaught of forbidden pleasure. His hands, too, were busy, stroking her jaw, her neck and arms, and then skimming her side from ribs to waist to the flare of her hip. Murmuring with pleasure, she let him push her backward. Then she drew him closer, ever closer, needing to feel more of him, by her, over her. *Inside her… please, yes. Hurry.*

A cold chill fell over her instead, a ghost of shame and fear. A memory of the terrible names Jeremy had called her, the accusations, her denials that she'd done the things that she was doing, was inviting now, with her students and her colleagues. *Cheating bitch. You little whore!* She heard the crack of a hand on flesh, felt the sting against her cheekbone, the shame of a morning after when she'd covered it all up with makeup and excuses, the lies she'd told herself. *He's under stress, about the business and with the baby coming, too. He's promised that he'll stop.*

Struggling to push past self-loathing, she willed herself to focus on Beau's kisses, on the knowledge that she was safe here in this fortress. Rebelling against the idea that her body and her choice in what to do with it belonged to anyone but herself, she grasped him by the wrist and dragged his hand to her breast. Arching her neck backward, she moaned as he squeezed, setting off a tingling that reached her curling toes.

"Emma," Beau murmured, his mouth transforming her name into a carnal promise. "Emma, I want this... I want you, like I've never wanted... It's been so damned long and you feel so very right."

His other hand pulled up the hem of her shirt, and he dropped to one knee between her parted legs to land an openmouthed kiss midway on the prickling pale flesh of her stomach. She felt herself melting with the heat of his mouth, writhing beneath the teasing of his tongue against her skin. He trailed more kisses upward, raising her shirt farther and deftly unhooking her bra from behind. He cupped both breasts then, thumbs flicking over hardened nipples.

She arched her back and groaned, wriggling to move closer. Aching to feel his lips, his tongue, the sweet pull of his mouth on her heated flesh. Instead, with a barely audible intake of breath, he hesitated, even though her thigh, where it slid against his, grazed the length of his erection, a discovery that had her hot and wet and anxious. Could that really all be him?

Opening her eyes, she looked up into his face, saw a look of hunger combined with reverence give way. The first crack appeared at his forehead, a horizon line soon joined by others. What followed was his sigh as he pulled down her shirt and pushed himself up off her, his face full of regret.

"I'm sorry," he said, shaking his head and reaching to help her sit up. "I do want to—you can't imagine how I want you, but this isn't— This wasn't what I meant to happen."

"It wasn't on my radar, either," she said, her body weeping with his absence, her mind reeling even more as the full intensity of her aloneness crashed down like a wave, reclaiming its patch of briefly dry shore. "But that doesn't necessarily mean it's—it's such a terrible idea." *Please.*

"Taking advantage of you while you're recovering here, with nowhere else to go? And with my family outside—hell. What kind of man—"

"Taking advantage? What kind of old-fashioned, paternalistic bunk is that? Wasn't I the one who suggested that you kiss me? The one who placed your hand on my—"

"You've been through a lot," he said.

Stinging with his rejection, she said drily, "Thank goodness I have you and your cousin to keep reminding me of that."

"Don't do that. Don't ever compare us, especially not when I'm trying to—"

"I'm not one of those local gold diggers gunning for your fortune," she said, wanting—no, needing to see this through, to break the hold that her ex-husband had on her. To finally evict Jeremy and all his horrible names for her from her head. "But I'm single. You're single. There don't have to be strings attached."

Beau shook his head. "Is that ever a bunch of bull." His voice softened. "You aren't a no-strings person, Emma, any more than I am. You can try fooling yourself, can talk any kind of game you want, but I've seen how you are with your work and your students. I've heard it in the way you've interacted with my aunt and kids. You're all about commitment, Emma, a forever kind of woman. And I'm not the man to give you that, not now and not ever."

She stared off into the middle distance, trying to figure out whether to be more hurt, furious or flattered by what he was saying. It was nearly impossible, with so many emotions competing with the craving to feel more of what she'd been feeling when his mouth, his hands, his skin had come into contact with her own. A firestorm had ignited inside her, but as powerful a force as her need was, his words still somehow cut through. His reminder of who she was and the things that truly mattered right now. Things far more important than the clamor of her hormones or her need to prove that Jeremy no longer controlled her.

Closing her eyes, she swallowed hard, fighting to pull herself together. The threat of tears stung but she forced them back, willing herself to be stronger.

"What are you thinking?" Beau asked. "Because if I've hurt you, that wasn't my intention."

"No, it's not that. It's—you're right. This—this was a terrible idea. I should pack my things and find another place to stay."

"You don't have to do that. In fact, I wish you wouldn't."

"This thing, my being here—" Her gaze lingered on his eyes, his lips, her body tingling with memories that refused to fade. "It's not just us who could be hurt. We're adults, and I'm sure we can figure out a way to make sure that what happened here this afternoon isn't repeated."

Rising from the cushions, he paced a few steps into the room, his muscles flexing as his crossed his arms. "I swear to you, it won't be."

"You're sure? Because those boys of yours—I can already see the wheels spinning in their little brains, and they're far too precious to hurt."

"You have my word." His words had the ring of an oath, serious and solemn. "I'll be your host, your protector, your friend if you need one. But as for any more than that—"

She frowned at him. "What if I need a partner instead?"

Chapter 12

I had a partner once. I killed her. Beau swallowed hard—the sounds of breaking glass and crunching sheet metal a distant echo. He saw on Emma's face that she hadn't meant "life partner" and couldn't understand why his mind would go there, leaping miles ahead of the lust his body was still working to extinguish.

"I found something I copied from the memory card," Emma said. "A photo I need to show you, to see if you might recognize him."

"Recognize who?" Beau asked. "From when?"

"It's a terrible picture, and just a partial image," she admitted with a shrug, "taken after three in the morning of the day Russell died. But you could definitely make out that this person's armed."

"Did you show the deputy?"

She waved off the idea. "I didn't trust him enough, and after what you just told me about those secret campaign contributions, I'm doubly glad I didn't."

"You don't suppose it could be Wallace in that picture, do you?" Beau asked.

"I—I can't begin to say. The angle's poor and the lighting's worse yet, so let's not get ahead of ourselves with wishful thinking."

Straightening his spine, Beau shook his head. "When it comes to defending this ranch and my father's wishes, I'll fight Wallace 'til the last lawyer's come down with laryngitis. But if you think for one minute I'm *hoping* he's the one that murdered Russell, you seriously misunderstand me. That jackass is still family, after all."

The look Emma gave him paired well with her snort of disbelief.

"I know. Surprises me, too," Beau admitted. "I guess some of my aunt's lectures on family loyalty must've sunk in somewhere along the way." More to the point, he hated thinking of Wallace's most-likely-blameless wife and daughters destroyed by such a discovery. "That doesn't mean I'll give him a pass, though, just because he has Kingston connections."

"I hope you're not imagining that I'd l leave that choice in your hands," she said, eyes narrowing a fraction.

"I wouldn't expect it of you."

"Good." She nodded crisply. "Then you won't be surprised to hear I've already left another message with my Ranger contact. I only hope Lieutenant Williams is busy investigating the matter and not just ignoring me."

"He's probably still reviewing his own copy of those photos."

She sighed. "That could take forever. There were hundreds of image files in that folder. And for all I know, there may still be more out there on other cameras no one's found yet. If we're really lucky, maybe we'll find one aimed directly at the turbine's base. Then we can turn it over, too, when we let the Rangers know what your PI friend's found out about the sheriff's campaign contributions."

Beau hesitated, the thought of his own signed lease deal with Green Horizon flickering like a prairie fire just over the horizon. A wildfire threatening to burn through any hope he had of saving the ranch's finances. There were other considerations as well. "It might be better to hold off on that, Emma, and let the Rangers collect that evidence themselves so it'll be admissible in a court of law, in case it happens to contain important evidence."

"Wait, and let someone else—whether it's the sheriff or whoever Russell was threatening—discover and destroy it first?"

"If they haven't already," he said.

"You're absolutely right. The cameras may be long gone, or at least their memory cards. But maybe they missed another one and we'll get lucky, especially if we can go by daylight," she said, her eyes alight with excitement. "We could find the proof we need to finally prove exactly who it was who—"

"All right, all right," he relented, worried that if he didn't help her, she might try to sneak off again, hobbling around on crutches to search on her own. "We'll go this afternoon, as soon as I touch base with my family. But first, let's head down to your room and see what you've got."

Their gazes connected, lingering long enough that her color deepened.

"I—I meant the photo, not—" he stammered. "Hell's bells. That did *not* come out the way I meant it."

She laughed awkwardly. "I know. It's just—it's—This feels a little…"

"It does," he admitted, praying that talking with her would get easier in time. Because for all the reasons that touching her had been a terrible idea, the back of his brain—and a good portion of his body—burned for the excuse to do it again.

Maybe she'd been right about needing to find another place to stay. But thinking of the evidence she might have found of murder, along with the threat posed by her ex-husband, had him immediately backing off the thought. Or was he worried more about himself, about never seeing her again?

"Fortunately, we're both adults," Emma assured him, "and if there ever comes a time that one of us forgets it, then it's time to pull the plug on this arrangement and send me packing, pronto. Deal?" With a tentative smile, she stuck out her hand.

"You've got it." Beau shook on it, wondering where, if the time ever came when he did feel ready to get to know another woman, he'd ever find these brains, heart and fierce determination, all wrapped up in such a gorgeous package. "Now let's go and see that *picture*. River here can chaperone."

Feeling fortunate but a little guilty that neither his suitcase nor the truck had been spotted by his family yet, he put off his reunion to head to the guest wing, walking beside Emma on her crutches.

"So how'd the rest of your trip go?" she asked as she made her way over the tiles. "Your ex-partner have any helpful suggestions for you?"

"None that don't involve time, money and a lot of lawyers," he said ruefully.

"Because of Wallace, right?" The glance she cast his way was sympathetic.

Beau sighed. "Even without him, I'm afraid, I would have trouble enough on my hands. The ranch has got some issues, financial challenges my father did a damned good job of hiding."

"So this new deal you have going with Green Horizons Energy…?"

"I won't lie. It could make or break us," he admitted, "which is one reason I damned well need to know if anyone from the company had a thing to do with Russell's death."

She stopped her awkward shift-swing forward on the crutches to look him in the eye. "And if they do? What will you do then?"

"Start scrambling for all I'm worth, I guess. Try to find a way to expand our sales of breeding stock."

"That doesn't sound like a half-bad idea. With average temperatures rising worldwide, I'd imagine the kind of heat- and disease-resistant cattle that do so well in south Texas could help those struggling with change."

"That's an interesting angle," he said, never having considered the way a scientist might view a business rooted in the past.

"I'm no expert on the industry, but if you ever want to bounce around ideas—" she shrugged "—I'd be happy to serve as a sounding board."

"I appreciate that." He felt a rush of warmth at her offer. "Especially from someone dealing with the problems you are."

"Maybe we ought to try trading troubles some time," she suggested with a wry half smile, "just to switch things up."

"I might take you up on that," Beau deadpanned, "with the possible exception of the potentially murderous ex-husband."

"That's fair," she agreed, moving her laptop to the room's writing desk, where she sat down and unlocked the secured screen. Watching her take that commonplace security precaution got Beau to thinking as he stood behind her while River lay nearby.

"Did you ever get to look at Russell's computer after his death?"

She shook her head and glanced up at him. "I turned it over to the sheriff, but it was locked." Keeping her gaze glued to the screen, she opened up a folder. "And I'm not volunteering to try to crack the password in case Fleming decides to destroy evidence he doesn't approve of. Or worse yet, try to somehow pin it on you."

Beau grimaced, fearing she was right. And wishing the state authorities would hurry up and take over this investigation.

"Here it is," she said as an image filled the center of the screen.

He bent over, bracing a hand on the back of the chair where she was sitting. "Can you enlarge it any more?"

"Not without losing all definition." She shook her head. "Not a lot to go on, is there? Too close, too much light from the flash, and—"

"He's armed. That's clear enough," Beau said, though it was impossible to discern more than the fact that the intruder was carrying a handgun, "and I can see he's wearing dark clothes. Long sleeves, even in the summer heat, and— Did you find another shot? One taken before or after this one?" Because Beau couldn't begin to be sure, not from this angle with this partial view. But there was something about the body shape, the way the man held himself, that nudged a suspicion. A suspicion chewing around the edges of his consciousness like rats gnawing at an engine's wiring.

Shaking his head, he dismissed it, certain he was wrong.

"I've gone through all of them, and this is it," she said. "Our only other chance is finding another camera out there that may have captured the same person when he stepped out of this lens's range."

"Then we'd better get on it as soon as we can. I'm going to need to see my family first, though, and grab a little lunch. Have you eaten?"

"No, but food can wait."

"It'll be hard enough getting around on that leg. We don't need your energy flagging, too, so what about this? I'll meet you in a half hour with some drinks and sandwiches to take with us. Sound good?"

She nodded. "Sure, but is everything okay, Beau? Ever since you I showed you that photo, you seem a little... You didn't know who—"

"I have a lot of my plate, that's all, and a hell of a lot of ranch business to deal with before the day is through," he insisted, unable to keep himself from sounding hurried and impatient. "So the faster we can collect any evidence you might've missed and get it safely into the right hands, the happier I'll be."

Something was wrong with Beau. She heard it in his voice and saw it in the way he rushed off, promising to be back for her again in thirty minutes.

Emma's gaze went to the open photo, and she wondered if, unlikely as it seemed, he had seen something in it. Something that explained how a man who'd been kissing her so passionately, holding on to her as if he'd never let go only minutes earlier, had cooled so abruptly. Or maybe it wasn't the photo but the lie he'd told her weighing on her, the one where he'd implied that he would give up on the deal that might be his only chance to save his legacy if he learned that Green Horizons was somehow wrapped up in Russell's murder.

Was that it, then? Had he recognized—or thought he

might—someone from the company? And was Beau, for all the doubts his cousin was spreading around about his parentage, really willing to give up his hold on power, privilege and all the trappings that went with being the sole heir to the ranch and the fortune that came with it?

Did those born and raised to wealth and power ever willingly walk away? Her own modest background might not offer much of a frame of reference, but the history books and the news were both brimming with examples of rich men and women willing to lie or cheat, even kill, to hang on to what they had. Was she foolish to believe that Beau was any different...or that she'd gotten any better at judging men by what they said or how they looked?

All she know was how she'd felt when he was kissing her, when their eager bodies began an interrupted conversation... She closed her eyes, catching her lower lip between her teeth before her thoughts were interrupted by her ringing cell...

Stomach clenching, she reached for it, the throbbing of her heartbeat drumming in her ears. Would it be Jeremy again, out to fool her into answering another of his calls? Could he somehow know, or guess, that she'd had another man's hands on her?

In an instant, the ugly names rushed through her brain again, the terrible accusations she had heard so often. Forcing herself to slow her breathing, she whispered to herself, "Stop it. Stop this right now," angry that she was doing her tormentor's job for him.

Blinking back tears, she glanced down at the phone's screen and blew out a long breath. "Lieutenant Williams," she said as she connected with the Ranger, "I'm so glad to finally hear back from you."

But once he started talking, her relief wouldn't last for long.

* * *

Aunt Alicia gave Beau a concerned look from her favorite lounge chair on the lanai, where palm-leaf fan blades spun lazily above to stir the warm air. "I've done my best to discourage them, but I'm afraid that the boys have been going on nonstop about our visitor, begging me to wake her up and make her come to breakfast, lunch, out to the Crazy Cow for ice cream sundaes…"

Beau winced, though he kept his eyes on his two sons, who were shouting, "Daddy, look what we taught Maverick!"

Cort stood by the poolside as the smaller Leland floated in the center of the pool, one arm over a lime-green noodle, though after years of lessons, both boys swam like minnows.

"Ready, Leland?" Cort directed while the oversize pup trotted around the pool's edge, looking anxiously from one boy to the other.

Leland gave his freckled brother a thumbs-up before sucking in a noisy breath and then relaxing, face-first, into a dead man's float. When he didn't stir for a few seconds, Maverick barked frantically and then leaped into the pool to splash toward him. Beau watched, smiling to see Leland sneak another breath while the young dog completed his rescue mission, grabbing the boy by the swim trunks and towing him back toward the poolside.

"Hey, let go of those!" Leland sputtered as he grabbed on to the edge.

Maverick raised his sodden head, coming up with the dripping swimsuit while Cort howled with laughter. "Oooh! Leland's skinny-dipping!"

"Hey! Give those back!" Leland yelled.

"Excuse me," Beau said on his way to head off Maverick at the pool steps and rescue Leland's trunks before the dog could begin a game of keep-away sure to give his aunt conniptions.

Handing the suit back to Leland, he ordered, "That's a pretty neat trick. Next time, though, we'll need to work out a G-rated version. Put it back on, or wrap up in a towel at least because it's time for you guys to run inside and get dressed. You're starting to get burnt."

Both boys complained about leaving the pool, as they always did, but he could see that they were exhausted from their time out in the sun.

After they headed inside to dress, with Maverick trotting at their heels, Beau sat down across from his aunt and poured himself some lemonade from the pitcher on the small table between them.

"So this woman," his aunt said carefully. "You're taking her for a private tour of the ranch this afternoon. Could that mean—"

"It means I'm doing the bare minimum as a host by taking her to look for one last piece of missing equipment from her study," he assured her for the sake of lowering her expectations. "That's all, truly. I know the boys have taken a shine to her, and you like her as well."

His aunt smiled up at him from behind a pair of outsize rhinestone-rimmed sunglasses. "She's an engaging young woman, with the loveliest manners."

"Wallace sure doesn't think so. She's been aggravating the fire out of him about her student's death investigation."

Aunt Alicia raised her own lemonade as if in tribute. "No wonder you're so taken with her, then."

"I wouldn't put it that way." His brain called him out on the lie, replaying the encounter in the den in excruciating detail.

"And so good with the children," Aunt Alicia went on.

He raised a palm in protest. "Please stop."

"Pretty, too, with those green eyes and a figure I can't imagine any man would find fault with."

"Her figure's got nothing to do with anything," he said irritably, trying desperately to get Emma's body off his mind, the heated lushness of her mouth when she had kissed him... "You have to understand. And make the boys understand, too. She's only here until she's well enough to return to her job and her life in Austin."

"It's not like that's the moon. And anyway, in this day and age, distance isn't something a couple can't overcome."

He shook his head. "That may be true, but we are *not* a couple. And we won't be. Can't be. Ever."

"You don't like her, then? Because I know for a fact you've spent time with her at the hospital, sent her flowers—roses."

"Have you been spying on me, Aunt Alicia?"

Her eyes widened in a look of wounded outrage. "*Spying?* Really, Beau. The things you say. You know I would never intrude on your privacy, but you are a Kingston after all, the head of the ranch and family—"

"For now, at any rate," he grumbled, thinking about Wallace's newly authenticated will.

"So you should know that people can't help taking note of what you're doing. And some of those people happen to consider themselves my friends."

Beau rolled his eyes at the way she talked about the family as if it were some sort of Elizabethan dynasty. Unfortunately, some of the suck-ups in this community subscribed to the same theory, including those who'd previously made his life hell because they didn't feel he was deserving of the honor.

"I should have never brought her here," he said. "I should've known you'd only start again."

The subject had come up several times since Beau's return, especially since his father's death. How it wasn't right for a man in his prime to spend his life alone. How his sons were not too old to learn to love another woman. *And it's a fact*, his aunt had told him after they'd picked out his father's gravestone, *that I may not always be around to help you raise them. With my brother and my sister both gone now, I can't pretend any longer that I'm going to live forever.*

He'd assured her that she absolutely would, if he had anything to say about it. But he wondered if her less-than-subtle nudges were her way of letting him know that the care of two lively boys, regardless of how insistent she was about doing so much of the work without help, was getting to be too much for her.

"If I've made a few suggestions," she said, "it's only because I want you to be happy. And if pretty Dr. Emma isn't for you, I know of any number of nice young ladies, beautiful, accomplished women who would be absolutely thrilled for the chance to meet the—"

"Anointed one?" His voice dripping with sarcasm, he scarcely registered the clicking of the dog's nails on the tile. "They *wanted* what my brother was, not some bastard whose father could barely stand to be seen with him in public."

"Please don't say that," his aunt pleaded, a note of frailty in her voice. "It's not true. Your father was grateful to have your help. He told me himself he'd underestimated how much of a rancher and a businessman you are."

"And they sure as hell don't want a man who's about to watch his one-hundred-forty-seven-year-old legacy crumble into dust."

"You *won't* fail this ranch." Aunt Alicia pulled off her sunglasses to blink at him with watery blue eyes. "You'll be the one to save it."

"Even if I do manage to save this place from Wallace's scheming—" the harshness of Beau's voice elicited a distressed whine, following by an insistent nudge at his leg "—that woman, the same damned woman you're suggesting that I invite into our lives, our hearts, my damned bed, could easily prove to be the final nail in this ranch's coffin."

When the dog licked his hand and nudged him harder, Beau said irritably, "Knock it off, Maverick. Enough with the clingy act."

Annoyed, he pushed the shaggy head away, only to realize that the dog so distressed by his tone and volume wasn't Maverick, but the far more sensitive River looking at him with anxious brown eyes.

River, whom he'd left down in the guest wing with—

Beau looked up sharply, toward the patio door entry leading into the pool area. The gaze he met there was green and stricken, the face pale as Emma stammered, "Ex-excuse me. I didn't mean to intrude," before turning on her crutches and thumping back inside.

Chapter 13

About twenty minutes later, Emma opened the door of her guest room to a knock to find Beau standing before her, his straw hat in his hands and a soft-sided cooler slung over one broad shoulder.

"I'm so sorry," he was quick to say, his eyes like bitter chocolate. "Sorry you happened to overhear my conversation. I didn't mean—I had no idea you were standing there."

She jerked her chin a little higher. "So you're not sorry you said it," she challenged, "only that I happened to embarrass you by showing up while you were being honest."

Upset that Lieutenant Williams had told her it could be several weeks before his current caseload allowed him to complete his review of the evidence, she'd been rushing to find Beau to vent her frustration. Instead, she'd run headlong into the truth about the rancher. He might have shown her and River kindness, might even be attracted to Emma on a purely physical level. But he had his own priorities, and they had nothing to do with her.

He raised his palms, as if in surrender. "Of course I am. But you have to understand. My aunt, my sons—they're all pushing for something I can't have. Not even if I start to—"

Cutting himself off, he shifted his gaze and shook his head. "You know what? We ought to get going. We can finish this conversation on the way or over lunch."

"Not until *you* finish your sentence. 'Not even if I start to' *what*?"

His dark eyes found hers once more. "Not even if I start to forget," he said, his voice a low rumble, "all the reasons why wanting you is a terrible idea..."

He reached for her, his hand rising toward her cheek.

Exasperated with his moodiness, she stepped back out of range. "Not a good idea. Remember?" she asked, glaring. I'm out to destroy you—or your ranch, at any rate."

He sighed and shook his head. "I know you'd never do a thing like that," he admitted, "not intentionally. When you overheard me, I was only worried, that's all, and trying to deflect my aunt's—"

"I just got off the phone with your friend Nadine at the motel," Emma cut in. "After I explained the situation to her, she insisted I come stay with her at her place, with her and her family for a few days."

When Beau stiffened, she thought he'd argue. Instead, he swallowed audibly. "They're good people. You'll be safe there."

Forcing herself to press on, Emma said, "She can come by and pick me up tomorrow morning. Or if you're especially eager to be rid of me, you can drop me off there any time after eight tonight."

"Is that what you want?" he asked.

It's not. She wanted to shout her admission, to pull him back behind this door and lock the world away awhile. To lock away the fear and stress she had been feeling, along with all the uncertainties over whom to trust and whether she was doing the right thing being here. To let pleasure rule the day for once, to allow her body's needs and the aching chasm of her loneliness to be assuaged for a few hours, even a few minutes, before reality set in again.

Then Jeremy's voice returned to her again, shuddering through her like a sick chill. *Spread your legs for him, why don't you, slut? But he'll never love you the way I did.*

"I want to leave as soon as possible," she managed to tell Beau, the quaver in her voice the only sign of the turmoil inside her. "I think it's best for both of us."

Beau hesitated, the look that passed between them so weighted with temptation that for a moment her heart lifted, thinking that he would try to change her mind. Or better yet, that he would reach for her, unable to resist.

She was still working through how she would react when he nodded.

"All right, then," he said. "Let's get going."

"You stay here this time," she told River, deciding there was no need to subject the dog to the afternoon heat.

Though River whined and laid her ears low, Emma was able to convince her with a few pats and a fresh bowl of water that it was a good time for a nap instead.

Afterward, Emma and Beau headed to his truck in grim silence. He stepped in front of her to open the passenger door and stowed her crutches with the cooler.

She thanked him as he helped her with her seat belt and then climbed behind the wheel.

"Any time," he said. "But before we head to the turbine, we'll stop by the equipment shed and grab one of the MULEs to make getting around a little easier for you."

"A *mule*?" Her sore leg gave a pang of protest. "I don't think I'm up to riding."

He grinned and shook his head. "Wrong kind of mule. This one's a brand of ATV. All-terrain vehi—"

"I know what an ATV is," she said, her face heating. "I just had a mental image of me prancing around the turbine, mounted on a jackass."

He grinned. "I'm afraid you'll have to settle for riding on a padded bench seat next to one instead."

She laughed, unable to stop herself. "You said it, not me."

He shrugged. "I happen to admire mules as saddle animals. They're tough, agile and resilient."

"I picture you more as the black stallion type. No, a stallion's too impractical for a man with your responsibilities— a big, solid quarter horse—a sensible brown with a sensible name to go with your big hat and the tall boots."

He looked sharply her direction. "You're good. I usually ride a cutting horse named Toby. He's a bay quarter horse gelding, and the smartest, toughest animal I've ever ridden."

Smiling to herself, she didn't tell him that she'd seen a framed photo of him aboard just such a horse while he'd been showing her the house and that one of his sons had mentioned the name Toby while describing their own Rascal and Pippin as the three had chatted after lunch the day they'd met.

It hit her then that she was going to miss Beau, miss having him to talk to…and share advice with and even tease, something she hadn't dared try with Jeremy in years.

As Beau backed the truck up to a small trailer toward

the open bay of a large beige metal building a few minutes later, a fit-looking older man with a thick black-and-silver mustache, light brown skin and darker eyes strode out, stiff-legged, his jaw set and his teeth gritted as he jammed a Panama hat back over his short, thick hair.

"My ranch manager, Fernando Galvez," Beau explained. "If you'll excuse me for a moment, I'd better check and see what's rattled his cage."

"*Who*, I think you mean," she said, gesturing toward a slim, far younger man stalking out behind the first, waving his hands emphatically as he shouted—though his words were muffled from inside the truck's cab—at Fernando.

Even in his anger, the young man was strikingly good-looking, with a thick sweep of shiny jet hair and flashing teeth so white against the warm golden-tan face that drew her gaze, making her wonder where it was she might have seen him.

"The fireman," Emma blurted, surprised that she recalled anything from those first awful hours after discovering Russell's body. But the memory of the two strapping firefighters, carrying the cooler of water between them to the back of Beau's pickup, was seared into her brain. "What would he be doing here?"

"Antonio's Fernando's youngest," Beau said. "Let me see if I can sort out these two hotheads before they come to blows."

Seeing the family resemblance between the two now, she impulsively reached for the door handle.

"Why don't you hang out here for a few minutes?" Beau suggested. "There's no need for you to get involved in a minor family squabble."

Emma nodded, though the way the two Galvez men

were glaring at each other, she wasn't sure about the "minor" part of Beau's assessment.

When Beau closed the truck's door behind him, she could see the pair abruptly went silent, both of their dark brown gazes shifting to look at her.

Unease rippled through her, a shiver sparked by the lack of welcome in eyes that were hard and flat with anger. Looking away, she sighed, feeling nothing but relief when all three men disappeared inside the metal building.

They're angry at each other, not you. But as true as she knew this to be, she berated herself for her tendency to cringe at any sign of a man's anger. When confronted face-to-face, she'd taught herself—over the course of months—to stand her ground and speak up. But inside, she realized she might never stop waiting for the next man or the one after to turn on her, just as the man she'd trusted most in this world had.

Would she ever get beyond it? Or had her mother been right, all those times she'd pleaded for Emma to see someone in the months after she'd filed for divorce. *A counselor can help you with your grief and pain, keep you from making the same mistakes with another man down the road.*

I don't have to worry about that, Emma had responded bitterly, *because I'm never getting that close to another man again.*

"I just came around to grab an ATV, not get into your business," Beau told Fernando, who kept glaring at his son. The thick atmosphere of his disdain, along with the way the twenty-year-old seemed to study the laces of his own tennis shoes, took Beau back uncomfortably to far too many arguments he'd had with his own father. Arguments that would have driven him from the ranch even sooner than he'd left had it not been for Fernando's calm and reliable influence.

Why couldn't Fernando see that his own son needed the same thing now—and more than that, needed the love and acceptance of the man he most respected?

"This boy of mine," Fernando all but spat out, "has no consideration, no pride in his family history or honor. And no care for his sick mama."

"Papa, please," Antonio told him. "Of course I care about my mother. Haven't I cleaned the house, cooked the meals, driven her to treatments?"

As Antonio—or Tony, as his friends called him—was the only one of the couple's children still living at home, Beau could see how many of the daily tasks might fall to him. Especially since it would never occur to the traditional Fernando that he, too, was capable of loading a dishwasher or pushing a vacuum.

"Then why abandon her now? To go to *Dallas* of all places." At the mention of the metropolis six hours to the north, Fernando narrowed his eyes. "You trade your family for what? Cars crawling everywhere, houses one on top of the other, strip malls and pollution and—"

"And the job I've been dreaming of and working for my whole life," Tony ventured. "An exciting, challenging career rooted in the future, not stuck in some dusty past—"

Advancing on his son, Fernando shouted, "You talk about this ranch, this life, like it is dead already, right in front of Señor Kingston?"

"It's all right." Beau stepped between them, afraid the two might come to blows. "He's young, Fernando, and he has to find his own way, just like you and I did.

Maybe someday, if things work out, Tony's path will lead him home."

"And I'll come to visit, Papa, as often as I can," Antonio offered.

"Your mother cried all night the last time you walked out of our house," Fernando accused, scowling over the top of Beau's shoulder, "and then I find your things in the storeroom here, where you're been sleeping like some bum."

"In the storeroom?" Beau echoed, thinking of the cold comfort offered by the glorified closet area, with its concrete floor, its bins of parts and equipment, and the tiny, Spartan half bathroom tucked into one corner.

"For the last time—" Antonio shook his head "—I would never touch the security cameras, and those things aren't mine. You know that. I've been—I've been mostly staying at the station or with Carlos," he explained, naming an older brother who lived in one of the modest homes that made up the ranch employee housing area a few miles away.

"Why do you lie to me?" Fernando demanded. "Do you think I don't talk to Carlos?"

"All right." Tony's shoulders sagged. "It's not him. It's Felicity. I've been staying with my girlfriend—"

"This rich white girl who goes with all the firemen? The one you are too ashamed to introduce to family?"

"She's not like that, Papa. You don't under—"

"Bah! We have seen you, driving this girl's fancy car around town like you're the big man, sleeping through Mass because all night you have been—"

"This stuff—I'd like to take a look," Beau interrupted, far less interested in who the kid was shacking up with than he was the night that Emma had nearly been run down. "And I'll be bringing Dr. Copley inside to check it with me—*if* I can trust you two not to embarrass all of us."

"I'm sorry, Mr. Kingston," Tony said, shaking his head. "It's bad enough he dragged me down here without bringing you and your guest into our family squabble. But if I came across as disrespectful, especially after everything you've—"

"We're fine, Tony." Beau shot a look to the kid to shut him up before he mentioned that Beau had served as a job reference for Antonio's employment applications. Fernando would feel even more betrayed to learn that Beau had given a nervous Tony some advice about his interview and sprung for his hotel room when he'd traveled for it a couple of months before.

A few minutes later, Beau was standing in the storage room with Emma, who seemed fascinated with the ranch equipment hanging from wall racks or heaped into bins. "What on earth is that thing?" she asked. "And this?"

"A cattle oiler for parasites, and that one's a broken head chute that needs welding. But I wanted to show you this." He walked over to the spot he'd gotten Fernando to describe and crouched beneath a bank of wall-mounted bins, where he pointed to a sleeping bag and several items of men's clothing.

"It seems we've had an unauthorized squatter," he said, looking up at her, "and I need to know if you recognize any of these things."

Emma's face went ashen, her eyes rounded with alarm. "You—you think Jeremy could be *here*?"

"I can't say. We don't know how long this has been here." Beau pulled a penknife from his pocket and used its blade to lift a dark gray T-shirt, gritty with dust, and a single crumpled sock.

"I—I don't recognize those things, but—but I was always on Jeremy for taking off his socks and leaving them balled up like a slob."

"That narrows down our suspect list to—half the men in this state," he said.

"What's the shirt size?" she asked. "Is there a tag?"

"It's hard to read. Large, maybe?"

"Jeremy wears a large," she said uncertainly, her gaze darting around as if she half expected him to still be here, hiding somewhere.

"So do a lot of guys," Beau said.

"It's Jeremy. I know it's him." Emma hugged herself. "He's killed Russell, and he'll kill you, too, if he's seen us together."

"We don't know for sure this is even connected to the attacks on you or Russell's death," Beau said. "The ranch has had other visitors in the past. Undocumented migrants looking for a safe place to spend the night as they pass through." Though he and his employees tried to keep the outbuildings secured at night to discourage such intruders, along with the occasional theft, Beau suspected it was one more area where procedures had grown lax.

He pushed at the surface of the blue sleeping bag, which was grease-splotched, worn and lumpy. And unaccountably bulky in spots, with several solid items hidden inside. Coming to his feet, he grabbed the bag's corners and shook it in the hope that something would fall out, preferably something like a wallet or a driver's license. Instead, something heavier fell, clunking against the concrete at his feet.

There was a second thud, and then a third, a wicked-looking knife landing beside a set of brass knuckles and a palm-sized revolver. And the last item that came sailing out, so light that it wafted downward, was a photo. A photo of Russell Jorgenson grinning, one hand lifting what looked like a margarita as he stood behind a bar hung with colorful paper fiesta banners. The other arm, tan and muscular, was draped over the shoulder of a slender woman in a summer dress, her sun-streaked hair shining and her head tipped back in laughter.

Beau was jolted to realize it was Emma, looking far more like a girlfriend than the grad student's professor.

Emma tilted her head forward, groaning as she covered her face with one hand. The crutch she had let go of crashed to the floor, but the sound barely registered over the roar of blood in her ears and the wave of dizziness that threatened to cut her legs out from underneath her.

"Emma, are you all right?"

Beau's voice seemed to float toward her from a great distance. Was he, like Jeremy, cursing her as a whore now, too?

"This—this was taken last spring at a private party celebrating a colleague receiving a prestigious fellowship at a university in—" She shook her head, clenching her teeth so hard that tears came to her eyes. "Russell and a group of grad students performed some ridiculous song they'd made up about bat species—my colleague's area of study—and we all took pictures after. Everyone was laughing, and—and I—"

"You don't have to explain," Beau said as he gently helped her to metal folding chair along one wall. "You don't owe me that."

"We were all only having fun," she said. "I wasn't—I never did anything more with Russell or any other student."

"If it helps, I believe you. I can see that photo's been cropped, other people removed from it to zero in on you two."

"That's what people do when they're obsessed," she

said, rubbing at the eruption of chill bumps along her arms. "What *Jeremy* does. It has to be him. But how could he get this picture? If he'd been anywhere near that night, I would've had the police on him in a second. Could he have hired someone? A private detective?"

"Maybe, but look at this photo paper—" Lifting it for her to see, he thumbed the flimsy edge. "Someone's printed this at home, probably off social media."

"I blocked Jeremy everywhere I could, deleted all of my accounts, too, so people wouldn't tag photos of me or…" She pressed her fingertips to her aching forehead. "I've made an effort to disappear online."

"Staying invisible is easier said than done these days," Beau said, the weight of his hand on her shoulder comforting. "And if it was your ex, he could've easily tricked someone who attended that party into accepting a request from a fake profile. You said he's good at conning people."

"Apparently, far better than I am at keeping a low profile." Shaking her head, she grabbed her crutches and pushed herself up from the chair. "But you know what? I'm not hiding any longer. I can't—I absolutely won't—let that man keep killing people."

People? He stared at her intently. "Wait—are you telling me that Russell's not the first person you believe your ex has murdered?"

Unable to look at Beau, she closed her eyes but couldn't stop the tears that leaked out from beneath the lids. "The law might have thought otherwise, but he's no less responsible. And I swear someday he'll pay for the child we lost."

Chapter 14

The shock of her statement cracked through Beau's composure. His gut clenched in response, his arms aching to pull her into an embrace, but the hard look in her eyes warned him she wouldn't welcome his touch. "You've lost a child? Emma… I'm so—I'm sorry. When did this—"

Green eyes flashing open, she slashed the air with her hands. "I don't—I can't talk about this. Please, forget that I said anything about it."

But Beau knew that he wouldn't. How could he, with the pain he'd seen in her face forever branded into his brain? Whatever had fractured Emma's marriage had clearly left deep wounds. Wounds that did much to explain her brittleness and apparent isolation. It partly explained, too, why he had been so drawn to her from the start. Had the damage he had buried so deeply and borne in silence for nearly three years recognize her scars?

"I just—I need that gun," she stammered, "to take care of this. To finally end this when he comes back for me."

Beau was shaking his head before she'd finished speaking. No way could he be a party to anything like that. "That's not going to happen. For one thing, that gun's evidence."

"Evidence for whom? The sheriff? Because that's who we'd have to call on this."

"It is Wallace's jurisdiction," Beau said uncertainly. "But you're right. We can't trust him not to make it disappear. Especially if he figures it might somehow implicate his friends at Green Horizons."

"So what, then?" she asked. "Surely, Jeremy will come back for these things. Those things he brought to hurt me."

"First off, he's not hurting you again. We'll see to that, I promise, one way or another."

She released an audible breath and nodded her agreement, though the apprehension in her eyes said she didn't quite believe it.

"Secondly," Beau continued, "if he does come back, I have an idea…an idea that might even help Fernando and his son pull their family back together."

To Beau's relief, both of the Galvez men were able and willing to pitch in, recruiting Fernando's elder sons, trusted friends Beau had grown up with, to assist with the round-the-clock stakeout of the weapons—though he'd used a bandanna to remove the revolver's bullets. Beau insisted the men work in pairs, and that they photograph the approach of any individual—and if they could safely do so, detain him and call Beau.

"We'll have to notify the sheriff, too, of course," Beau explained to Emma as they finally headed for the turbine about twenty minutes later, the ATV rattling on its trailer behind the truck. "But first, we'll get some answers of our own—and record whatever he'll tell us."

When she only continued staring out the window, he prompted, "Sound good? Are you going to be all right?"

"To tell you the truth," she said, "I feel sick, seeing that photo and all those awful weapons."

"I'm sure it has to be unsettling, especially after everything that's happened."

She sighed. "I've been getting by these past few days by convincing myself that whoever's tried to hurt me, whoever's killed Russell, must have moved on by now. But this—this looks and feels too personal to me to be anyone who'll give up. Or anyone but *him*…"

The man she blamed for the loss of her child. No wonder she looked so pale and shaken.

"No one would think any less of you if you went home," Beau told her as they came around a curve and Turbine Number 43 loomed high above them.

"It's what everyone expects of me," she said, her voice so low, he had to strain to hear it. "What everybody wants."

"The question is, Emma, what do you want?" he asked. "And where, if anywhere, would you feel safe?"

He pulled up in the shadow of the turbine, which remained shuttered and motionless, despite the steady coastal breeze. From where he parked, he could see that the padlocked chain remained in place, too, as he knew it might for months, or even permanently, depending on the outcome of both the safety and any further criminal investigations.

Emma released a shaky breath, but her voice sounded strong when she said, "Let's focus right now on why we came here. If there's another camera anywhere, that'll be a whole lot more helpful than running and hiding from the problem."

"What about a sandwich first? I know it's gotten kind of late, but—"

She speared him with a look. "You go ahead if you want, but I'm not in the mood to make a picnic of a murder scene. Or a search for evidence, especially with Jeremy somewhere close by."

"As long as we stay hydrated, I can wait to eat, too," he said. "And I didn't want to make you nervous earlier, but you need to know I didn't bring you out here unprotected."

Opening the console between the seats, he pulled out a pistol. "I've got a rifle in a case in the back seat, too. If push came to shove, do you know how to shoot?"

"The handgun for sure. I've never fired a rifle."

"With any luck, we'll have no reason to worry about either."

For the next two hours, they searched without interruption, the wind depositing sand over every inch of flesh grown sticky in the heat. But for all their hopes and preparations, the effort proved fruitless. Other than the one camera Emma had found and stripped of its memory card the night she'd been out here alone, they located only one additional game camera—only to find its inner compartment hanging open and its contents missing, too.

"The question is, who took this one?" Beau asked Emma. Back in his MP days, he would've called in an evidence team, but at this point, all he could do was photograph the find and leave it in place.

"Whoever forced Russell up that turbine would've certainly had a motive."

"Sure," he said, "but if it was really your ex-husband, acting on some jealous obsession, how would he have known to look for the cameras? How would anyone unless he'd had some knowledge that Russell had set them up?"

"You don't know what Russell might've told him as he was being forced to climb that turbine. He had to have been desperate, willing to do or say anything that might save his life."

She was right, he realized, but her certainty that her ex-husband was nearby didn't rule out someone Russell may have threatened to expose as a suspect. Someone who might feel that the woman who'd worked so closely with the dead man also constituted a threat.

Finally conceding defeat, he cranked up the engine and started the air-conditioning for Emma while he loaded the ATV back on its trailer. Once inside the truck, he passed her some fresh water. "I'll drop you off at home to get cleaned up for dinner before I take the MULE back to the storage unit."

"Dinner? I thought you'd want to take me to Nadine's right away, get me away from here, especially since it looks like Jeremy's been hanging around the ranch."

"For all we know, whoever was hiding in the storage area was scared off days ago."

"So he could he could be long gone?"

"That would be my guess. Maybe he caught wind that you were in the hospital and then skipped town. I can't think he'd want to risk hanging around here, where my men would surely recognize a stranger if they saw him, very long."

"I don't know. It's not that far from the house. If he comes back to get his things…"

"That's why I have my best vaqueros, friends I'd trust with my life, watching for him. You'll be safe here, one more night. I promise," he said, "Stay. Please."

"I don't—"

"I'm grilling steaks this evening," he rushed to add,

"and it's an unwritten rule that you can't leave this ranch without a bellyful of good Kingston beef."

"Really?" she asked. "What about your vegetarian guests?"

"We're polite that way and humor 'em, but they don't know what they're missing."

"All right, then," she agreed. "But only because I'm too hot and tired to argue and I feel like I'm carrying around half the outdoors on my body." Wincing, she waved a hand to indicate her tangled hair and sweat-stained clothing to her dusty boots. "It'll be such a relief to get it off."

Grimy and windblown as he felt himself, his brain went there anyway, picturing that gritty ribbon of sand sluiced from her body and circling the drain. Imagining using the shower wand to rinse it from her, then soothing her sunburned skin with cooling cream...before heating it again with nips and kisses, forgetting for a short time—making both of them forget—the grief and stress they lived with and their uncertain futures.

Stifling a groan, he hurried back to the house, the trailer skipping sideways as he took the turn too quickly.

"Are you all right?" Emma asked him, glancing over with a strained look.

"Just hot and hungry myself," he admitted, looking straight ahead as he pulled up to the mansion.

Because if he looked her in the eyes, he feared, she'd know damned well how close he was to admitting that she was what he hungered for.

"I can't believe he's taking another call from that fool lawyer over dinner," Aunt Alicia complained as they sat around the table later, where Emma had just polished off a grilled veggie skewer, a helping of potato salad and the most amazing rib eye steak she'd ever eaten in her life.

The older woman, dressed in cheerful multicolored pastels this evening, frowned at the half-eaten remains of an even heartier dinner on her nephew's plate. "Now it's gotten all cold. And Leland, you hand over that skewer right now, young man."

Sticking out one gnarled hand, she fixed the younger boy with a look she'd given him and his brother earlier, when they'd been badgering Emma to come to the pool with them later or let them show her the frog pond in the morning.

Leland caved to his great-aunt's stare, surrendering the makeshift sword he'd been using to poke at his brother under the level of the table's edge.

"Sorry, Aunt Alicia," he said glumly.

"*Sorry, Cort*, you mean," she said with a sniff of disapproval.

"Don't worry. I have my trusty shield," his freckled brother held up the book—something with an armored knight on the cover—he'd been reading whenever he thought no one was watching.

Emma, who had gotten into trouble for doing exactly that as a girl—though she'd preferred horse stories at that age—had caught him at it earlier and given him a wink of approval.

"I'll take your skewer, too, sir," Aunt Alicia said, apparently deciding on a course of prudence. "Then if you two are finished eating, you may be excused now."

"But what about—" Leland shifted a reluctant look toward Emma. "Isn't there going to be dessert?"

"Maybe some chocolate ice cream later," his great-aunt allowed. "For now, though, why don't you take the dogs and play ball in the courtyard before it gets too dark?"

After the boys had gone, Emma and Beau's aunt talked for while longer, each occasionally glancing to the door behind which Beau had disappeared. At times, his raised voice could be heard, its harshness making Emma's stomach clench.

Though Emma tried to keep the conversation light, focusing on the ranch, the boys and possible rain in the forecast, Aunt Alicia continually peppered Emma with polite but increasingly probing questions about her background and upbringing in suburban Houston.

"And your father, what was it he did? Your real father, I mean?"

As much as she understood the woman thought she was looking out for her beloved nephew, Emma felt her patience fizzling at the awkwardness of this obvious vetting process. She began to sympathize with why Beau had said what he had earlier to put her off the scent.

"My father's been gone twenty years now," she said, injecting a note of surprise into her voice. "I can't imagine why such a thing would matter." She still remembered that agonizing day he'd been struck by a car while running with the track team he'd coached for the local high school. The idea of having his career—a career her family and the community she'd grown up in took such pride in—judged, and most likely found wanting, by a woman born into a fortune had Emma losing patience.

"I also gather," Beau's aunt said in hushed tones as she glanced from door to door to be sure she wasn't being overheard, "there's been a divorce in your past? Only the one, I take it? You'll forgive me for asking, but in this day and age, a person can't afford to assume—"

Shaking her head, Emma said, "Thank you for the

lovely dinner, but this inquisition ends now. Beau might not have mentioned it to you before, but I'll be leaving the ranch first thing in the morning. I appreciate the hospitality, but you need to know I won't be back."

Before reentering the breakfast room, Beau fought to still the turmoil roiling inside him. Though he knew that everyone else would have finished and his dinner would be cold or cleared away, he'd lost his appetite only seconds into the call with his lawyer.

"I've hashed things out with J. Armstrong Pinckney, and we can make this go away now, but only if we do it before the judge's ruling," Ed had rushed to say before naming a figure that Beau couldn't believe he'd heard right. His father's longtime attorney had gone on for some time, explaining the structured settlement that would cripple the ranch financially for decades and force him to sell off assets held intact for nearly one hundred fifty years.

"If I agree to that, Ed, what the hell's the point of anything?" he'd demanded, thinking of all the ranch's history, a past built from almost nothing into a juggernaut that Beau's father, the vaqueros who had helped to build it and the people of this community had always been so proud of, crumbling into dust on his watch. "If I take that deal, the ranch will be nothing but a shadow of its former self, one its debts will inevitably chip away at until, by the time my sons inherit, there'll be nothing left at all."

"But you'll still have years to enjoy it. Don't you see that?" With the strain in his voice making him sound even older, Ed struggled to strike a consoling tone, as if he hadn't just ripped Beau's heart out. "A lifetime in the mansion your great-grandfather built, time to build memories with your boys at your side and to help your people transition into other fields. Or at least you'll have that if you take this deal now. If not, you could lose everything within a few months, every dime, every calf and every acre. Not to mention what it's going to do to you, watching Wallace Fleming take everything and run it into the ground."

"You really think I'll lose it, don't you? That the probate judge is going to overturn what we both know my father wanted."

"Did he?" Ed had asked pointedly. "Because I think if that were really true, he never would have drawn up a will naming Wallace as his heir in the first place. Or at least he would've fixed things legally after you came back home and resumed working on the ranch. He wasn't a stupid or a careless man, your father."

Angered by his lack of support and dejected with the choice that Ed insisted he must make by morning, Beau had ended the call. But the atmosphere inside the breakfast room, where his aunt sat crying quietly over an empty table, seemed no less upsetting.

"What is it? What's wrong—other than my going missing through another meal?" After grabbing a box of tissues from the buffet, he hurried to stand beside her, where he laid a hand on her thin shoulder to still its shaking. Had she overheard part of his conversation? Did she guess the way of life she'd known since childhood was about to come to an abrupt end, all because his father hadn't been able to overcome his fears that Beau was another man's son?

"I'm nothing but an old fool," she cried. "I'm afraid I've said the wrong thing, peppering her with far too many questions. Now I've ruined everything. Your Emma's leaving in the morning."

"It was nothing you did," he assured her, though he

knew all too well that his aunt could be like a dog with a bone once she got it into her head to start prying. "Emma was leaving anyway. She was always going to leave. I told you that from the start. I only wish you hadn't gotten your hopes up so much."

He plucked a couple of tissues from the box and gently pressed them into her hand before kissing the top of her blond head.

"Maybe it's for the best, after all," his aunt said as she daubed at her damp eyes. "We don't need a girl like that, from heaven only knows what background. Certainly nothing she was willing to answer any questions about."

"I'm not sure we can hold that against her," Beau said, "especially considering all the stress that she's been under."

"And when I asked about past marriages, you would've thought I'd put her on the rack."

"Aunt Alicia, her ex-husband—we think he's been stalking her."

She straightened, her eyes widening. "*Here*, you mean? But I thought—didn't Wallace arrest some dreadful deviant after she was assaulted?"

"He's not the man, it turns out, and I didn't mention it before because I didn't want you to worry, but that night when her Jeep stranded her out here, someone tried to run her over. For all we know, her student might've been deliberately killed by this same person."

Aunt Alicia gasped, her face draining of color. "And you brought this woman into this home with your sons? Whatever were you thinking, Beau?"

"You were the one who insisted she stay, if I remember."

Anger burned in her blue eyes. "Only because you didn't inform me that she could pose a danger to us all."

"If I didn't think I could keep her safe—keep all of us safe—I would never have allowed it for a minute."

"You weren't thinking at all," she accused. "Certainly not with the head that's on your shoulders, anyway."

He gaped, shocked by his normally prim aunt's innuendo. But she wasn't finished with him.

"You've gone off to see Fernando, and then to San Antonio, leaving your family, your *little children*, alone with a woman whose very presence is a danger."

"I'm sorry." She did have a point. He'd allowed himself to count too much on this house's security, its history and the power of the family name to safeguard them. "I should have told you everything instead of trying to protect you by holding back the details."

Yet even as he said it, Beau found himself doing it again. Keeping what he knew of the ranch's future, which seemed bleak no matter what his choice, from her for a little while more.

"She needs to be removed immediately, Beau. This evening," his aunt insisted.

He shook his head, looking at the dimming sky outside the window. "I know you're upset, Aunt Alicia. And maybe a little embarrassed because of how this evening went. But Emma's had an exhausting day, and mine's been hellacious. So yes, she's going, I promise you. But not until first thing tomorrow."

Tonight, he told himself, would have to be completely dedicated to the most painful decision of his life.

Chapter 15

Sitting on the guest room's bed, Emma tried to focus on the avalanche of e-mails clogging her laptop's inbox. There were routine bills to be paid and urgent inquiries from her department head that she couldn't put off much longer. She even received a message from her mother with several photos of her and Emma's stepdad smiling in front of European landmarks. But after dashing off a quick reply, Emma soon lapsed back into misery, her brain squirming with embarrassment over the way she'd snapped at Beau's aunt Alicia. Yes, the woman had been annoyingly intrusive, but Emma regretted not deflecting her questions more gently, perhaps with a joke or by excusing herself to elevate her leg.

In truth, the injury was healing nicely, the bruising and soreness so much reduced the she was able to move from the bed, where she'd been working, to the bathroom if she took things slow and easy. But as she downed an over-the-counter painkiller to counter the ache from the day's activities, she couldn't help but wonder if Beau would show up to take her to task for repaying his family's hospitality with rudeness.

Instead of walking down to the guest wing, he only sent a text, apologizing for once more getting called away from their meal and asking whether it was okay that the boys were holed up in the family room snuggling with both dogs watching movies.

No problem about the business call, she replied carefully, followed by, River will love the company.

After a moment's hesitation, she sent another message. Is your aunt okay? Afraid I've hurt her feelings. Will come apologize if it will help.

For some time, he didn't respond, leaving her to wonder if Beau had gone to ask his aunt what happened. For several minutes, she listened anxiously for his footsteps in the hallway.

About the time she figured that he'd gotten side-tracked, her cell chimed again.

Better let it rest, I think. Breakfast in town in the morning around seven thirty and then Nadine's?

So that was it, Emma realized. *He's being polite enough, but he's washing his hands of me, leaving me alone the way I wanted.* Ignoring the sense of loss welling up inside her, she replied, Thanks and have a good night, before turning back to her computer.

As she responded to a colleague's email sometime later, her cell rang. She caught her breath, seeing it was someone from the sheriff's department calling. *What now?*

Knowing she would never sleep tonight unless she found out, Emma swallowed back her fear and answered.

To her surprise, Wallace Fleming's greeting sounded almost cheerful, with some lively music playing in the background. "My deputy tells me there's been a little misunderstanding, Dr. Copley. I just figured that since we've gotten on so well in the past, I'd give you a call personally this evening and see if I can ease any worries you might've had regarding the return of your handgun."

"We *have*?"

"Have what?" he asked, his confused tone overriding a country singer's muffled voice.

"'Gotten on so well,'" she quoted. "Is *that* what you would call it?"

"I know we've had our ups 'n' downs," he said, "but what two strong-willed people don't, from time to time? The point is, I wanted you to know that Jim Kendall may've misinterpreted my wishes. I never meant for him to take that danged gun over there, only to remind you that you could come on in and sign for it any time you wanted, in case you felt the need."

She made a face. "So you're throwing him under the bus now, in case the Texas Rangers end up getting interested in your behavior?"

"Anyone ever tell you you've got a hell of a contrary streak? Especially in a woman, it's not the most attractive quality."

"I've found it beats being a doormat…or a punching bag."

"There's a happy medium, you know."

She rolled her eyes. "So did you call for any other reason, Sheriff? Other than advising me on how to become more attractive to men?"

"That's not what I meant and you know it." Met by her frosty silence, he laughed and added, "My wife and my girls would probably advise me to shut up now before I get another taste of my own boot leather. But as I'm a glutton for punishment, yes, I did have something else to tell you."

"You've found Jeremy?" she asked, feeling a flutter of hope that he would confess to everything and this nightmare could be over.

"We're still working on that, but with a statewide BOLO out on him now, it's only a matter of time."

She wished she could trust the sheriff enough to tell him about the items Fernando had found in the equipment building. But between Wallace's feud with Beau and his possible conflict of interest over Green Horizons Energy, she couldn't afford to take the chance.

"What about Russell's laptop?" she asked instead. "Have you found anything useful there?"

"I've gone ahead and turned it over to the state boys. They've got their best geeks workin' on that password, though it could be a while."

"That seems to be a common theme, things taking forever."

"Welcome to the real world of law enforcement, missy. Nothing like you see on TV, is it? I did check out that memory card you got me from the game camera, though."

"So you saw him, then? The armed man near the turbine a few hours before Russell died."

"I did," he admitted, sounding none too happy over the development.

"So you finally believe me? You see what I've been saying all along about Russell being murdered?" she asked, unable to keep the hope from flooding her voice.

Wallace hesitated, the only sound the hum of what she was now certain was his car radio. Finally, he said, "I've got to admit, this raises one hell of a lot of questions. Questions I'll be asking when I have him brought in tomorrow."

"Him? You mean you *recognized* him? From just that one lousy photo?"

"Not well enough to satisfy a judge, maybe, but yeah, I think I might've. Something about the shape of the ear and that jawline—which is why I've called to warn you."

"Called to warn me about what? Did you compare it with those photos I sent you earlier?"

"It's definitely not your ex-husband, because it was Beau Kingston out there that night. I'd swear on anything it was."

A beat passed before she blurted, "Oh, come on. The guy you're out to get this ranch from?" As obsessed as the sheriff clearly was with his rival, he would probably pick Beau out of a lineup while standing in the dark, blindfolded.

"I know how it probably sounds, but yeah," said Wallace. "I'm serious enough that I'm on my way to get you. You can't possibly risk your life by staying another night in that house."

"You might as well turn around now," she told him. "I'm locked into my guest suite for the evening, and I'm not coming out until I'm ready to leave first thing tomorrow for new accommodations."

"Dr. Copley—Emma, I'm serious about this. If anything happened to you, I'd never forgive myself for—"

"Nothing's going to happen, and I'm serious, too, Sheriff, when I tell you that when it comes to Beau, you've lost all perspective."

"You wouldn't think that if you had any idea—"

"Save it," she said before it hit her that, as deluded as the sheriff was, he was truly concerned about her safety. "But if it makes you feel better, I'll check in with you in the morning. But right now, I'm turning off the light and going straight to bed."

"If I don't hear from you by no later than eight, I swear I'm personally coming out to get you."

"Make it nine," she said irritably. "And in the meantime, I'd suggest you get some sleep. And maybe switch to decaf."

After ending the call, Emma closed and set aside her laptop on the bedside table. Realizing she was missing River, she told herself the hairy traitor must be conked out next to Maverick in the family room. Or maybe she'd sneaked into one of the boys' rooms to indulge in a little stealth bed snuggling. Emma told herself it was no big deal, sleeping without the presence of her beloved companion for one night.

Still, she lay there for a long time, missing the reassuring sound of soft canine snores on the floor beside her. And struggling to put Wallace's warning—and the memory of the weapons that had clattered to the floor of the equipment shed—out of her mind.

Sometime later that night, hot tears soaked Emma's pillow. She lay on a bed in the hospital's ultrasound room, where the technician's face had gradually turned ashen, her reassuring patter giving way to silence with her failure to detect a fetal heartbeat. *I'll be just a moment.* The young woman avoided Emma's eyes as she spoke. *I—I need to get the doctor.*

Instead, it was Jeremy who burst in, Jeremy, screaming into Emma's burning face, *Why so upset? We both know that kid was Russell's bastard anyway, not mine!*

It's not true, she screamed, desperate to wake up from this horror, to open her eyes to a time when her baby was okay, when Emma herself could still pretend that she was.

Instead, Jeremy pulled out a fine straw cowboy hat from somewhere—Dream Emma recognized it instantly as Beau's—and laughed, *So you were sleeping with that rancher then. I knew it—but don't you worry. I've taken care of him, too, you cheating bitch.*

Only then did she notice the bullet hole that pierced the hat's crown and the dark blood dripping from it. So much blood that she jerked awake, her stomach lurching with the knowledge that, because of her, Beau Kingston, too, was dead.

Disentangling herself from sweat-soaked sheets, she hugged her knees to her chest and tried to rock her body past the terror of what she told herself was just another nightmare. This one lingered, though, the vivid memories leaving her jumping at every sound, from the air-conditioning switching on to the faint swish of the tall ornamental grasses planted outside the window in the wind.

Knowing she wouldn't soon risk sleep again, she decided to shower away the acrid clamminess that coated her body like a second skin. Maybe afterward, she'd manage at least a few hours of blessed, dreamless sleep.

Stripping off her damp nightshirt, she crumpled it into a ball and tossed it toward her packed bag before limping to the shower. She stood beneath the spray a long time, allowing the warm water to her shaking body and soothe her frazzled mind. Steam billowing around her, she at last began to feel her eyelids drooping. By the time she shut off the faucet and blotted her body with a thick white towel, she could no longer hold back a yawn.

But when she opened the bathroom door, she froze, sensing something in the air before the wrongness of it hit her. Hyperaware with the adrenaline flooding her brain and body, she took in the scene in an instant: the humid breeze, the rumbling of thunder, and the window standing wide open, though she was sure she'd left it closed and locked. Then came a heavy clatter as a silhouetted male shape exited the opening, at the last instant sending something heavy crashing to the floor inside.

Before she could scream, the figure vanished into the inky darkness, leaving the window open in its wake. Desperate to close and lock it to keep the intruder from returning, Emma wrapped the towel around her body and surged forward, her sore leg forgotten in her hurry.

Or at least it was forgotten until she heard the horrifying sound rising from the floor.

Chapter 16

Beau hadn't been asleep long when the sound of a phone woke him. Not his cell, but the landline, which scarcely anyone used since they'd signed up for a service that blocked nearly all their nuisance calls.

Determined to give what he felt certain was a telemarketer a piece of his mind for calling in the middle of the damned night, he reached for the handset—only to see from a flashing button that the call was coming from one of the mansion's in-house lines.

"Everything all right, Aunt Alicia?" he asked as he picked up, praying that she wasn't ill.

"He was—he was here! In my room!" cried Emma. "I—I tried to—"

Springing from his tangled sheets, Beau heard a shriek and a clatter. It sounded as if her handset had fallen to the floor.

"Emma?" he shouted. "Emma, can you hear? Pick up. Pick up!"

His mouth bone-dry, he strained his ears but heard nothing but muffled sobbing in the background and a peal of thunder from outside. But it wasn't the forecast storm that had his pulse crashing in his ears.

He switched on a bedside lamp, the marine in him forcing him to take stock of his options, to plan the best way to neutralize any threat and keep it from coming upstairs where his aunt and his children slept.

Barefoot and clad only in the boxers and black tee he had worn to bed, he headed downstairs to the den, where he unlocked the gun safe and took out the big revolver that his father had favored for home defense.

Closing the safe behind him, he exited the room and sprinted for the guest wing hallway, where a series of motion-activated night-lights flared like fireflies to dimly light his passage. A few doors shy of Emma's room, he paused to catch his breath and listen for any steps behind him that might indicate that a family member had heard him and come running to investigate.

Hearing only the faint patter of rain outside, he fought to quiet the questions running riot in his brain. Was Emma being hurt—or even killed—now? Could she be dead already? How the hell had an intruder defeated the mansion's security system, and how well-armed might he be?

Looking up and down the curving hallway, Beau saw nothing out of place, and heard nothing to indicate that the call he'd gotten had been anything but a particularly vivid nightmare. But the memory of Emma's panic kept him moving forward, his gun raised and his heart pumping like a piston.

Though muffled by the closed door, he heard the sound of her voice, high and tight with fear.

"Beau? Are you out there? Please be out there. Please!"

"I'm right here," he called to her, hurrying to key in the master code to disengage the lock. "I'm coming inside."

As it chirped and the tiny light flashed green, she cried, "No! You can't! Don't open it!"

"What's going on?" he demanded, stopped cold by the terror ringing in her voice. "Emma—are you alone?"

"N-no! I'm afraid that I have company—except—except it isn't human."

"Isn't—what the hell?" Ignoring her directive, he pushed the door inward, hard enough that it banged against the wall. Inside, he could see a section of wood flooring lit by a slanted rectangle of light coming from the bathroom. Beyond that, he made out the room's small desk and the window to its right. Wide open, it looked out onto a swath of darkness where a security light should have illuminated a landscaped area.

From outside, thunder rumbled, and he could smell as well as hear the rain.

"Don't move. It's on the floor," Emma warned from somewhere out of his line of sight—the bed maybe, he thought.

"What is?" he asked, leaning far enough to reach a wall switch that flooded the entryway with light. Gun aimed toward the floor, he caught a movement out of the corner of his eye as something brownish-gray and mottled made for deeper shadow.

"S-snake!" Emma said just as he realized what he was seeing. And hearing. The warning rattle of a diamondback far longer than the one that had bitten her before.

"It's under the bed," Emma told him as the tail disappeared from view. "If it climbs up here with me—I can't do this again! I can't!"

Entering the room farther, he saw that she was standing on top of the bed, her hair damp and her nude body wrapped only in a towel. He spotted, too, the phone's handset on the small rug near the bed's edge, where she must have dropped it earlier.

On the floor close to the window, a wooden box lay on it size, its hinged lid broken open. He quickly decided that the man who'd come to terrorize Emma must have used the container to transport the rattler.

"I know this is hard, but you're a tough woman and I need you to pull yourself together. Right now, Emma," he said in his firmest voice. "I'm here for you. All right? And the only way you're going to end up hurt is if you panic. And panic's what whoever came here wants from you. That's why he chose the snake instead of attacking you directly."

"I don't care why that lunatic did it—or how he even knew how much this would freak me out. I just want it gone. This minute!"

"I need you to slowly crouch down." Beau deliberately infused his words with a sense of calm authority. "No sudden movements, Emma. I just want you to lower your center of gravity so you don't fall down."

"What if it comes up here?" she asked.

"Rattlesnakes can't climb," he lied, worried because she looked to be balancing on one leg and, with the wall so far from the bed, she had nothing to brace herself against.

She made a huffing sound. "Next time you want to patronize a woman with some made-up nonsense about reptiles, don't pick a wildlife biologist."

"I'll tried to remember that if it comes up in the future," he assured her, coming a step closer, yet keeping about a body's length of distance between himself and the bed. "Now crouch down, before you end up falling on your charming new friend—and getting bitten again."

This time, she complied, slowly bending her knees to squat as she complained, "If that thing slithers up here and fangs me on the fanny, I am never going to let you hear the end of this."

Snorting at her phrasing, he cautiously knelt about six feet from the bed to look beneath it, only to find the snake escaping out the other side. Wishing like hell he weren't barefoot, he scrambled around the bed to see where it was heading, only to shout in surprise, stopping short to avoid stepping on a second, somewhat smaller snake.

"There's two of them?" he shouted as he jumped onto the bed next to her. "Why didn't you tell me there were—"

"I didn't see it! Look! The big one's getting away!"

"The hell he is," said Beau before the sound of the first gunshot boomed like thunder in their ears.

"You're sure you got them all?" Emma asked as she looked up from the big plush sofa in the bedroom sitting area where she'd sat quivering for the past fifteen minutes, her knees drawn nearly to her chest and a blanket covering her bare shoulders.

"There were just the two." Beau nodded as he closed the door behind him. The door of *his* bedroom, upstairs where he'd carried her to wait while he checked things out and made some calls.

Outfitted with a comfortable sitting area, expensive-looking rustic furnishings and fixtures, and a king-size bed with a headboard artfully inlaid with veins of turquoise and silver, the spacious suite was as solid and masculine as the man who'd just reentered, now wearing a pair of worn jeans and boots to go with the long day's worth of stubble and the big revolver in his hand.

"'Just the two,' you say—" she shuddered "—as if that's not enough to warrant years of therapy. Even worse, I saw him, or at least his silhouette, as he was scrambling out that window."

More than anything, she wished she'd gotten a better look. Or that she could be as certain of the identity of the intruder as the sheriff had been about what he'd imagined he had seen in the game cam photo. But one thing she knew for certain. When she'd been frightened nearly out of her mind, she'd reached out without thinking for the one man her instincts insisted she could count on.

And once more, without hesitation or any thought for his own safety, Beau had rushed to her aid. But not even blasting the two snakes—themselves blameless victims of her tormentor's machinations—had served to stop her shaking. Or the nausea that struck each time her mind replayed what had happened.

"What if he's still hiding nearby," she asked, looking over to where Beau set the gun down on the dresser, "waiting for his chance to finish what he's started?"

Crossing the room to her, Beau touched her hair, gliding his fingers over the still-damp strands. "He's long gone. I'm sure of it. After checking out the house, I went outside and found fresh tire tracks where a vehicle had pulled up off the road behind some shrubs not far behind the guest wing. I called Fernando, too—"

"This guy didn't show up for his cache, did he?" Emma felt her stomach give a queasy slide.

"No, and I doubt he will. But our security cameras there are all back online now, so I've asked Fernando's older sons, who were pulling the night watch over there, to secure the weapons he left and hightail it over here to patrol the perimeter around the mansion."

"What about your family? Is everything still—"

"Sound asleep," he assured her. "I checked on them." A smile warmed his brown eyes. "Gave me a little scare at first when I couldn't find Leland, but it turns out he and his brother are on the floor of Cort's room, camping out with their sleeping bags on the floor with both the dogs."

"I'll rest easier knowing they're together," she said, certain the animals would sound the alarm if they heard anything suspicious. "That is, if I can ever bring myself to sleep again."

He dropped his hand to Emma's bare shoulder, giving it a squeeze. "You're stiff as a board. Can I get you something to drink? A glass of wine, maybe? I'm sure we have some in the—"

"Don't leave me alone again." She grabbed his hand and held on for dear life. "Every time I close my eyes, I keep seeing his shape in my window and imagining I hear another snake rattling on the floor."

Sitting beside her on the sofa, he pulled her into his arms. While she rested her head against his chest, he gently stroked her hair, her back, until the tightness in her body eased.

"It's all right, Emma," he said, in a voice as smooth as the finest of aged whiskeys. "I'm right here, right with you. And I'm not going anywhere, except maybe to my closet over there to grab you one of my shirts. You must be cold in just that towel."

She reached to adjust the light throw that had slipped off her shoulders. "Not cold now. Don't move. Please," she said, opening her nostrils to the clean, outdoorsy smell of him as she snuggled closer, matching her own breaths to the movements of his warm and solid chest.

Finding in him a slower, calmer rhythm. A pace that felt as right, as natural, as the ebb and flow of tides.

"Before he came," she said, barely speaking above a whisper, "I had a nightmare. A nightmare where he—where Jeremy said he'd killed you just like he'd killed Russell. And like he killed our baby."

"You had a baby," he said quietly.

"I was pregnant, almost five months along when I—when Jeremy burst into the office of my department head with his wild accusations. He claimed that everyone at the school knew, that they were all in league, covering for the fact that the baby wasn't his."

"Sounds seriously paranoid."

"The pregnancy—he was so happy when we first found out, enough that I began to hope we might have some chance, some path back to the way we'd once been. But over time it seemed to magnify all his insecurities, which only made him drink more and take—I'm not even sure what he was on that day, only that he was—I was humiliated by his raging. And terrified he'd scare Dr. Lee into a stroke with all his shouting." She shook her head, fighting back the tears. "When I tried to interfere after he'd cornered the poor man in his office, he shoved me—hard enough that I fell into some cabinets, cracking a few ribs in the process. He ran out then. I think he'd scared himself. But with all the pain and the—the emotional upheaval came the cramping...and a rush of blood."

In her worst moments, she still saw it, shockingly deep and red and spreading far too quickly.

"There's nothing I can say except—I'm so damned sorry, Emma." Beau's voice roughened. "And if I ever get my hands around the son of a bitch's neck, I swear I—"

"And the worst part?" she went on, lost in the pain spilling from her like the tears she could no longer hold back. "The worst part was the doctors saying that the miscarriage was unrelated to my injury. That there was some kind of issue with—with the placenta—that it might have happened any time, as if what Jeremy did had not a thing to do with losing her." Her. Jaime Lynn. That was the secret name Emma had given the impossibly tiny daughter—so very pink and inconceivably fragile—who had come into a broken marriage and a broken world too soon.

"So your—your husband got off scot-free?"

"Thirty days in the county lockup, and after that probation. And I filed for divorce the first moment I was able."

"How long ago was all this?"

"Ten months, but it still feels like—" She laid a hand over her heart, which staggered on as always despite the pain she carried. "It feels like yesterday inside me. If only I'd thought first of protecting her, called security instead of barging into Dr. Lee's office and intervening that day. Or if I'd really understood how much I wanted her, how much I already loved her, instead of worrying all the time about how things with Jeremy were—"

"Don't do that," Beau said. "Emma, please. Don't put this on yourself. I know it's tempting to turn your grief and anger inward. God knows that no one's more aware of that than I am, but in the end it doesn't change things. Or leave you anywhere but aching and alone."

She looked up into his face, where she saw a bone-deep weariness that had nothing to do with the late hour. A twinge of sympathy loosened the past's grip and reminded her of the gossip she'd overheard in the café. "You're talking about your wife, aren't you?"

She felt, as well as heard, his sigh.

"You weren't—you weren't with her, were you," she asked, "when it happened?"

"It was a Friday afternoon, and I'd gotten a call at work. Melissa hadn't shown up to get the boys from day care the way she'd promised. I asked our babysitter to pick them up and went to find her. To confront her, because I figured she'd gone to happy hour with her work friends and gotten carried away with the wine and lost track of the time."

"She'd done it before, I take it?"

Beau nodded. "I don't want you to get the wrong idea. Melissa was my best friend—and a great mom, a wonderful woman who juggled two little ones, our household and a high-stress job without nearly as much help as she deserved from me. But every so often, things got to her and she had to blow off steam. Sometimes in a very big way."

"So she was a binge drinker?"

He shrugged. "I guess that's what you'd call it, dating back to her college days. She'd go months and months without slipping up and then…"

Emma squeezed his hand to let him know she understood.

"But that day," Beau continued, "I'd had a big ski resort security job I'd worked for weeks to set up fall apart while she was out at this little hillside tavern that was popular with both the tourists and the locals. So I was plenty ticked off when I found her sloppy drunk, cutting up with a couple of her coworkers. Angrier still when she refused to leave with me, insisting she would keep her keys and drive herself home. It was an awful scene."

"Sounds like it."

"Yeah, but there was no way I was leaving her there, staggering and slurring, so I got one of her more sober friends to help me force her into my truck. Once we got her buckled in, I took off with Melissa, with her screaming over how I'd embarrassed her for the last time and she wanted me out of her life."

Emma hugged him tighter, feeling his distress in the pit of her stomach. And dreading the rest of the story, for all that she was certain of his need to get it out.

"I wish I could say I'd handled it better in that moment, that I'd told her I would always love her. I've wondered ten thousand times what would've happened if I'd tried a little harder to make her understand. Or if I hadn't let my hurt or the ugly words I was shouting back take any of my attention from the road. They say it wasn't my fault, that I was still inside my lane as we rounded the curve heading toward home. They say it was just bad timing, our being there at the same moment the driver of that logging truck had some kind of seizure and—and—"

"Oh, Beau. Oh, no," she said, her throat closing as tears choked her. "You couldn't have possibly known that driver would lose control of his vehicle in that place at that moment."

"You're right about that. But I could have—I could have sat in that parking lot a while longer, tried to talk things out with my wife instead of being in such a rush to get her back home. I could have made her understand that I was willing to make changes, to spend more time and take on more responsibility at home, to do whatever I had to to make her happy."

"It doesn't sound as if she was in the frame of mind to listen right then."

"At least I could have make sure the last words she heard from me, the last words she heard on this earth, weren't me—me telling her that the boys and I would be better off without her."

"You were *there* for her, Beau," said Emma, her tears now flowing freely as she reached up to turn his head toward her and felt that his face, too, was damp. "You went to find her because you loved her. To bring her home because you cared about the family you made together. And as hurtful as her words were, as both of your words were in the worst, most heated moments of your marriage, I know that in the end, it surely meant something to her that you were by her side in that terrible moment. That she didn't have to die alone."

He'd been only trying to comfort her, or at least to warn her away from the painful path he'd been stuck on for the better part of three years, a shame so deep that he had never confessed it to another living soul. But with Emma's willingness to listen, her kind words instead of judgment, he felt a weight slide from his shoulders, like a thick shell of glacial ice slipping down a sun-warmed mountainside.

In spite of every other burden he still carried, the shock of that relief was enough to take his breath away. Without further thought, he pulled her even closer, taking in the scents of soap and shampoo still clinging to her warm flesh and wondering why the hell he'd wasted so much time fighting what any fool could see both of them wanted. And needed, if they were ever to heal the scars that grief and guilt had left on their hearts.

Cradling her face in his hands, he kissed her gently, softly, a kiss she returned with a tentative sweetness that soon melted into something deeper, warmer, her hand sliding across his chest and a little murmur of encouragement rising from her throat.

It was enough that his hands dropped to shift her so that she sat astride his lower body. Where there could be no hiding the effect her nearness and his need were having on him. Yet instead of pulling away, she flexed her hips against him and in one deft move, loosened the towel from around her body, allowing it to drop.

Though his blood was rushing in his ears and his body aching for release from the clothing—far too much damned clothing, with his jeans now painfully restrictive—his gaze lingered on her eyes, whose lashes remained spiky with the remnants of her tears.

"You—you're beautiful, amazing—but are you sure you want this, Emma?" he asked. "You've had a hell of a scare tonight, and I don't want you to think for a single moment that this is—this is the price for staying safe here with me."

Reaching down to where his head rested, she straightened her back, looking sensual as a siren and proud as a queen as she placed a finger over his lips. "Enough with the noble self-sacrifice, cowboy. And the talking." Casting a seductive smile, she ran her fingertip along the seam of his mouth. "For one thing, I can think of better uses for this."

Bending forward, she kissed him, fully, firmly, and the last of his restraint snapped, his hands finding the soft mounds of her breasts, his fingers squeezing and pinching her erect nipples. As he slid lower to suck, one hand dropped to undo the torment of his fly. In a moment, she was helping him, and soon he was kicking off his boots and sliding free of pant legs, before peeling off the T-shirt that was now the only scrap of cloth between them.

"The—the bed," he managed, pulling her up with him from the sofa and leading her to the more comfortable expanse of smooth sheets and fluffy pillows—along with the bedside drawer, where in a rare, hopeful moment last year, he had stashed a box of condoms.

Because it seemed, against all odds, that he was going to have good reason to make use of them tonight. It was the last coherent thought he had before she reached down to touch him and all remaining doubt gave way to giving and receiving the rare gift of perfect pleasure…and laying down their worries through the darkest hours of the night.

Chapter 17

As Emma slept in his arms, her breathing easy and her body relaxed in the wake of their lovemaking, Beau fought his own need for sleep, unwilling to risk allowing one or both of the boys, who often barged in to jump in bed with him on those rare mornings when he slept in, to catch him with Emma in his bedroom. As bad an example as that would set—and as stern a lecture as he knew it would incite from his aunt—he was more concerned about Emma breaking Cort's and Leland's tender hearts by leaving…and likely disappearing from their lives.

But as hollow ache hit him, Beau faced the truth. *It's you you're worried for, not them.* Because he had no idea how what had happened between him and Emma had changed things for her, but in him, something critical had shifted. As precarious, as stressful as his future—as both their futures—might prove, he would face it gladly, if only he knew he had a woman as compassionate and lov-

ing as Emma by his side. Imagining the two of them together, with each watching for the other, nothing seemed
impossible...except, apparently, the fight to keep from
tumbling after her into a dreamless void.

He jerked in surprise at the sound of his cell ringing an hour or so later, his sleep-starved brain scarcely
registering where he was or what had happened. When
Emma stirred beside him, the memories rushed back in
a torrent. Pulse accelerating, he extricated himself from
her embrace and climbed naked from beneath the covers
before grabbing the phone on his way to the sitting area.

"Hold on, just a second," he told the caller, figuring it
was Fernando or one of the men he'd assigned to guard
the house. After grabbing a robe from the back of the
closet door, he shoved his arms into it before padding
out of the master suite.

"Sorry to wake you, Farmer Beau," a familiar voice
rasped as Beau headed for the den, "but I figured you'd
be up and at the milking by now, or whatever gets you
up so damned early in the morning."

"This is *not* a good time to mess with me, Pirate,"
Beau said. "We had a little visit last night from that son
of a bitch that *you're* supposed to be tracking for me."

"You're sure about that?" Ty said, clearly thrown.

"Not a hundred percent," Beau admitted, closing himself inside the den before laying out the evidence, from
the items found out in the equipment building to the bi-
zarre nature of last night's break-in.

"That sounds like a pretty personal beef to me," agreed
Ty, "exactly like something that obsessed SOB might do
to try to terrorize his ex. The only trouble is, I just got
word that he was picked up about eleven thirty last night
and thrown into an Austin drunk tank."

"What? You're sure it's him?"

"Sure sounds like it considering the guy was carrying Jeremy Hansen's ID, matches the guy's description and was hassling one of Emma Copley's students for information on her."

"Well, hell…" Beau said as he tried to make sense of that information. "So if it wasn't him here last night, he must not've been the one who murdered Russell."

"I'm not so sure you can rule that out completely. But I am sure that Jorgenson had other enemies. And Emma Copley, too."

"Emma saw some evidence, before it was stolen, that Russell was preparing to expose someone for tampering with the results of their study. She thinks he could've been upset enough about it to confront the guilty party. Or, hell, maybe he was up to blackmail. Why else keep what he was doing secret from her?"

"Why, indeed?" Ty rasped. "Listen, Beau. I know you don't want to hear this, but I have reason to believe that your new friend, Dr. Copley, knows a hell of lot more than she's saying. That's why I really called so early. To warn you, right away, to get her out of your house."

Beau swore under his breath.

"And your bed, too, man. I'm saying this as a friend."

Jolted, Beau asked, "How did you—"

"I hear it in your voice, man, and in the way you're clearly taking things she's told you at face value. Besides that, I know you, what you've been through these past few years. And how vulnerable that sort of thing can leave a man to a hot, smart lady who plays her cards close to her vest."

"I'm no freaking fragile flower, Pirate, and she damned well hasn't played me."

"See if you still think that after you check out the attached files on the email I just sent you."

* * *

Emma stirred sleepily, her eyes cracking open to the sound of the bedroom door closing shortly after she'd been roused by the muffled ringing of a cell phone. Blinking in confusion, she took in her surroundings, dimly lit by what looked like early-morning sunlight filtering past the edges of the windows' slate-blue curtains.

Memories had anxiety ripping through her: the intruder escaping her room into the darkness, the snakes he'd left to terrorize her, Beau's gun blasting in the guest room's close quarters.

But afterward, he'd brought her up here. To his room, his bed...

Her body tingling with the thought, a shy smile tugged at her lips as she relived the way he'd driven every other worry—every other thought—from her head to coax and tease and tempt her body to wave after wave of splintering pleasure. But it was the passion in his gaze as he'd looked down into her eyes, into her soul, when their bodies had finally joined, that made her shiver...and reach beneath the covers to feel the spot he'd just vacated, still warm from his body and smelling of the man she wanted.

Cuddling his pillow, she drifted off again. When she next cracked her eyes open, she noticed that the light was brighter. Beau, now fully dressed, stood nearby, threading a belt through his jeans. As he finished buckling it, he paused, freezing as he noticed her smiling up at him.

"Hey," she said, her voice a sleep-warmed rumble as she reached toward him.

Ignoring her proffered hand, he frowned at her. "It's high time you got up and dressed and out of here. I don't want my sons confused or frightened."

At the chill in his voice, her stomach plunged. *"Fright-*

ened? What on earth is wrong?" she asked. "Beau? Has something happened?"

He turned away, but not before she caught the mixture of fury and regret hardening his handsome face.

Shoving back the covers, she stumbled from the bed and walked up behind him. Ever atom in her ached to touch him, to soothe whatever hurt was making him act this way.

She had nearly reached his shoulder when she recoiled, her hand dropping to her abdomen at the thought of the last time Jeremy had looked so upset—and how he had reacted to her touch.

Backing off, she looked around for something to cover her nakedness until she found what must be his bathrobe draped across a nearby chair. She shoved her arms into the sleeves and tied it tightly around her shaking body, too bewildered to care that it was ridiculously large for her.

He flickered a look in her direction before ordering, "Now go to your room and pack your things. My boys are early risers, and I need you out of this room, this *house*, before they're up."

"I'll leave, Beau. I can do that," she said. "But what I can't and won't do is pretend that last night never happened. Or that it meant nothing to you."

"I never—I damned well never said it didn't, Emma. That's why this hurts so damned much. To know that you've been playing me. Playing every one of us for fools."

"Playing? What are you talking about? And why on earth would you imagine, even for a second, that I'm the kind of woman who would play with—with my own damned heart, my body. Because—Beau, you might not believe this, but other than my husband, you're the first, the only man I've ever—"

"The time for lies is over. Thanks to Ty's hard evidence, I know exactly who you are now. What you are. And I won't have a killer in my house for one more second than I absolutely have to, so if you don't want to be here when the sheriff comes to take you in, I suggest you get out while you can."

Less than thirty minutes later, Emma sat in her Jeep, which one of his men had delivered, her hands clenching the wheel as she pulled over outside the ranch gate and stared in a state of shock at the dusty road ahead. Though her injured right leg ached with the strain she was putting on it, she almost welcomed the physical discomfort. Anything to distract her from the searing shock of Beau's betrayal and his utter refusal to listen to anything she had to say.

Everything I need to know, he'd said icily, *came from the trash folder of your own email account. For future reference, the next time you want to cover your tracks, you'll want to empty that, too. Oh, and use a way more secure server.*

I have no idea what you're talking about, she'd responded, *but do you honestly imagine, even for a moment, that I could've murdered anyone, much less my own student? Surely you can't think that was me with the gun in that photo—or that I could have—*

I don't know about your accomplices, Beau said, *and right now I don't want to. I only want you gone from my sight, before I do something I regret.*

Behind her in the back seat with Emma's luggage, River stood and whined, circling repeatedly and looking back over her shoulder.

"Sorry, girl. We can't go back. Not ever," said Emma, wiping away her tears. "Now settle down. That's right. Lie down. Stay."

Because talking to someone, even the dog, felt good, she added, "I shouldn't even be surprised he wouldn't listen." Because when it came down to it, men didn't ever, did they? Or at least the men Emma had made the mistake of falling for—and she'd fallen hard and fast for Beau. "He was just waiting for an excuse to turn against me."

But what had been the trigger, transforming his caring and protective nature into a cold fury that had left her half-afraid he'd knock her off her feet?

One thing was for certain. She couldn't rest until she understood what had happened. And whether, somehow, Jeremy could have been behind it.

But where could she possibly look at those emails Beau had mentioned? She tried checking on her phone but quickly realized she would need her laptop and a decent Wi-Fi connection to get into the folders he had mentioned. This would mean a drive back into town, but there was no way she was heading to Nadine's place, since Beau might well have called to warn his friend not to harbor what he now thought of as the enemy.

Remembering the public library, where she'd worked this summer when the motel's Wi-Fi was on the fritz, Emma fought to compose herself as she drove. She headed into Pinto Creek and pulled into the nearly empty parking lot of the café. There, she took out a still-restless River before limping inside to pick up a large to-go coffee.

"You can't have that animal in here," the curvy brunette with the cat's-eye makeup behind the counter scolded.

"Please," Emma said, all too aware that her own eyes were red and swollen. "I couldn't leave her in the car, and if I don't get some caffeine, my brain's going to melt into a puddle."

"Aren't you—?" The waitress sniffed. "I thought I heard you were a guest out at the big house these days?"

"Where on earth did you hear that?"

"Guess he's still pining for the dead wife after all." Malice sparkling in her brown eyes, she leaned in to whisper, "The way I heard it, it was him that killed her anyway. Yanked the wheel into the truck's path so he wouldn't have to share his millions with some drunken who—"

"Yet from what I overheard out of your own lying mouth before," Emma fired back, enraged by the woman's cruelty, "you'd hop into his bed in a second for half a chance to cash in on the exchange."

As she fled with River, the waitress screeched in her wake, "Did you hear that? That little witch all but calling me a prostitute?"

An older man who'd been sitting nearby said, "I don't believe anybody caught it, Margie, but we *did* hear you runnin' that nasty mouth of yours again like always."

Shaking from the encounter—Emma still couldn't believe she'd stuck up for Beau like that—she drove to the historic one-story stone building that housed the library. Mindful of River's presence, she pulled into an area of the parking lot where she'd learned from working here this summer would offer her a strong enough signal to use the laptop from inside her vehicle.

Once more, River whined behind her, restlessly circling in her seat.

"For heaven's sake, girl, knock it off," she urged, realizing her dog was missing the chance to burn off energy with the Kingstons' puppy and the two boys she'd grown so attached to. Two boys that Emma ached to realize she might never see again.

Unzipping her day pack, she pulled out River's toy duck and gave it to the dog to chew and nuzzle. Then Emma shook two tablets from a small bottle of over-the-counter painkillers and choked them down without water to ease the pain in her leg, which ached from the drive.

After taking out her laptop, she glimpsed a sheriff's department vehicle gliding down the street. The flash of silver hair and fishhook-shaped scar had her ducking low in her seat. Her heart pounded as she imagined Deputy Kendall arresting her. Could Beau have reported the emails he'd been sent already?

But as she peered over the level of the door, she saw the deputy fiddling with his radio. He glided past without glancing in her direction. Sighing with relief, she fought to stop herself from shaking.

She sat up and forced herself to breathe again. Once she opened her computer, she quickly connected and logged in to her email. It took a minute to change the program's password. She hesitated, her finger vibrating above the laptop's trackpad. Her stomach cold and quivering at the thought of what she might find inside the trash folder Beau had mentioned.

Hard evidence. His contempt echoed through her memory, deepening the fault lines in her fractured heart. *I won't have a killer in my house for one more second...*

"Whatever it is, it isn't real," she whispered to River as she double-clicked the icon. "We both know it can't be."

Yet the three messages, ostensibly sent from her to Russell, were no less devastating for all of her brave words. Reading through tears, she cringed to see whoever had been impersonating her referring to a shadowy—and highly misguided group—called Animal Avengers, which had made the news several times in recent years, breaking into zoos and freeing animals from their enclosures, causing fatal traffic accidents after smashing down fences containing livestock, and breaching a cancer research facility, where a security guard had been shot down while attempting to stop the activists' mission to liberate a host of white mice.

According to the overwrought messages, Green Horizons had earned a place on the group's hit list for its casual destruction of protected birds. Determined to take down the company, Emma had supposedly conspired with Russell, whose responses were nowhere in evidence, to fake evidence to get the government to shut them down for tampering with the study.

The final message, dated the day prior to Russell's murder, however, had the phony Emma raging, accusing Russell of "betraying the animals—and me" by instead using the data to extort money from the company. As the language turned more threatening, Emma closed the message window, a sick headache pounding in time with her heartbeat.

She didn't need to read more to understand that failing to drive her away from Kingston County hadn't been enough for her stalker. The scheming sadist clearly wouldn't be satisfied until he'd cast suspicion on her for what he himself had done.

Chapter 18

For the past hour, Beau had been holed up in the den, obsessively rereading Emma's trashed emails, along with a few other, unrelated messages that had apparently been accidentally copied with them. With every moment, his nausea built, along with the fear that Ty had been too quick to send the warning, out of fear for Beau's safety. And that he himself—

What the hell have I done? Why couldn't I just talk to her—or better yet shut up and listen?

He cursed himself for a fool and shoved away his tablet computer, knocking the letter tray off the desk's edge and spreading important papers he'd been meaning to file everywhere.

Dropping to his hands and knees, he'd barely begun scraping together the signature pages from his lease deal with Green Horizons when his cell rang. He fumbled for the phone and answered without looking, "Emma, please come back. We have to ta—"

"Judging from the way she drove out of here," said Carlos Galvez, who'd been keeping watch on the house, "I very much doubt she'll be returning any time soon. But I'm pretty sure you have bigger trouble, jefe, heading up your driveway."

"What trouble?" Beau asked, his gaze snagged on the list of signatories of the lease deal. A name there jumped out at him, a name that caught him by the throat, far too similar to be coincidental. Or was he reaching too far in his desperation?

But as Carlos began speaking, Beau realized that the question would have to wait for now.

Moments later, he was hurrying down the hall to find a set of windows that would allow him to check the front of the house. His jaw clenched, he cautiously peered out from behind the heavy drapery of a window in the formal dining room, looking for the threat his vaquero had described.

"Daddy, w-why? Why would you—?" asked a small, strained voice behind him.

Beau jumped at the sound, allowing the curtain to fall as he turned to face Cort, who stood with Maverick at his side, panting and drooling on the Persian rug.

"How many times have you been told," Beau asked him sharply, "not to bring that dog into this room? Now take him up to your room—no arguments—and stay up there until someone comes to get you."

Cort's freckled face reddened, his brown eyes flaring at the unexpected harshness.

I'll make this up to you. I swear it, Beau ached to assure him. But driven by a more pressing concern for what his boys might see or hear, he channeled his own late father's stern tone. "Round up your brother, right this minute, and take him upstairs with you."

Sobbing, Cort turned. But instead of fleeing, Beau's normally soft-spoken son whirled and shouted, "She was going to be our new mom, but you ruined everything! We heard you!"

"What?" Beau asked before realizing that his sons must have been near the door of his bedroom this morning. And must have heard him telling Emma in no uncertain terms to leave. "Listen, Cort, you don't understand, and there's no time to explain."

"You made her go away! I hate you! I wish she took me, too!"

"Your room, son. *Move—and don't forget your brother!*" Beau shouted.

Cort gave him one last tearful glance, the pain and bewilderment in his small face reminding Beau of what he'd seen on Emma's when he had turned so suddenly on her. *God forgive me...*

He forced himself to peer out the window just as the black-and-white SUV pulled up and Wallace Fleming climbed out. His wide jaw set in a look of grim determination, his hand rested on the butt of his gun as he strode toward the front door.

He really means to do it, Beau realized, reading the hostility radiating from Wallace's stocky form, the sheer resentment as he pulled a pair of cuffs off his belt.

"Bad enough you've been plotting to steal this place your whole life," Beau said. "But there's no way in hell I'm letting you perp-walk me out of here in front of my family on whatever trumped-up charges you've invented."

Ignoring the strong knock, Beau headed for the back door. As he grabbed his hat and keys, he heard movement from up near the front atrium, followed by his aunt's annoyance. "Where on earth is everyone? Now hold your horses, Wallace, and give me a moment to unlock this."

Beau cursed, hated the thought of leaving Aunt Alicia to deal with whatever delusional accusations Wallace was going to level. Surely she would order him to leave, and even as angry as he was, Wallace respected the woman too much to defy her. Especially once he realized that Beau had driven off in his truck.

He wasn't going far, nor would he continue trying to avoid his cousin. If Beau wanted to fix the rest of his life—the mess he'd made with both his sons and Emma—he had to get the proof he needed that Ty had been right about this from the start. Many of his problems *were* related.

But he'd never put an end to them through lawyers or third parties. He'd have to do it face-to-face and on his turf, today, using the same allies he'd relied upon since childhood, after his own father had turned his back on him.

Forcing herself to reexamine the damning emails, Emma couldn't do a thing to stop the waves of pain. It wasn't so much knowing that someone had taken the time and effort to craft such an elaborate deception just to hurt her, but that Beau would toss aside what they'd shared, swallowing the hateful lies whole.

Maybe he was feeling panicked this morning, all too exposed by the unfamiliar intimacy. Willing to latch on to this convenient "proof" she was a monster as an excuse to push her away.

"Then you deserve to be alone," she said, voice shaking. "Do you really think a college professor would send emails filled with so many misspellings to a student? Such dreadful punctuation?" Not to mention the hysterical tone. But maybe those factors were only obvious to her, maybe the sheriff or a DA would argue that they'd sounded off because she'd been overwrought when they'd been written.

Exhausted and frustrated, she started to close the laptop screen to go hit a fast-food drive-through for another attempt at coffee. Instead, on impulse, she lifted the lid again and clicked on the image file she'd saved to her computer's desktop. Once again, the blurry photo of the armed man from the game camera popped up. Once again, she squinted at it, hoping to spot some resemblance to her ex-husband that she could take to the authorities.

But wasn't that the same thing Wallace had been doing? Trying desperately to force the evidence to fit the suspect of his choosing? She thought back to what the sheriff had told her, something about the ear, the hair, or had it been the jawline?

Closing her eyes, she focused on her breathing. On letting go of everything that had happened over the past few weeks—and the anxiety and sadness running through her.

It took a while, but gradually, the throbbing in her leg eased and the knot in her stomach loosened. Only then did Emma take a fresh look at the photo.

This time, she zeroed in on those details Wallace had mentioned, the facial features an experienced law enforcement officer had focused on.

And just like that, something clicked, bringing with it a swift intake of breath as Emma saw what she had missed before. And with a shocking jolt of intuition, she knew, too, why Wallace might've been misled and Beau had discarded what may have been his own first suspicion.

Behind her, River gave a little growl-yip, and Emma

scolded, "*Please*, dog! Will you stop pestering—" She then gasped at the blurred movement of something vanishing behind the rear seat back.

A small hand holding River's duck.

Her stomach somersaulting, Emma commanded, "Come out where I can see you, right this instant! What are you doing back there? Cort?"

"He was too scared. *He's* the baby." Leland's defiant face, with its missing front tooth, popped up from behind the barrier, where he'd clearly been hiding since she'd left the ranch. "If Daddy's going to be so mean, I want to stay with you now. You can be my mom and River can be our dog."

Emma closed her eyes and gusted out a sigh, praying this was a hallucination and she wasn't about to add a charge of kidnapping to her list of woes. But when she opened her eyes, the six-year-old was crawling over the rear seat and hugging River, who happily slurped the side of his face before reclaiming her duck.

"You can't run away from home. Your father and your aunt will be so scared."

For a moment, he looked doubtful. Then storm clouds darkened his expression. "They still have perfect Cort and all his dumb books."

"And what about poor Maverick? Won't he have hurt feelings if he finds out you like River better?"

"That dumb puppy chewed the heads off my favorite action figures!"

"He's still learning how to be a grown dog. Learning to forgive when the people who love him sometimes mess up. And to forgive himself, even when it's really hard, when he makes terrible mistakes, too." *Such as endangering a child's life by driving him all over without so much as a seat belt.*

"Do you think—" Lines of worry creased the boy's small forehead. "Do you really think, Miss Emma, they might miss me a little?"

"I think they're probably running around like crazy, looking everywhere, and calling your name right now. You aunt Alicia might even be crying. You know, she'll blame herself for—"

"It wasn't her fault. It was Daddy's, telling you to go away," Leland insisted. But his brown eyes pooled with tears as he suggested, "Maybe we should call 'em? Just so they won't be too scared."

"I think that's a very good idea," Emma told him. "You're a very thoughtful boy to come up with that on your own."

Chapter 19

"**Y**ou take me for a fool? Why the hell would I agree to come meet you alone?" Wallace demanded after Beau, sitting in his pickup, reached him on the cell phone. "And especially way out there, where nobody could hear a gunshot? You thinkin' to maybe solve your problems with an ambush, mongrel?"

"I'm thinking it would be a good place to finally hash this all out," Beau said, fighting back a red-hot surge of temper that would do him no good whatsoever. "A quiet place with no lawyers between us, no kids or aunt to interfere. Just you and me, talking like grown men, unarmed." *And recording every word you say.*

Out ahead of where he sat parked, the wind rippled over the seed heads of tall grasses, sparkling in the morning sunshine after last night's rain.

"I'm an officer of the law," Wallace argued. "I don't go anywhere without my sidearm. If you want to talk to me, you know where my office is."

"I don't think you'll want to have this chat there, on the record and in front of my attorney." Beau drew a deep breath, turning his head to take in that long strip of range darkened by the shadow of Turbine Number 43. Even from inside the cab, he could hear the low hum of its motor as the blades whirled slowly, once more producing clean, if not exactly bloodless, power. "And I don't think you'll want to explain the evidence I've brought to show you to your colleagues without having a chance to prepare."

"What do you have, bastard?"

"I suppose that's the fifty-four-million-dollar question," he said, naming the figure of the settlement offer. "And afterward, if you're still of a mind to haul me in in handcuffs, we can go that route, too. I swear it. I'll just be damned if I let you arrest me in front of *my* heirs."

Beau referred to his boys as such as a reminder that, even if Wallace chose to try to expedite his takeover with another murder, he'd still face a legal challenge on behalf of Cort and Leland. What Wallace couldn't know is that the boys' godfather, Ty Phelps, would stop at nothing to destroy him if that's what it took to protect the children's interest and avenge his friend.

Wallace sighed, "Well, we do need to talk. And this time you're gonna damned well listen to me."

"I'll be waiting," Beau said.

Wallace hesitated before saying, "Just make damned sure you're alone, and know that if you try pulling anything out there, that Kingston name of yours won't stop a bullet."

Once they ended the call, Beau whispered, "That name's never been a shield for me. It's a lesson that you taught me early, you and my father both…"

Along with the stupidity of playing by his cousin's rules.

* * *

After dropping off Leland and leaving both boys with hugs and a vague promise that maybe she would see them sometime, Emma left the mansion once more. But a lump rode with her, like a boulder in her stomach. Something hadn't been right. Something beyond Beau's absence and the coldness of her welcome.

She sensed it in the odd behavior of Beau's aunt, who'd seemed awkward and distracted as she'd curtly thanked Emma for returning her charge. Still dressed in her bathrobe and with her normally perfect dome of curls mussed, Mrs. Parker had seemed off, distracted. Normally the most vigilant of caretakers, she'd admitted that she hadn't even realized that her younger charge was missing until Emma's call.

Emma had tried apologizing, both for missing Leland when she'd left the ranch and for speaking so sharply yesterday when they'd talked. But the woman had all but pushed her out the door, saying, "I think it would be best if you're gone when Beau returns from wherever he's run off to. There's been enough upset around here this morning without— Just go now, all right?"

Emma had had no choice except to leave, but she didn't feel good about it. Should she reach out to Beau to suggest he check on his aunt? But at the thought of hearing his voice again, she tensed, her mind flooding with his angry accusations. With the lack of trust, the fear she'd felt mingling with bad memories from her marriage.

"He isn't Jeremy," she reminded herself. "You can at least text him."

Pulling over on the ranch road, she took out her phone and tapped out the message: Had to return your stowaway youngest to the ranch. Your aunt seems a little off. Maybe you should check on her? Looking awfully pale.

Once she sent the message, she noticed an unread text waiting for her from Lieutenant Williams, asking where in town he might be able to meet with her tomorrow. Only the text, she realized with a start, had been sent yesterday. She'd somehow missed it. Was the Ranger in Pinto Creek already, investigating Russell's death, after misleading her to keep her from giving anything away?

As she tried to think of a safe place where she could meet him, she glimpsed a silhouette on the horizon. It was the top of Turbine Number 43, a sight that drew a shiver.

Why on earth were the blades turning, along with the blades of the more distant turbines? Could the company's review already be over? She'd expected it would take months and have to be signed off on by the federal agency that oversaw workplace safety as well.

Or had the company found the way to gloss over that "minor inconvenience" To get its investment producing once again?

After texting the lieutenant to let him know she was on the Kingston spread but expected to be heading back to town soon, she abruptly turned toward the turbine in the faint hope of spotting the Green Horizons engineers who had restarted the windmill. But when she saw the pair of vehicles haphazardly parked near the tower's base, she startled, her instincts telling her there was something deeply wrong here. Something she couldn't, in good conscience, drive away from.

Not without checking to make certain the man that she couldn't help still caring for—no matter how he'd hurt her—was all right.

"Careful there," Wallace warned, drawing his gun as Beau reached into his back pocket. Both stood in the shade of the turbine's base, the pulsing thrum of the spinning blade like the breathing of a giant high above them.

"It's a piece of *paper*, that's all," Beau said, noting the sweat rolling down his cousin's face and the slight shake of his barrel. A barrel now pointed at Beau's own chest. "A copy of a contract I've left locked in the mansion's vault…*after* emailing a scan to my ex-partner. For insurance."

"Insurance against wha—" Distracted the sounds of hinges creaking, Wallace jerked his head to see the turbine's access door swing slightly open to his left, revealing a shotgun aiming at him. "Galvez! What the hell?"

"You will want to put away that weapon now," Fernando said with a hard stare that said he meant it, "and listen to your cousin, calmly and politely. This is surely what the old jefe, your uncle, would have wanted, would he not?"

Wallace took a step back, the color draining from his face and the barrel still aimed at Beau shaking. "Put that shotgun down right this second, or I'll have you in a cell faster than you can blink. Not only that, I promise you, I'll see the whole lot of your relations evicted from this property the second I lay claim to—"

Fernando nudged the door wider with a booted foot. "You dare to threaten *mi familia*?"

"And *you're* threatening an officer of the law? You do know that kind of killin's a capital offense in this state, don't you?"

"Nobody's killing anybody," Beau insisted, ignoring the rushing blood in his ears as he attempted to regain control. "Now both of you, lower your weapons. Yeah, like that. Fernando."

"Now put it down," the sheriff ordered. "On the concrete at your feet, Galvez."

When Beau said nothing, Fernando's silver brows rose as he stared the question. "Jefe?"

Beau hesitated, weighed his options. Prayed that his choice would lead to a de-escalation rather than dead bodies, since Fernando's son, Antonio, who was lying among the weeds not twenty yards away holding a pistol, was young and inexperienced enough to be an unknown quantity if he feared for his father's life.

"Go ahead, Fernando," Beau said, "and Wallace here will holster his gun, too. Right, Wallace? So we can finish *talking*."

The look Fernando gave him was full of disbelief, but Beau didn't waver. Finally, the ranch manager slowly and carefully laid down the shotgun, contempt plain on his face as he glared at Wallace.

Holstering his own pistol, Wallace told the older man, "There are damned well gonna be some changes around this place, startin' with a new crew that didn't grow up runnin' with this little bastard."

"Don't you get it, Wallace?" Beau asked, unfolding the paper he still held. "It's all over. You're not getting any settlement, and you're sure as hell not getting the ranch. But then, you never were, no matter what J. Armstrong Pinckney promised."

"What? What would your father's lawyer have to do with—"

"That's what I was wondering. Why would you ask the man who allegedly updated my father's will to bring *my* attorney a settlement offer?"

"I—um—I liked his style when I met him, that's all. And the lawyer I was usin' was a damned fool, with his cockamamie idea that a fraud suit might root you out of—"

"Lawman like yourself, I'm betting you took the trouble to check this Pinckney fellow out first, especially when he approached you out of nowhere with this second will, right?"

"Why would I—"

"Oh, I don't know," Beau said sarcastically, "maybe to catch wind of the fact that he's represented quite a few clients accused of fraud and embezzlement, even forgery." It had been right there for him to find, in a search of court filings that had taken only minutes.

"He's a lawyer, isn't he? I'm sure he's represented all sorts of crooks."

"You ever hear of a criminal defense attorney handling a will involving an estate the size of this one? And what's even more interesting, I happened to catch this name, right on my own lease agreement."

Beau pointed out a name low on the signature page he'd brought, belonging to Green Horizons' vice president of energy projects. "Edith A. *Pinckney*," he read aloud. "That sounded so familiar I couldn't help but get curious. Curious enough to do another quick web search."

Wallace was shaking his head, sweat trickling down the side of his face. "What's that have to do with some lawyer out of Houston?"

"The thing is, your new lawyer friend's not originally from Houston," Beau said. "He's from California, same as his sister, Edith."

"His sister? I—I don't know anything about that. Let me—let me see that," Wallace demanded, reaching out to snatch the copy from Beau's hand and scanning the names on it. "Are you—are you sure about—"

"What was it they promised you, Wallace, after they found out about your weakness? The jealousy poisoning you, the certainty that you deserved it more than any brown-eyed bastard? Did they offer you a cut if I jumped at that payout? Or did they know, just like you did, that I'd never break the ranch's back with that kind of debt, not even to save it? Did you really ever imagine that if you did win the ranch in court, they would ever let you keep it—after you'd committed murder for them?"

"I never killed anyone!" Wallace shook his head emphatically. "I don't have to stand hear and listen to this horsesh—"

"So all you had to do was what? Look the other way while somebody else took care of Green Horizons' little blackmailer issue? Then get it ruled an accident—and shut up Emma when she started making too much noise."

"What the hell are you going on about? After all I've done trying to bring in her attacker and keep that fool girl safe?"

"From who? When we both know you're the killer," Beau said.

"No, Beau. Wallace isn't," said Emma, who had appeared—using her crutches once more as she stepped from behind the turbine's base, the partially open door at her back.

Chapter 20

"Didn't I tell you to leave this property and not to come back?" The harshness of Beau's voice didn't hide the fear she saw in his eyes.

Fear for his own safety? Or is he more terrified that I'll end up with a bullet in me?

But Emma understood the risks, had known them the moment she had heard their angry tones and spotted the sheriff's right hand on his gun. Even so, she'd chosen to intervene—to go to the man who still held her heart captive—before the two destroyed each other, no matter what it cost her.

Terrified as she was, sounds filled her awareness: the rush of air in her lungs, the rapid-fire pumping of her own blood in her ears. The turbine thrummed above them, and River, tied by her leash to the Jeep's bumper, yelped at the sound of her voice, clearly upset at being restrained.

"It *wasn't* Wallace in the photo that night," she told Beau, "don't you see? He couldn't have been the one who climbed that tower to plant something—maybe a money drop to pay off Russell for keeping quiet—up there as a lure. The man who did that and sabotaged the harness— or maybe he forced Russell to go up at gunpoint. We might never know for sure—except whoever did it had to have been younger, fitter, a trained climber like a—"

"*You're* trained, aren't you, Doctor?" the sheriff asked, his eyes widening as it hit him that she might be something other than a victim. "Whoever your accomplice was, *you* were the one they paid to get Russell up—"

"Let her finish," Beau ordered.

"Trained like a firefighter," Emma said.

"You lie!" bellowed a deep voice about eight feet behind her, a voice that startled her into crying out and lurching forward, her legs tangling with her crutches.

Chaos erupted, measured in the splintered fractions of a second. Shouts came at her from all sides, commands to *Freeze*, *Shut up* and *Drop it* colliding in the air as she went down. She caught sight of the sheriff, pulling at his sidearm, Beau lurching forward, reaching for her, and finally—as her back smacked down—Fernando Galvez, raising a weapon in the turbine's doorway.

As Beau reached her, the air exploded. Sharp cracks of gunfire overlapped a deeper *Boom!*

Blood sprayed over her body. Beau's blood, hot and bright. She screamed as he fell to his knees, his hands rising to his neck.

As she reached for him she heard the unmistakable racking of the shotgun.

Raising her hands, she looked up. "Don't shoot! Please! I won't tell anyone about your son!"

A sharper crack, followed by two more, split the air around her. Fernando's head bobbed hard, the Panama hat flying. Slumping awkwardly in the doorway, the ranch manager's body sagged and pitched forward, the shot-gun falling from his hands and dark blood spreading from beneath him.

Wallace had dropped onto his knees. His arm bloody, he struggled to raise his gun hand, which he turned in the direction of the field behind them before another shot came out of nowhere and he flopped onto his side.

Panic ricocheting through her, Emma crawled to Beau. Shaking violently, he held both hands to the side of his neck as blood squeezed from beneath his fingers.

She wanted to scream her lungs out, to stop the world to tend to his wound and get help for all three men who'd been hit. But right now, the only thing that mattered was keeping Beau from being shot again by whoever had just fired on—and possibly killed—Wallace.

"We need to move, right now," she screamed near Beau's ear. "Get behind that door, inside the base!"

He didn't move at first, saying only, "Tony won't—h-hurt me."

As this name registered, she stood, abandoning her crutches to grab at Beau's arm, pulling on him before he slipped into shock. But no matter how she struggled, he was too far heavy for her to drag.

"Help me, Beau, or we're both dead."

"Antonio's…friend. H-help."

"Antonio," she insisted, "is Russell's killer!"

She looked up to see a figure rushing toward them—the same young fireman that she had just accused of murder.

"Tony would never—" Beau tried to argue. But with pain, shock and blood loss making speech nearly impos-sible, his mind flashed to the new car the kid had recently been seen driving, the *rich white* firefighter groupie girl-friend that the family hadn't met. How suddenly unconcerned the young man seemed about the cost of a move to Dallas.

Had Fernando begun to suspect? Was that why he had turned the gun on Emma when she'd named the son he was unwilling to give up on?

It was then Beau spotted Antonio, his hand still clutching his pistol and his face a mask of desperation as he charged toward Emma.

"Tony, no!" Beau croaked out, comprehension dawning that Tony meant to silence her.

Drawing from some unknown reserve of strength, Beau surged to his feet and shoved Emma toward the shelter of the doorway. Tripping over Fernando's body, she fell again, and Beau scrambled after her, heedless of the blood pouring from his neck.

Yanking her to her feet, he pushed her through and turned to face the threat. The young man he'd believed as good a man as his father and his older brothers, a young man who'd chosen a deadly shortcut to achieve his goals.

Now that he had shot the sheriff, it was clear that Tony wasn't going to let anyone stand between him and the woman who had named him for the killer that he was.

"I'm s-so sorry, Mr. Kingston," he said, his voice sounding impossibly young as he aimed his weapon straight at Beau's chest. "I didn't mean—I n-never w-wanted things to turn out this w-way. I wanted to prove that I could—"

"Stop this! Let him go, please," Emma shouted, struggling to push her way past Beau. "It's me you want. Don't—"

"Get back, Emma," Beau said, blocking her. Didn't she understand that Tony had no choice except to kill them both? Unless he could find some way to—

"Don't shoot your brother," Emma pleaded. "Yes, that's

right. Can't you see it in your faces? Your jaws? Your ears, your coloration? You're both your father's sons."

Beau stiffened, but Antonio bellowed, "No!" and dropped his gaze to his fallen father.

Their father, if Emma had it right—who found the strength to raise his shotgun and pull the trigger one last time.

Chapter 21

All he knew, obliterated. Shattered in a hail of gunfire, a waterfall of intermingled blood. Beau's, Fernando's and, most of all, Antonio's, as the blast from his father's shotgun, aimed upward at nearly point-blank range, blew out the juncture of the twenty-year-old's hip and thigh.

Beau lay in the dimness of his hospital room, clinging to the raft of painkillers he'd been given. The screams replayed in his mind, the desperate, all-too-brief cries not of a monster, but of a young man barely getting started, confused by how things could have taken this ungodly turn.

My half brother—could it be true? And did that mean Fernando was my— Did he even guess? Or had he known all along, while he'd advised Beau, taught him and watched his cousins call him bastard while his legal father's contempt had torn his soul to ribbons?

As questions spun through his brain, Beau squeezed

his eyelids tighter, his throat tightening and his stomach contracting to a hard knot.

"Hey, are you awake in there?" a soft voice said beside him. Emma's...

He forced his eyes open, and relief flooded through him, gratitude to see her rising from a bedside chair in a room softly lit by sunlight filtering through the window's shade. Though she appeared unhurt, clean and wearing a fresh set of clothing, there was no disguising the fatigue and strain in her pale face.

She leaned to kiss his forehead and then insisted on getting him fresh water. "I'm so glad you've finally come around. It's been two days, Beau. Two of the longest days of my entire life."

"Days?" He fought to push himself upright, but the room spun and pain surged where the movement pulled at his wound.

"Easy there." She gently pushed him back down, careful not to disturb the tubes sticking into his arms. "The transfusions helped, but you still have a ways to go to get your strength back."

"My family—are they—?"

"They've been here day and night, waiting, praying. When the doctors said the surgery to repair the artery in your neck was a success and you were out of danger, I finally convinced your aunt to take the boys home so all of them could get some rest."

He felt a pang, imagining how terrified Cort and Leland must have been, thinking of their mother. Thinking what he'd put them and his poor aunt through with his terrible miscalculation about meeting Wallace at the turbine.

He heard the shots again. The screaming. Feared that he would always hear them.

After easing the dryness in his throat, he ignored Emma's queries about how he was feeling.

"Fernando?" he asked. *Please, God. I have so many questions.*

She shook her head and squeezed his hand. "I'm sorry, Beau. Fernando and Antonio—they were both gone before help arrived. But Wallace—your cousin was taken to San Antonio for spinal surgery. He may not walk again, but I'm told he'll survive—and he's facing charges as soon as he's sufficiently recovered."

"They're—they're both dead?" Beau echoed, stuck on the first news she'd broken.

"I'm so sor—"

"Because *you* barged in after I sent you away—" at the thought of how close he'd come to watching her die, too, fear and grief roared through him, morphing into anger "—and flat-out accused Fernando's son of murdering—"

"I had no idea he was hiding there," she said, her voice thick with emotion. "No idea that either he was or his father—"

My father...

"Of course you didn't know. You couldn't have," he said, his head clearing as it came back to him how both armed men had been hidden on his orders. "Instead of yelling at you, I should be thanking you for—for saving my life."

She shook her head, deflecting. "Not me. You're a strong man, and you must've had an angel on your side, to catch only the smallest portion of that shotgun blast in your neck."

"My angel, yes…" If Beau lived a hundred years, he knew he would never forget seeing her rise, covered in his blood and Tony's. Shaking off her shock, she'd kicked away all three men's weapons before calling 911. Afterward, she'd rushed to Beau's truck to retrieve the first aid kit there, which she'd used to pack his wound before...

The rest faded into murky grayness, a windswept void where the rhythmic rush of the turbine deepened into the thrum of a medical helicopter's blades.

"Lieutenant Williams has been here," Emma said. "He tells me that as the result of an interagency investigation, several arrests have been made. Two top executives from Green Horizons, which has a history of padding the pockets of local law enforcement wherever the company's projects started running into trouble."

"So they really were paying off Wallace?"

"It started with some pretty low-key influence peddling, the campaign contributions your ex-partner discovered that were meant to convince the sheriff to look the other way whenever the occasional violation came up. Lieutenant Williams discovered some incriminating communications referencing one of their employees getting pulled over for expired plates—and caught with a bunch of bloody carcasses of hawks and eagles wrapped up in his back seat."

"But Wallace wouldn't have turned a blind eye toward murder."

"Apparently not, which is why they upped the ante after Russell decided to try his hand at blackmail—the state techs found the proof after they opened up his laptop." Emma rubbed her temples, her eyes filling with regret at her student's fateful choice. "Then Green Horizons came up with the golden ticket to buy the sheriff's cooperation—"

"That phony will."

She nodded. "The lawyer Pinckney and his master forger client are both in custody."

"So how did Tony get mixed up in all this? He was

just a young guy with big dreams." Beau still couldn't wrap his head around it.

"Big enough that he was always training, trying to get a leg up on other big-city firefighter candidates, which led him to start climbing the turbines with a couple of gung-ho Green Horizons techs—who must've realized how hard up he was for money. And how eager to prove he wasn't afraid of anything."

Beau's heart broke a little more. "Including jumping you, after the memorial service?"

She nodded. "The lieutenant says his blood type matched the splotch that was found on my clothing from that night, and his prints were on the weapons and photo from the storage shed, too. Green Horizons really wanted to convince me to leave town and back off Russell's murder, but they were afraid that if I turned up dead, too, the kind of outside authorities they couldn't pay off were sure to come down on their heads. That was their biggest fear, you see, because the wind farm on your spread isn't their only project that's come under scrutiny just lately."

"So they decided to terrorize you instead," he realized.

She shrugged. "It must've seemed like the perfect plan after Wallace told them my ex was threatening me, especially after he went missing."

"Jeremy's in jail now?"

"For the time being, yes, for violating the terms of his parole and for tearing up the bar where my student Lucie works in Austin. Once he's released, his family's promised to get him into a supervised residential rehab program for his issues."

"Good news for you."

"I hope so, but the fact remains that he had nothing to do with anything that happened here."

"So the snakes placed in your room—that was Tony also?"

"His prints were on that box, too."

Beau realized Tony could have learned to disable the security systems at both the equipment shed and the mansion during the years he'd spent tagging along, learning the business while his father worked.

Our father... The very thought still left Beau reeling. Or could Emma have been wrong about that? A resemblance—what did it prove? Didn't his Sicilian great-grandfather's photo prove that?

Beau decided he didn't need or want to know, because he refused to allow whoever he was, whatever he'd become, to be defined by the actions of others instead of what he made of this life he'd been given. How he treated others, what he built and how he loved.

"I know it's a lot to process," Emma said gently, "but right now you should focus on resting, getting better."

"I've been down too damned long already." He elevated the head of the bed, an action that sent fresh waves of dizziness breaking over him.

"You nearly *died.*" She squeezed his hand. "Another half inch to the left, and— You have no idea how frightened I was out there, how terrified I was that I would never get to tell you how I—"

"Except you did," he said as it came back to him, those terrible moments when she'd crouched over him, the pressure of her hand on a wad of bandages the only thing preventing the life from leaking from him. His vision might have darkened, but he'd heard the tears in her voice. Her fierce determination. *You're not leaving me, Beau Kingston. You're not going anywhere without ever hearing me say how much I love you.*

"I heard you out there, heard you in that moment when

I figured everything was lost. My life, my chance to raise my kids and make something of my legacy, the people that lay bleeding, dying all around me. And I thought— I thought if you could take a chance on coming back for me, could risk your life fighting to save me after the things I'd said, the way I'd hurt you— I feel like a world-class fool, believing for a second that those emails could've been yours."

"Shh." Sniffling, she leaned closer, the light, sweet scents of soap, shampoo and something he recognized as uniquely Emma—something he could never get enough of—wafting toward him. "Please don't beat yourself up for that. You couldn't have guessed that Green Horizons would get so desperate to discredit me, they'd find a way to hack into my—"

"I was scared to death I'd die right there, before I could tell you how very sorry I am for the way I hurt you. When I took a second look, I knew damned well I'd made a terrible mistake. And I was as sure as any man alive that a woman who'd already had the precious gift of her trust destroyed once would never in a million years give me another shot."

"You were right before, Beau, back in the ravine that day you said that I know who you are. I *know* you. And if I didn't think that you were worth it, I wouldn't have gone back, just like I wouldn't have begged an extra week before I have to go back to start my new semester—"

"No, Emma. Please stay here. Stay with me."

"Beau—"

"I love you—I'm in love. With you. With every single thing about you, from your passion to your courage to the way you never seem to know when to back down from a fight. And I want more of that, of you—even though I know I'm being selfish."

"You are the least selfish person I have ever known."

"You're wrong there. I am being selfish. Because I don't know what my life will be—whether with Green Horizons' crimes exposed, I'll be running what I can salvage of my ranch or supervising its dismantlement and then looking for some other way to earn my living. I'm not asking you to give up your life in Austin and stay with the rich ranching heir who runs Kingston County. I'm asking you to stay with *me*, simply because I know damned well that whatever I end up with, whether it's the mansion my great-grandfather built, a house somewhere in the suburbs or a ramshackle log cabin on the edge of nowhere, holed up with our family, it'll be a paradise if I have you by my side."

"Oh, Beau," Emma said as she wrapped her arms around him. "You had me at 'our family.' It's all I ever needed…to be right there in the thick of it, with you."

Chapter 22

Seven months later

Of all the things Emma had expected, three days before they were scheduled to be out of the mansion ahead of the ranch's sale, Beau's suggestion that they get out for a short drive had been the last.

"But the packers will be here any minute," she said, exasperated to see him looking all fresh and crisp and handsome as the devil after a meeting with his attorney, where they'd been hashing out final terms of a deal to save as many local jobs as possible, while she was a hot mess from boxing some of the boys' things while they were at school. "I can't just drop everything and—"

Taking her gently by the wrist, he swung her past River and Maverick, who wagged their greetings, and into his arms, his smile welcome after all these months of uncertainty and loss, months in which she'd learned that not every man crumbled before adversity or blamed others for their setbacks.

"Aunt Alicia's got this covered. Believe me, she's a five-star general when it comes to ordering people around."

"But I promised her I'd—"

"She's aware you're being abducted by your husband." His voice was a sexy rumble as he drew a strip of deep blue silk out of his rear pocket. "So play along now, Emma, or you'll spoil the surprise."

His gaze latched onto hers, those deep brown eyes she loved so much lit by a playful spark. Was he putting on a good face, attempting to hide what it would cost him walking away from the work of generations? She knew full well how many nights of late he'd spent tossing and turning as he'd worried over returning with the family—minus Aunt Alicia, who'd chosen a move to the new active retirement community all her friends had been gushing over instead of relocation to Colorado—to run his security business, with all the memories, good and painful, that his former home entailed.

"Playing along," she agreed, trusting him enough to allow him to blindfold her. "But if this is one of those sexy kinds of surprises, you're going to be sorry you didn't give me time to shower first."

As he tied the cloth, he kissed the top of her ear, sending delicious shivers through her body. "If you think I'd be put off by a little sweat and grit and dog hair, you don't know me at all."

Laughing, she trusted him to lead her, half expecting that, as early as the hour was, he'd take a detour to their bedroom. Instead, he carefully guided her down the staircase and toward what she was certain was the front door, where he told the dogs, "Sorry, you two. This part of the journey's exclusively for humans."

"Where on earth are you taking me?" she demanded as their footsteps echoed beneath the portico.

"Patience, Emma."

"Since when has that ever been my strong suit?"

He chuckled. "You've shown a lot of it of late. With me, especially. I just wanted you to know it's been appreciated. Here we are, at the truck. Now don't forget to duck your head when you step up."

Burning with curiosity, she allowed him to help her buckle in and somehow managed to contain her questions—and keep from fretting about all the other things she should be doing. Things like grading midterms for the online classes she'd started teaching part time this semester and finishing a grant proposal for a local nonprofit she'd become involved with, which rehabilitated injured wildlife.

But when the truck slowed to make a turn, the chassis jolted three times on the right side. It was enough to goose her heart rate because she knew that set of potholes. Knew the place where he was taking her. A place of blood and death.

"No, please." She shook her head as her shaking hands fumbled with the silk cloth. "I don't want to play—to play this game anymore."

"It's all right, Emma," he said, slowing as he reached out to touch her knee. "I just need you to trust me—"

"I almost lost you here, Beau," she said, pulling off the cloth. Yet her eyes remained closed tight because she didn't want to see it. Couldn't bear to again. "Don't you understand? I still have the nightmares sometimes. The ones where Russell's hanging body wears your face, where those gunshots exploding all around us leave you as dead as—"

"Another few minutes, Emma. That's all. Just keep your eyes closed that much longer and we'll be past Number 43. I promise."

She sat stiffly in her seat, still shaking with emotion. As much as she loved these low hills and swales and all the hidden life that thrived here, she would be glad to put this blood-soaked corner of this land in the rearview of her life.

The pickup slowly climbed onto a ridge before Beau braked and stopped the engine. Leaning to kiss her temple, he whispered, "I sorry we had to pass through that place to reach this one, but I hope you'll find the view worthwhile."

Drawing a deep breath, she opened her eyes to see that they were on the area's highest ridge, looking out over a vista dotted with the shadows of the puffy clouds above and herds of cattle fattening on pastures replenished by the winter's rains. Realizing that she would never again take in this view, she stepped out of the truck and saw, to their east, the once-proud Kingston lands extending as far as the sparkling blue Gulf. But to their west, the coastal plains rolled out for miles more, studded with the many turbines that had once been Green Horizons'. And all of them, to her shock, were alive and spinning once again.

"What on earth?" she asked. "I thought Green Horizons was finished—that they'd never kill another bird or hurt another soul." At last count, half of the company's leadership was under indictment.

"Oh, they're finished." Beau moved to her side. "You're right about that. But—I didn't want to say a word until the deal was final, but another company, Living

Winds, has bought up all of the company's obligations on this site—with significant concessions."

"What kind of concessions?"

"They've had to retrofit every one of those turbines with state-of-the-art bird strike mitigation technology, which will have to be tested and signed off on every year. By you."

"By *me*? But won't we be in Colorado? The buyers for this place have made it abundantly clear that they don't want us around interfering with how they do things on their property."

"That's very true." He shrugged before casting a boyish grin in her direction. "Or at least it would be if I weren't about to pull the plug on this whole godforsaken deal."

A deal, she knew, he hated, since it would result in the ranch being carved up into dozens of pieces for commercial and residential development by a conglomerate of foreign investors. The mansion itself, they'd been told, would have an airstrip put nearby, along with an eighteen-hole golf course and boutique shops to support its use as an executive conference center.

But as distasteful as he—and especially his aunt Alicia—found it, the project would at least bring jobs to local residents, including those employees whose welfare meant so much to Beau.

"Don't you remember all the work, all the months you've spent hammering this deal together?" she asked him.

"I remember every agonizing minute," he said. "Especially how they've kept trying to back out of their obligations to pay benefits and a living wage. So that's why, now that we have Living Winds on board and Ed tells me we'll be getting a financial settlement from Green

Horizons' parent corporation, I want to make a change of course. To take a shot at saving all this." His gesture swept the land around them, the sky above and Gulf beyond. "But only if you're with me."

Emma's heart broke wide open, knowing that he meant it, that if she said the word, he would close the door on this dream. He would find another, smaller challenge, one they could more easily shoulder. If she asked him to, he'd come with her to a different place, a different future than the one he'd tentatively planned, so she could follow whatever opportunity ignited her passions.

But at the moment, the only passion she was thinking of stood right in front of her.

Laying her head against his chest, she said, "Of course I'm with you, always. Where else would I be?"

As he embraced her, Emma smiled, her fingers brushing just below her navel, touching on the memory of sorrow. And on that place where fresh hope nestled, new and fragile as the first green shoots of spring.

* * * * *

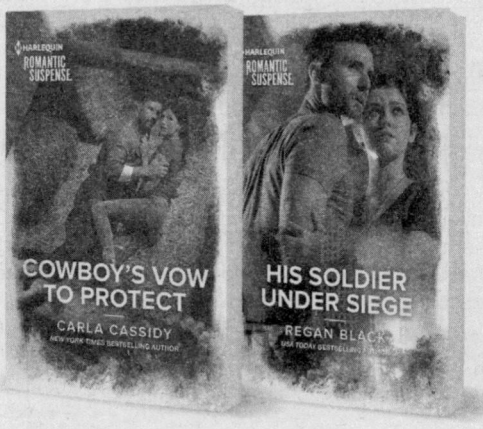

A.L. rode shotgun while Rena drove. He liked to look
around, study the landscape. Jane Picus had lived
within the city limits of Baywood. The fifty-thousand-
person city bordered the third-largest lake in west-
central Wisconsin, almost halfway between Madison
and Eau Claire. While the town was generally peaceful,
that many people in a square radius of thirteen miles
could do some damage to one another. Add in the
weekend boaters, who were regularly overserved, and
the Baywood Police Department dealt with the usual
assortment of crime. Burglary. Battery. Drugs. The
occasional arson.

And murder. There had been two the previous year.
One was a family dispute, and the killer had been quickly
apprehended. The other was a workplace shooter who'd
turned the gun on himself after killing his boss. Neither
had been pleasant, but they hadn't shaken people's
belief that Baywood was a good place to live and raise a
family. People were happy when their biggest complaint
was about the size of the mosquitoes.

Now for-sale signs were popping up in yards. There would likely be more by next week. Four unsolved murders in forty days was bad. Bad for tourism, bad for police morale and certainly bad for the poor women and their families.

In less than ten minutes, they were downtown. Brick sidewalks bordered both sides of Main Street for a full six blocks. Window boxes, courtesy of the garden club, were overflowing with petunias. The police department had moved to its new building in the three-hundreds block over ten years ago. Even then, it hadn't been new, but the good citizens of Baywood had voted to put some money into the sixty-year-old former department store. There was too much glass for A.L.'s comfort on the first floor and too little air-conditioning on the second and third. But it beat the hell out of working in the factory at the edge of town.

Which was where his father and his uncle Joe still worked. The McKittridge brothers. They'd been born and raised in Baywood, raised their own families there and had never left.

A.L. had sworn that wouldn't be his life. Yet here he was.

Because of Traci. His sixteen-year-old daughter.

Don't miss Ten Days Gone *by Beverly Long,*
available February 18, 2020 wherever
MIRA books and ebooks are sold.

MIRABooks.com